D1741078

Hugh Mackay is the author of three previous novels, *Little Lies* (1996), *House Guest* (1997) and *The Spin* (1999). He is a psychologist and social researcher, and writes a weekly column for the *Sydney Morning Herald*, the *Age* and *West Australian*. He is also the author of four best-selling books in the field of social psychology: *Reinventing Australia* (1993), *The Good Listener* (1994), *Generations* (1997) and *Turning Point* (1999). He lives in Sydney.

Winter Close

HUGH MACKAY

HODDER

Every effort has been made to contact
the copyright holders of material reproduced in
this text. In cases where these efforts have been
unsuccessful, the copyright holders are asked to
contact the publishers directly.

A Hodder Book

Published in Australia and New Zealand in 2002
by Hodder Headline Australia Pty Limited
(A member of the Hodder Headline Group)
Level 22, 201 Kent Street, Sydney NSW 2000
Website: www.hha.com.au

Reprinted 2002

Copyright © Mackay Research Pty Limited 2002

This book is copyright. Apart from any fair dealing for
the purposes of private study, research, criticism or
review permitted under the *Copyright Act 1968*,
no part may be stored or reproduced by any process
without prior written permission. Enquiries should
be made to the publisher.

**National Library of Australia
Cataloguing-in-Publication data**

Mackay, Hugh, 1938- .
  Winter close.

  ISBN 0 7336 1548 1

  I. Title.

A823.3

Text design and typesetting by Bookhouse, Sydney
Printed in Australia by Griffin Press, Adelaide

For Adèle

Contents

PART ONE

The Talk of the Street

ONE

Chika is a picture of wounded innocence

Like a hand raised at an auction, any vehicle moving at a hundred and twenty in a sixty zone—especially one with a faulty muffler—is bound to attract attention. Chika Frost's BMW thunders down Eastern Valley Way, throbbing like a bush ballad, and brakes sharply for the left-hander into Winter Close. A police motorcycle attaches itself to the BMW's tail. Viewed from the discreet eyrie of my front balcony, the familiar ritual of cop-issues-speeding-ticket-to-dumbstruck-motorist is curiously reassuring. Chika is perfect in the role, having played it often. Both men are clad in black leather jackets. The policeman's head is almost as bald as the helmet now resting on the saddle of his bike. Chika's spiky black hair is so heavily gelled it reflects the still-flashing blue light of the police bike.

The policeman is nodding in response to Chika's long-winded tale of woe. From this distance, it looks as if he might almost be persuaded to sympathise. But he keeps writing the ticket while he nods, then tears it from his pad and hands it to Chika, whose body language eloquently expresses his resentment.

This is the moment for the policeman to mount his motorcycle and roar off. Instead, he is walking to the rear of Chika's car, looking at the tyres, maybe, or checking the tail-lights. Now he is signalling Chika to open the boot and Chika is becoming agitated. The policeman is insisting. Chika is a picture of wounded innocence. From where I stand, I can almost hear his sigh of resignation.

Chika swings open the lid of the boot and the policeman leans over, out of my line of sight. Chika's wife Alex, their baby on her hip, has emerged from the front door of number seven and is marching towards the BMW, demanding to know not what is going on, nor what a police officer wants with her husband, but why Chika is running so late.

'Chika, your mother has been on the phone three times already. Where in God's name have you been? There is no way we can get to her place on time. Chika!' Then, more quietly, '*Chika?*'

It is as though Alex has only just noticed the police motorcycle with its light still flashing, just noticed the large policeman straightening his back behind the car, just noticed the green plastic garbage bag in the policeman's hand, and just noticed that Chika is trembling. Even from my balcony I can see he is trembling. Chika can shrug off a speeding ticket—he has shrugged off many speeding tickets—but not this. Whatever it is, this has made him tremble.

'Chika?' Alex's voice, sounding flat, repeats her question.

'It's nothing, lover. A speeding ticket, that's all. I was in a bit of a hurry to get home to take you and the baby over to Mama's. It's nothing.'

I can't hear what Alex says in response, but she is pointing at the plastic garbage bag which, it seems certain, does not contain garbage.

The policeman, bag in hand, goes to his motorcycle and calls someone on his radio. I can hear the voices, but not the words. Chika looks edgy, wild, almost like a man who might be thinking about making a run for it.

Tiny Enid Riley, full of concern, has emerged from her front door and is leaning on the front gate of number five. Rich Abel has arrived home in his black Volkswagen and is standing in the driveway of number eight, half-watching the constabulary tableau and half-waving to me on my balcony.

'Evening, Rich. Chika's been booked for speeding.' I try to keep my voice down but there's a sudden lull in the roar of traffic on Eastern Valley Way and Alex, hearing me, looks up. I wave.

Now I'm unsure how to proceed. I feel as if I've been caught out, watching too intently. I was already standing on my balcony before any of this happened, though Alex wouldn't know that. Enid at her front gate seems somehow less intrusive than me peering down from my balcony. I step inside, saunter downstairs, take two beers from the refrigerator and untwist the tops. I pause at the front door, then emerge to offer Rich a beer and a little conversation across our dividing fence. Chika is still trembling, glancing nervously in all directions; he is ignoring Alex, whose shoulders have drooped with disappointment or distress, or perhaps both. They stand together like strangers at a bus stop, one agitated, one resigned to the wait.

Each of us steals occasional glances at the unfolding drama, talking about everything except what's going on; talking about nothing in particular. The unwritten rule of the street is: the less said about Chika the better. More flashing lights arrive atop a police car with a male and female officer on board. The plastic bag is handed over and Chika is ushered into the back of the police car.

The motorcycle cop walks Alex back to her front door as Chika is driven away. The BMW stays where it is. It looks as if Chika's mother won't be seeing her boy tonight.

TWO

Although we live in the same street, we inhabit different worlds

At our annual street party—held, according to Rich Abel's careful formula, on the Monday night of the week before the week in which Christmas Day falls—we all get along famously, though it's clear we have nothing in common beyond the fact that we've chosen to put our roots down in Winter Close. We're neighbours, not friends; for most of the year, we're content to leave it at that. Although we live in the same street, we inhabit different worlds.

I once came upon Mrs Spenser from number nine sitting on the flight of concrete steps outside our local supermarket, hunched over a magazine in which she appeared to be filling out the answers to some quiz. At a glance, you might have taken her for a vagrant: dumpy figure, greasy and unkempt hair, skirt awry, blouse less than pristine, purple socks folded down over the top of shabby joggers. Now well into her seventies, she's lived in Winter Close longer than anyone else: she remembers, as a teenager, seeing US

Army blitz wagons on Eastern Valley Way and double-decker buses painted in the khaki camouflage of World War II. Although she has long since retired from whatever work she used to do, she is clearly not short of cash: charity collectors are often so moved by her generosity that when they reach my front door they are still talking about the size of her donation.

Mrs Spenser appears not to care about most of the things that might normally preoccupy a householder in a suburb like ours. She speaks her mind, offends people by her directness, is careless about grammar and syntax, never washes her car and is an equal-opportunity gardener, refusing to discriminate between weeds and flowers.

She often sits down on the kerb, or a step, or someone's fence, because that's where she happens to be when she feels in need of a rest. The day I saw her on the supermarket steps, she was licking the lead in a remnant of pencil and scribbling with zest. I found it hard to imagine what kind of magazine article might have had the power to engross her so totally, even to the point of extracting written responses from her. 'How to rate your love-life', perhaps? (That was an uncharitable speculation, Mr Spenser apparently having pushed off more than twenty years ago. Mrs Spenser still lives in the house built by her parents, both of whom died when she was a young woman. At some point, Mr Spenser came, and subsequently went.) When I expressed interest in what she was doing, she held out the page to show me: 'Win a trip for two to Bali'. If she won, I wondered who she would take. She never has visitors, and rarely goes out. Yet she seems irrepressibly alive and alert.

Filling in the answers to a magazine quiz is the kind of thing Mrs Spenser likes doing, especially when perched on concrete steps in the middle of our shopping centre. It's not an affectation exactly, but she takes a certain sly pleasure in the raised eyebrows of her neighbours.

My neighbours in number eight, the house between Mrs Spenser's and mine, wouldn't be caught dead participating in magazine contests, or even buying magazines of the kind Mrs Spenser thrives on. None of them, not even the children, would sit down on the supermarket steps. For the Abels, slaves to perfection and loveliness, such things are simply not done.

Doctor Rich Abel and his wife, Doctor Ruth Abel, have three adorable, precocious, and oh-so-carefully-spaced children: Laura, nine, Ethel, seven, and Humbold, five. Neat timing, but what about the names? The Abels are the kind of family who want to be memorable as well as wonderful. Rich is Richard, but there's no way you'd ever call him Dick. And Ruth, a general practitioner, is generally known as Doctor Ruth—even Rich calls her that, though possibly not in private. (A PhD in chemistry and once a renowned whiz kid, Rich likes to play the humble academic: 'I'm not a real doctor, of course. My wife's the real doctor.')

They admit they wanted their children to have unmistakable names which, on reflection, makes Laura's the hardest to understand. Perhaps hers was the result of a brief lapse into sentimentality on the part of her parents. Rich frequently manufactures opportunities to remark that sentimentality is a substitute for real emotion among the uneducated and unsophisticated, but the birth of their first child may have tapped into a rarely mined substratum of soppiness in them. (Laura has a similar effect on many people—including me, I must say.) No such lapses, though, with Ethel or Humbold.

I admit I'm quite sentimental, though I try to hide it from Rich. Doctor Ruth is neither so vigilant nor so judgmental, except when Rich is around and she feels the need to support his ceaseless struggle to lift us all out of the cultural slough of suburbia. For people living on the fringe of a suburb like Castlecrag, the Abels are an enigma. Rich, in particular, appears to hate everything the place stands for, yet he eschews the postmodern chic of a cluster-housing development on the campus of the university where he works.

Demographically, they're a bit odd, having three children and an intact marriage. Rich frequently reminds me that they represent a mere eleven per cent of the households of Australia and that Mrs Spenser and I, living in single-person households, are more mainstream. So there's a kind of eccentricity—pleasing to Rich—in having created a family that is almost anachronistic. They drive an old car, too, though not just any old car: a beautifully maintained 1974 Volkswagen practically qualifies as a fashion accessory.

Rich is fond of saying that the thing about Winter Close is that it fosters a real sense of community. That's a big claim and I wish I could share Rich's confidence in making it. Now that Sydney has grown to four million, communities are hard to come by: a common complaint among Sydneysiders is that 'we don't know our neighbours'—as if that's the neighbours' fault. I've given up saying, 'Why don't you knock on their door and introduce yourself?' The puzzled looks I receive make it clear I've missed the point: plenty of people *like* not knowing their neighbours and only pretend to complain about it. Suburbia offers a wonderful cloak of anonymity for those who want the security of proximity without any of the demands of intimacy.

Some of the peninsula suburbs around the harbour—places like Balmain and McMahon's Point—feel a bit like suburban villages, though almost all their residents go somewhere else to work, and there's an uneasy alliance of old, local families and blow-ins who've gentrified the place.

There are some suburbs, though, landlocked between arterial roads and railway lines, indistinguishable from the acres of bungalows and apartment blocks that surround them, crisscrossed by overhead power lines and pay-TV cables, roads clogged by snarling traffic, where, for no apparent reason and with no encouragement from their environment—not even a delineated boundary to mark them off from the next suburb and the next and the next—people have satisfied their herd instinct by forging strong links with their neighbours and developing a palpable sense of pride in the place. With no visible charm to help them along, such suburbs can still work beautifully.

Castlecrag has no such natural disadvantages to overcome. It straddles the ridge of a peninsula jutting into Middle Harbour, the value of real estate rising steeply the closer you get to the water's edge. Once a rather bohemian place where writers, artists, actors and assorted celebs coexisted with people living more conventional lives—at least on the surface—Castlecrag has gradually given way to rich dentists, merchant bankers, marketing directors and IT professionals. But the original spirit of the place survives in pockets of raffishness, and Walter Burley Griffin's flat-roofed homes, built from the local sandstone and designed to blend with the surrounding craggy bushland, are a startling reminder of the area's radical roots. Most of the street names are borrowed from the vocabulary of castle architecture—The Parapet, The Rampart,

The Bulwark, The Postern, Sortie Port—and there are crescents and cul-de-sacs everywhere.

Although our postal address is Castlecrag, Winter Close can hardly claim to be part of the cultural or aesthetic heritage of the place: we cling to the very edge of it, grateful for the impact of its cachet on the value of our homes, but we would probably feel more authentic if we were part of Willoughby—a sprawling, unpretentious, comfortable suburb to the west, separated from Castlecrag by the width of Eastern Valley Way. We're an undistinguished street—not a flat roof in sight and no local stone either. All the houses were built in the thirties and forties; our rather nondescript double-fronted brick-and-tile bungalows have mean porches at the front and generous verandahs at the back. No one could call us stylish.

The concept of the urban village is all the rage—there are even office blocks, not far from here, being converted into 'vertical villages'—but the claim that we're a village would seem a bit far-fetched to anyone who had ever lived in one. The dynamics of a traditional village, where frequent, incidental contact fuels a sense of neighbourliness and keeps people closely in touch, can hardly operate in a suburb like this, where most people come and go by car, serious shopping is done elsewhere and few people would travel for less than half an hour to get to work or school. But the magic happens in little pockets—a street here, a street there, or even one end of a street.

Perhaps it's happening in Winter Close: Rich Abel certainly keeps the dream of it alive. Our annual street party was all his idea, and he invariably describes trips to the local shops as 'going down to the village', though it's uphill all the way.

THREE

'I sometimes wish I'd known your mother'

There is a loud crash from the outer office. Madeleine, my loyal receptionist and secretary, is renowned for her calm disposition, but when she's roused anything can happen. It rather sounds as if she's been roused.

I peep around the door that connects our offices. 'Everything all right, Maddy?' There's no sign of broken furniture.

Maddy looks up from her computer screen and smiles without much conviction. 'Sorry, Tom. I slammed the filing cabinet drawer shut with a little more vigour than is strictly necessary, that's all. I've had Harl on the phone. It appears our fiscally challenged daughters have extracted the promise of a return airfare to London from him. Contrary to my clear instructions, needless to say. Instructions repeated on several occasions, I seem to recall.' She shrugs. 'I'm afraid they've taken that Oscar Wilde line to heart: "The longer I live the more keenly I feel that whatever was good enough for our fathers is not good enough for us". I wish I'd never quoted that to them—it was meant to amuse, not inspire. I think it's become their mantra.'

The smile has faded. 'Your four-thirty isn't coming, by the way. She rang just before Harl, sounding quite bright. I wouldn't be surprised if we never hear from her again. It's a funny business you're in—losing customers is the surest sign of your success. I predict you'll get a chirpy postcard from her in about a month, telling you she's worked everything out and she hopes you're as happy as she is. They never give you much credit, do they? Maybe you should send out recall notices for half-yearly check-ups, like my dentist does. Anyway . . . you can have an early mark if you like. There's nothing else in the book. Can you sign these letters before you go?'

I work as a counsellor in North Sydney and Maddy has been with me since the day I began in private practice. Our office is in the front half of a converted railway-workers' cottage. The owner lives in the back half and, although he pays too much attention to Maddy for her liking, the rent is reasonable, there's no agent's commission and he's a handyman who rectifies any problems promptly.

Maddy and her husband have recently moved into a city apartment. Harley is about to retire from a career that made him fabulously wealthy when he sold his small IT company to his major competitor in a very smart cash-and-equity deal. The new owner went public at precisely the right time, the value of Harley's shares increased tenfold and he sold them at their peak. The company subsequently collapsed and Harley stepped away from the wreckage into a comfortable, half-hearted consultancy. It's a very Sydney story and Harley never tires of telling it. In spite of all this wealth, Maddy, a vibrant fifty-four, is desperate to keep working.

Their twentysomething daughters seem to be causing Maddy more grief than they did as teenagers. At about the time Maddy started working for me, her younger daughter, Fiona, had quit school halfway through her second-last year, dyed her hair blue and moved in with a guitarist who was living in his parents' garage in the eastern suburbs. Both sets of parents finally objected to this arrangement and Fiona was brought home. She didn't speak to Maddy for six months.

'I know you'd love to have children, Tom, but have you thought it through? Littlies can be cute and charming, primary-schoolers can be sweet and earnest, teenagers are hair-raising but kind of fun . . . kind of. But young adults are a species of an entirely different order. We thought these two were up and away about five years ago. Now they're telling us thirty is the new twenty. Susie wants to go back to university next year to do her master's and Fi has just split up with a perfectly wonderful man whose only crime seems to have been that he admitted, under close questioning, that he wanted to marry her. Now she and Susie are off to London for a friend's book launch. Did you catch that, Tom? A friend's book launch. Knowing the friend in question, I have a feeling this event will redefine the meaning of "book". And probably "launch", as well. Harl must have rocks in his head. Well, he does have rocks in his head. We know that.'

'Any desire I might have for children is purely theoretical, Maddy, as you know. Clare wouldn't have a bar of parenthood and, well . . .'

'I know. There's no woman on your copulatory horizon. You're a mystery to me, Tom. The world is full of women looking for someone like you—warm, caring, reliable, good sense of humour, straight teeth. I don't get it.'

'Thank you, Maddy. I'll ask you for a reference if I ever need one.'

'No problem. Look, Tom, do you mind if I say something? I mean, something rather frank?'

This is unexpected. Maddy is always frank, in my experience, and never particularly reticent about speaking up. We've worked together for ten years, and she's the closest thing to a mother-figure I've got, though she'd be appalled to hear me say it. She is quite beautiful, with close-cropped grey hair, pale green eyes, and a figure that must be the envy of her own daughters. She dresses with the impeccable taste that Harley's wealth permits—stylish suits, mostly, but all carefully understated so as not to intimidate my clients, many of whom are young and far from affluent. I love her with unbounded affection, yet there's never been a hint of sexual tension between us. Maybe that's our secret.

'Go ahead. When didn't you say exactly what you think?' (Maddy was urging me to end my marriage months before Clare packed up and left.)

'I'm worried about you and that Alex woman in your street.'

'Me and that Alex woman? We happen to live in the same street, true, but we don't belong together in a sentence like that. She's married, for a start. What are you getting at?'

'Come on, Tom. You talk about her every single day. There's always something. The baby. The hopeless husband. The swishy skirts. I've never met the woman and I can tell you she's trouble.

She's playing with you. I know the type. I suspect Fi might have the same gene. It's all a game to them, Tom. You don't seem to understand that. You take everything so seriously where women are concerned. I sometimes wish I'd known your mother. She must have been a bit . . . what? Severe? Demanding? Remote? You don't seem able to handle women lightly.' Maddy pauses and unleashes one of her trademark high-voltage grins. 'Have I gone too far?'

'I think you're being a bit harsh on my mother. I was only twelve when she died, remember, and I hadn't discovered girls by then. So I don't think we can pin too much of the blame on her for whatever's supposed to be wrong with me. My memories of her are quite pleasant, quite warm. She was a nice woman, though she was a bit . . .'

'Go on. A bit what?'

'Well, I was going to say aloof, but that might be unfair. I was always being told how frail she was, so I think I learned to keep my distance too. Her death wasn't a shock. Dad and I got on with our lives.'

'But there was never another woman in his?'

'Not that I knew of. He would have been better off with a new wife, or a new someone, and I often used to wonder what it would be like to have a female in the house—especially one who was cheerful and robust, like the mother of one of my friends. I thought it would have been rather nice. At least, I think that's what I thought, but I might be projecting backwards from the present. Anyway, it didn't happen. He . . . well, he seemed almost to worship the memory of my mother. He once said he'd promised her he'd look after me, which was a strange promise to be asked to make, don't you think? What did she think he'd do? Turn wild and neglectful the moment she dropped off the twig? Or did she fear the prospect of him looking at another woman and liking what he saw? The melancholy truth is that life became easier for both of us after she went. We made more noise, went out more, ate meals on our knees in front of the TV and generally pleased ourselves. I don't know what else to say.'

Maddy smiles. 'Sign these letters and ask me out for a drink. That's something else you can say. Harl is working late—or he says he is. I think he's scared to face me after what he's done. Two tickets to London for a book launch? Those girls will take it as long as he'll hand it out. I've been telling him that for years. Why do I bother?'

'Why *do* you bother, Maddy? Come and have a drink with me and I'll explain to you why nagging never works.'

FOUR

When the hormonal tide is running, the brain is mere flotsam

My wife left me for a squadron leader, and then left him for a middle-aged hippie. The squadron leader lost his appeal when he was promoted to a desk job in Canberra and started wearing a business suit to work. Mutual friends reported that Clare couldn't stand the prospect of living in Canberra, though she and I had explored that very possibility ourselves when I once toyed with the idea of taking an academic job. So she moved to Byron Bay and has been seen by several of my friends in the company of a man in another kind of uniform: caftan, sandals and a beard. Earrings and beads have also been mentioned in dispatches.

The switch from military officer to hippie made a rough kind of sense to me, though I was irritated at the time by the intensity of my interest in the matter. Clare always said she hated war, but the squadron leader evidently managed to help her overcome any squeamishness on that subject, at least for a while. I always thought she hated beards, too, but what would I know? Ex-spouses are a notoriously unreliable source of insight into the tastes and preferences of their former partners. The filters of indifference, resentment, disappointment, grief or bewilderment effectively distort every memory: even the attractions that once drew people to each other are mostly thrown into deep shadow by the glare of rejection. It doesn't seem to matter whether you're rejecting or being rejected, those unhappy distortions still occur.

Still, I am sure of this: Clare and I were finished long before she joined forces with her squadron leader. I had known that from the moment when she stood in our kitchen, arms akimbo, eyes blazing, shouting at me that I ought to be angry with her, considering the way she had treated me, and that my continuing to behave lovingly towards her was a sure sign of mental illness.

She may have been right, by the way. When the hormonal tide is running, the brain is mere flotsam. Whether it's the rampant lust of a teenager on heat, the wild mood swings of a woman temporarily disorientated by menopause, or the seemingly inexplicable philandering of a man who, in his middle years, takes his eye off a lovely wife and children and follows his prick to the ends of the earth, the proposition that man is a rational animal is constantly challenged by the evidence of people's love-lives. My own persistence with our relationship, in the face of Clare's obvious contempt for me, arose from my unquenchable desire for her, and there's no rational explanation for that.

Even before we parted company, Clare's view of me was blurred by her simmering rage, alternating with bleak depression, that made it hard for me to recognise myself in her attacks on me. I began to wonder whether I was living in the right house, or even in the right body. Night after night, I would come home from work feeling uneasy about the kind of reception I was about to receive. By the time she left, I was postponing my homecomings for as long as possible, finding any pretext to stay late at the office, having a drink with anyone who asked me, even allowing myself to doze on the bus so I would be carried past my own stop to the terminus, where I would cheerfully pay a second fare for the pleasure of wasting time in an empty bus on the way back home.

When Clare finally left, after months of threatening, it was a relief of sorts: I don't believe anyone could tolerate, indefinitely, the strain of not knowing what kind of reception might be in store for them when they returned. But her leaving also generated a sense of failure that has shadowed me ever since—not only the obvious failure of the marriage, but my more personal failure to convey to Clare the depth of my devotion and my willingness to go on living with her, in spite of everything, in the hope that one day she would show me a flicker of corresponding tenderness. Stating it even now, I know it's absurd. I don't believe in unrequited love; love needs to be nurtured by some degree of mutuality. So how could I have maintained such a forlorn hope in the face of such relentless discouragement? Clare said it wasn't love at all: just another of my obsessions.

The most awkward aspect of all this is that, although Clare packed up and moved on more than three years ago, I still experience a dull ache in my chest when I talk about her. So I daresay she was right: I was crazy about her. Goodness knows what she thinks of me now, if she thinks of me at all.

FIVE

'That's a plastic bag, young lady. Seen one of them before?'

Winter Close hasn't escaped the impact of the regulatory mood of this society. We're as hidebound as anyone else by the need for children to wear crash helmets when they pedal their bikes around the Close, though they can hurtle up and down the street far more riskily on their skateboards and rollerblades without fear of prosecution.

We're all fully conscious of our social obligations in the matter of multiculturalism, too. We go out of our way to avoid any hint of racial overtones in our comments about Chika, or about the Nguyens in number three. In any case, the Nguyens are such a charming, exemplary family, it would be hard to think of anything unkind to say of them; though their immediate neighbours—the unflappable Joe and Enid Riley in number five—have occasionally been bold enough to describe their feelings of relief as the Nguyen girls' gradual mastery of the violin allowed their practice sessions to progress beyond endless repetitions of 'Twinkle, Twinkle, Little Star'. (Rich Abel did once remark—but only in the most general and theoretical way—that he harbours some reservations about the Suzuki method of learning to play a musical instrument.)

Our sensitivity to the new social order can also be gauged by our positively religious devotion to the recycling of garbage. Our local council has issued us all with four bins: grey for regular household garbage, to be put out weekly; green for garden waste, fortnightly; yellow for newspapers and cardboard boxes, alternate fortnights; black, for plastic and glass bottles, same schedule as the yellow. It doesn't seem particularly challenging when you spell it out, but memories are short: offhand, I couldn't tell you whether next Sunday is garden waste or papers and bottles, but the contents of the bins themselves can be a useful pointer. ('I couldn't have accumulated this many papers in one week,' you say to yourself, boosting your confidence as you gather yourself up for the trip to the front gate. 'There's a fortnight's worth there, surely.')

Observance of these rituals makes us all feel virtuous: such comprehensive regulations spark some instinct for obedience in us, and we sometimes wonder whether the garbage is handled at its destination with the same degree of finesse as we use in its sorting. This is an occasional topic of conversation on Sunday nights as we all trundle our wheelie-bins into the street at about the same time, glancing at each other's loads to check whether we've got the combinations right. A mistake by whoever gets their bins into the street first can lead us all into error: social pressure is a powerful persuader and we have occasionally received corrective phone calls from a council officer urging us to be more conscientious in our adherence to the bin roster.

Late on a Sunday evening a shadowy figure can sometimes be seen flitting from bin to bin, looking for one that's empty enough to receive the phantom dumper's overflow. We're strangely reticent about this. It would be easy enough to ask each other whether there's any excess capacity available, on occasions where one of us might have had an unusually heavy week, garbage-wise, but we prefer to leave this particular matter uncanvassed. As far as I know, no one has ever objected to having a bin topped up with someone else's garbage, but the subject is never mentioned.

But when it comes to questions of moral imperatives—to say nothing of obedience to regulations and the imposition of social constraints—dogs and their owners are unquestionably the most contentious topic around here. Years ago, when I was living on a few acres in Megalong Valley, one of my neighbours told me that the greatest single source of trouble between farmers in the district was goats. They are so hard to contain, and so destructive when they wander onto someone else's property, he had long since rid himself of his own goats because he couldn't stand the strain.

There was a murder in the valley not long after I moved out. A man's head was blown apart by a shotgun blast. Although the police were convinced there must have been a motive buried in the murk of an illicit love affair, or a business deal gone badly wrong, they never managed to cobble together any basis for laying charges. My former neighbour believes it was a simple case of a farmer's patience expiring in the face of repeated incursions by his neighbour's recalcitrant goats.

In my experience, dogs are the urban equivalent of goats. Barking, biting, jumping up and planting muddy paws on clean clothes, crapping on footpaths or neighbours' lawns, burying bones in precious flowerbeds, stealing other dogs' food . . . the scope for irritation is broad.

As far as Winter Close is concerned, no moving object attracts as much attention as a dog—on or off its leash, but especially off. These days, an unleashed dog so obviously spells trouble that you're inclined to feel sorry for the creature in case it's impounded before its hapless owner can be identified and charged with canine neglect, or social irresponsibility, or cultural degeneration, or sedition—however harshly the crime of letting a dog roam free is being defined this week.

There's an uneasy truce between Mrs Spenser (first name unknown) in number nine, golden retriever, and Samantha (surname unknown) in number four, poodle. The conflict between them erupted, as these things do, over a pile of dog turds.

I saw it all from my balcony.

Mrs Spenser, walking her retriever, Harold, spied some dog droppings on the pavement outside her house. Mrs Spenser is herself far from either fastidious or conformist, so, in the ordinary course of events, you wouldn't expect her to be too concerned by such a discovery. But there are few more potent symbols of the threat to suburban order—to which even the subversive Mrs S has adapted—than a mound of dog droppings lying unattended in a public place. If it's right outside your own house, questions form: Whose dog did this? Where is the offending animal now? More to the point, where is its owner? Where was the plastic bag when it was needed? (The plastic bag is to dog ownership what quality time is to parenthood—a symbol of commitment and acceptance of responsibility. Among dog owners, the plastic bag has been rescued from its mean status as an environmental disaster and has become a universally recognised badge of a dog owner's good breeding.)

Those are all coded questions. What they mean is: where is civilisation heading? Is urban decay inevitable?

Faced with the offending pile, Mrs Spenser didn't hesitate. She fished a plastic bag from the pocket of her tracksuit pants, bent down and scooped up the droppings, walked to the gate of number four and emptied the contents of the bag onto the footpath. She then held the soiled bag open and carefully placed it upside down over the gatepost, like a shroud. As she did so, Samantha emerged from the sideway of number four in black leather pants and a stretchy black T-shirt, an unruly mane of red hair falling around her shoulders and her poodle on its leash.

Samantha and her friend Jodie are renting number four from the Fidlers who are overseas for six months. We haven't had much of a chance to get to know them yet. That's the sort of thing we leave to the street party: by Christmas, they will have become part of the scene. When the Fidlers return and it is time for Samantha and Jodie to move on, we'll be out on the footpath—Rich and I, at least, and probably Alex too—waving them off like firm friends and declaring we'll keep in touch, though that won't be how it will turn out and we'll all privately recognise our declarations as hollow. That will be apparent from the brevity of our waving and the speed with which we turn our attention to other, more pressing matters: a flapping newspaper needing to be retrieved from the gutter, a fallen branch waiting to be snapped into pieces small enough to fit in the garden-waste bin, or local news needing to be exchanged: 'The fish shop has been taken over by a Lebanese family'. Former neighbours rarely work out as distant friends. They move on, while expecting us to stay as we were, locked in their past like photos in an album.

'What *is* that?' Samantha had stopped and was staring at the plastic bag neatly placed over her gatepost. Her poodle was leaping up enthusiastically, trying to get a better fix on the rich aroma coming from the stains inside the bag. Neither Samantha nor her dog had yet noticed the material lying on the footpath.

'That's a plastic bag, young lady. Seen one of them before?'

'I know it's a plastic bag. But, like, what's it doing there? Like, what *is* this?' Samantha looked bemused. She hadn't yet detected the anger seething in Mrs Spenser, either.

'It's so you can scoop up your dog's shit. I'm doin' you a favour, givin' you a bag.'

Samantha's gaze drifted across Mrs Spenser's face, down her arm to her pointing finger and came to rest on the little brown mound, squashed into a less well-defined shape than before, but still of unmistakable composition.

'My dog? *My* dog?'

'There are only two dogs in this street, young lady, and this ain't Harold's work.'

'Harold?' Samantha stopped short of laughing out loud at the name of Mrs Spenser's dog, but it was clearly a struggle and Mrs Spenser sensed it. Each of them had now offended the other. 'Any number of dogs walk in this street. Why pick on Zorro?'

'Zorro? You call that thing Zorro?' It's one-all in the game of what-a-silly-name-for-a-dog. Mrs Spenser no longer cared what Samantha thought of her, if she ever did.

Harold, meanwhile, had begun to show some interest in the pile of squashed turds, perhaps seeing it as a welcome distraction from the tedium of human conversation. Though it always disgusts Mrs Spenser when it happens, it's not unknown for Harold to eat his own excrement, a practice the vet has assured Mrs Spenser is both normal and harmless, and might even be healthy. She is somewhat reassured by this information, but remains utterly unreconciled to the idea of her dog eating the droppings of some unknown, alien creature. Noting Harold's mounting interest, she jerked his lead and pulled him to her other side.

Gradually, it dawned on Samantha that the pile on the path was once in the bag and that this woman standing before her had actually emptied the bag outside her front gate. The enormity of the act was difficult for her to grasp.

'You *put* that there? Like, *deliberately*?'

'Your dog, your responsibility. Clean it up.'

'I will not clean it up. You're a disgusting, *disgusting* old woman. You put it there, you clean it up yourself. It's not Zorro's. Couldn't be.' Samantha advanced through the open gateway and swung her leg as if she might be about to kick the offending matter in the general direction of Mrs Spenser.

Mrs Spenser, though poorly educated, is not unintelligent. She realised she had weakened her position by moving the dog droppings from their original position. Whoever might have been responsible for their being left on the path in the first place, she was responsible for their current position.

She narrowed her eyes. 'Are you sure?'

'Positive.'

'Well, do you have a plastic bag with you? If that dog of yours does anything, you're obliged to pick it up, you know.'

'I know.'

'So, do you?'

'What?'

'Have a plastic bag.'

'Yes.'

'Show me.'

'I'm not going to show you. What *is* this? You're unreal.'

Mrs Spenser hesitated, perhaps deciding she'd gone too far, even for her. 'Well, make sure this doesn't happen again.'

'It hasn't happened once. It can't happen again if it hasn't happened once. You're absolutely unreal. Now, would you please remove this mess you've left outside my gate . . .'

Both women looked down, but there's no mess. Harold had already cleaned it up, polished it off. The discussion had become academic.

It's hard to see how two women could become friends after such a start to their relationship, but stranger things have happened in Winter Close.

SIX

Every life is a
complete life

The great stories of human existence hum beneath the surface of every single life. Sometimes we choose to amplify them; sometimes we try to ignore them. Sometimes, foolishly and at our peril, we struggle to suppress them. If you work at it, you might achieve a pretty good imitation of a tranquil, stable, uneventful life . . . but in my experience, that's never the real story, never the *inside* story. The big themes—love, pain, chronic insecurity, growth, disappointment, disillusionment, hope, faith, loneliness, tenderness, courage, frustration, betrayal, despair, joy, death—are always there, lying in wait, ready to seize the right moment to claim our attention.

A tax accountant feels everything a poet feels, even if the emotional hues are not labelled with as much facility in one case as the other. The subtleties and varieties of the emotional life are as rich in a jockey as a judge, the foibles as irrational in a banker as a priest.

Every client who comes to me for counselling—like almost everyone I meet—carries their shadow with them, though the presenting problem may not be consciously tragic or seem particularly serious. Even when the person has a bubbly disposition and the capacity to see the funny side of life, the unfolding story invariably exposes a substrate of grief or distress, yearning or despair. Sometimes it's the death of a child; sometimes the anguish of estrangement from a loved one; sometimes—often—the sense of never being taken quite seriously enough. The calibrations of grief vary from case to case, and so do its consequences, but there's a central story that almost always emerges: the story of people searching for ways to live with private pain.

It's so fundamental, it might be an inescapable consequence of the human sense of mortality. But, mostly, you don't have to aim so high for an explanation; you can find its cause in quite specific events in people's lives. The mystery is not usually why they are troubled, but how they managed not merely to absorb the blows that life has rained on them, but to triumph, to strike out in new directions, to keep smiling at people who lie beyond the horizon of their grief. For instance, how do you learn to live with the memory of a child who suicided on the very threshold of adulthood? How do you rebuild your life, as one of my clients has done, after losing first one, then another wife to cancer?

I'm never much help with any of this. I mostly feel like a bystander—interested and supportive, but ultimately powerless. I'm constantly amazed, though, by the strength of the human spirit.

My neighbours in Winter Close are at least as fertile a source for these reflections as any cases that come to my consulting room: the Stuthridges, for instance—long-term residents at number one.

Brian Stuthridge is more reclusive than his wife, but neither of them seems comfortable with the rest of us: they've not attended a single street party in the eight years I've been living here. Although Mrs Stuthridge will pass the time of day with you if you meet her at the local shops, she fends off even the most tentative enquiries about her husband. Brian himself leaves the house each morning by car—his driving calculated to achieve the opposite effect to Chika's—and returns home after dark, summer and winter. He sometimes appears in the front garden on weekends, head down and a beanie pulled low over both ears, but he scurries inside if anyone approaches.

The Nguyens, in number three, seem perplexed by the remoteness of the Stuthridges. Their next-door neighbours on the other side, Joe and Enid Riley in number five, are closer to the Nguyens' ideal of Australian neighbourliness: warm, accessible, responsive, but never intrusive. Mrs Nguyen, in a disarmingly self-deprecatory moment, once told me she would be quite pleased if Brian would complain about her children's violin practice: at least that would be a form of contact. But he's never complained about anything to any of us. Most of us have never even heard the sound of his voice.

Walking home from the shops together, Mrs Stuthridge and I occasionally engage in some inconsequential chat. Reacting to her wariness, I try to stick to safe, neutral topics. But on a recent Friday afternoon, she is far from wary. Dressed in a claret-coloured overcoat that seems too hot and heavy for this early summer evening, and wearing a matching beret reminiscent of Brian's beanie, she fixes me with a searching gaze, as if she'd never taken in my appearance before.

'You're a counsellor, aren't you? People talk to you about their . . . difficulties?'

The knowledge that I'm a counsellor encourages all kinds of people—even the most casual aquaintances—to unburden themselves to me at inconvenient times and in unlikely places. At least Mrs Stuthridge is a neighbour; the thread of connection is often more tenuous than that. I was once pinned to the wall in the change room of the local squash courts by a man wanting to give me his side of a very messy divorce story. Rich had introduced us and happened to mention my line of work. Do people who have chance encounters with accountants describe their financial affairs with the same recklessness? Do they bare their teeth to dentists they meet on a train? My mother used to say she was the kind of person people often spoke to spontaneously—at a bus stop or in a supermarket queue or sitting in the cinema—and she found it a bit of a burden. Perhaps I've inherited that talk-to-me look from her, or perhaps it's one of the professional hazards of the counsellor.

I usually try to deflect these overtures by suggesting that personal matters are better discussed in the context of a proper professional relationship, but Mrs Stuthridge gives me no time for such niceties. She is quickly into her story.

An old school friend had called on Brian, without warning, the previous weekend. Brian was in the garden and when he saw someone coming along the footpath, he ducked inside as usual. It's unclear whether he had recognised the visitor or not: slithering out of sight is his standard response to the sight of anyone approaching his front fence. It was left to Mrs Stuthridge to answer the door.

Brian had retreated to his workroom (his wife's rather ambiguous term), locked the door, and flatly refused to emerge. The friend had been understanding, according to Mrs Stuthridge; he remained seated in the lounge room, reading a magazine, while she busied herself with the preparation of afternoon tea, knocking on the bedroom door at intervals and softly entreating Brian to come out. He neither answered nor appeared.

Mrs Stuthridge had explained to the friend that Brian was unwell, but she knew he was unconvinced. Brian's behaviour must have suggested to his former friend that he was very unwell indeed, though perhaps not in the way Mrs Stuthridge had meant to suggest. Eventually, the friend wrote Brian a note, sealed it in an envelope supplied by Mrs Stuthridge and left. He gave no reason for making the visit and made no proposal for any further contact.

Mrs Stuthridge has not learnt what was in the note. Brian has not referred to the visit and refuses to say anything about his relationship with the visitor.

'I know what this is about,' Mrs Stuthridge says to me, her voice heavy with resignation, distress or embarrassment—I can't tell which; it might be all three. She stops and places a plastic shopping bag on the ground while she wipes her nose with the back of her hand and tugs at her beret. 'He's ashamed. Ashamed of everything. He's ashamed of his missing teeth but won't do anything about it. He's ashamed of his career, considering he was one of the brightest boys in his class at school. He's ashamed of me—oh, yes, that's nothing new. He makes no secret of his loathing. But I'm nothing. What he's really ashamed of is his life. No, that's not right either. He's ashamed of . . . himself. Yes, that's it. Himself.'

'Yet you stay together. There's something . . .'

'Why would I stick around when I know he loathes me? Is that what you're asking?' She picks up the shopping bag and we walk on.

'Well, it's none of my . . .'

'I think we need each other. That's all. Who else have we got? Brian hasn't got another living soul in the world, apart from me. I've got a few cousins somewhere, but Brian—zilch. Never knew his father. His mother died when he was still a little boy and his grandmother cared for him until he left school and got a job. Then he was on his own. No parents or grandparents. No brothers or sisters. No uncles or aunts. No cousins. And no children of our own. One of us couldn't have them and we were never interested enough to find out which, to tell you the truth Once I realised what Brian was like, I became terrified of the possibility of children. I took steps. That all seems a very long time ago.'

We have arrived at the gate of number one and Mrs Stuthridge is weeping silently but copiously. Both hands are weighted by plastic shopping bags and her tears course down her cheeks without restraint, dripping off her chin. I reach out to put a comforting hand on her arm, but she backs away and pushes the gate open with a practised thrust of the hip. I wait on the footpath and watch her walk to her front door. She puts her shopping bags down, fishes for the key, opens the door, and carries all but one of the bags inside. A moment later she reappears, picks up the remaining bag and closes the door behind her without looking in my direction. She is firmly back in her world.

SEVEN

Australians like to pretend their hearts are in the bush

Most Australians live in the suburbs. We might dream of the rural life and we might like to pretend our hearts are in the bush, but the truth is that Australians are a suburban people. The sooner we admit it, the sooner we can get on with making the most of it.

Rich Abel doesn't agree with any of that. At least he says he doesn't agree, but where does he live? Where does he *choose* to live, in spite of his endless talk about moving to the bush? He would say he is forced to live in the suburbs, because of his job, but he would prefer to live in the country. He hates it when I suggest we choose to live wherever we're living.

He's standing in the middle of his backyard—tall and solid with lush, wavy hair that's prematurely white—revelling in his mastery of the rituals of a Sunday barbecue. This is an unexpected situation for me: Rich and I occasionally meet somewhere for lunch, but

I've never been to his home for a meal. We're neighbours, not the kind of friends who visit each other by invitation.

'Doctor Ruth is tossing a salad. Why don't you drag the cork out of that bottle for me, and I'll focus on the serious business of the steaks. Rare or medium? Don't say "well done". This is a barbecue, not a crematorium.'

'Medium is fine. The dark side of medium, if your imagination can stretch that far,' I say, wondering where the little Abels are hiding. I was looking forward to seeing Laura especially, though there's always a certain pleasure in saying Humbold's name out loud.

Rich is showing off a handsome new barbecue unit, set in a red cedar trolley that can be wheeled to any part of the garden. He claims that's why I've been invited, to christen it, but it's clear something else is on his mind. Rich is rarely edgy, but something is troubling him this bright Sunday.

I can't help speculating. Perhaps Rich and Ruth have hit a turbulent patch in their marriage: almost everyone does, sooner or later. They know I'm in the counselling business and they might be planning to ease the conversation around to an enquiry about whether I'd be prepared to take them on as clients (I wouldn't: next-door neighbours as clients would not be a good idea) or, if not, whether I could recommend someone sensational. It would have to be someone sensational; this is Rich Abel and Doctor Ruth we're talking about. Perfection in marriage, perfection in divorce, if that's what's looming. But what might the trouble be? Has Rich grown tired of marriage? Or is he ready to put his longstanding threat to move to the country into practice, solo? Has suburbia finally ground him down, as he always said it would if you didn't fight it? Possible. Unlikely.

Perhaps it's Ruth. Perhaps she's met someone else. Hard to imagine, though. Wife and mother is such a big part of who she is; what makes her proud. When it comes to The Family, I'd have said Ruth is a believer. Could be something unexpected, though, like . . . a woman. Perhaps Ruth is having a sexual identity crisis. She's in love with a woman, wants this woman to move in with her and the kids—perhaps even with Rich too—and Rich is shattered. That would be enough to unsettle even the unflappable Rich. Wife runs off with lesbian lover. Not uncommon, in my professional experience. Certainly not uncommon in the circles Rich moves in, though maintaining a spouse and a gay lover, simultaneously, is more the go. (A friend who was born in Hobart used to enjoy saying that homosexuality was illegal in Tasmania, but compulsory in Sydney.) Come to think of it, last time we had lunch together in North Sydney, Rich was ruminating at length about the effect on a colleague of the discovery that his wife of twenty years had fallen in love with another woman and 'come out' as a lesbian. Perhaps that's where I got this idea from.

'Better than having her go off with another fella, I suppose,' Rich had said to me, hoping to sound rational, though his heart didn't seem to be in it. 'If a wife swapped sides, that'd be a whole lot better than . . . well, I don't know. Mike says it's easier to understand, so I guess I can see his point. It's not as if she grew tired of one man and fell for . . . well, I don't know.'

But Doctor Ruth? Anything's possible: who knows that better than I? My files are choked with the stories of people who thought this—whatever 'this' might turn out to be—could never happen to them.

Perhaps she's fallen for a patient. Wife runs off with lesbian lover *and* doctor has affair with patient. Double whammy. Could be. Why not? That would be enough to explain Rich's uncharacteristic edginess.

Settle down, Tom: this is too fanciful by half. If it's a marital problem, it'll be a boringly predictable one. Rich wants sex more often than Ruth does. Or Ruth wants more 'space'. (I'm no stranger to that one, in and out of the consulting room: for 'space' read 'distance' and preferably lots of it.) Ruth feels she's on the up escalator while Rich is on the down—the famous oestrogen effect. Once they're released from the grind of producing it, many women feel as if they could fly. But is Ruth old enough to be menopausal?

Rich could be a cross-dresser. That's too heavy for a lot of women to handle. Or it could be drugs. It would be a miracle if Rich didn't dabble, and Doctor Ruth would never approve. Rich is usually the fascist, Ruth the bleeding heart. But drugs would be different.

No, it's probably something about fairness. Managing their money, perhaps, or the division of domestic labour, or the length and frequency of holidays and whether one or other of them is entitled to an occasional break away from the kids. ('But I thought you loved the kids. I thought we were a family. Since when are we slinking off by ourselves for a break from the kids? Is that what you mean, or do you *really* mean a break from *me*? If that's what you mean, why don't you have the guts to say so? Why hide behind the kids? Anyway, the kids will be grown up and gone before you know it, so don't talk about having a break from them. Any minute, they'll be wanting a break from *us*.' I can hear it now.)

Those are common enough stumbling blocks. The stuff that seems trivial and easy to fix often turns out to be lethal to a marriage. It's surprising how often people seem to take the big problems in their stride—the glaringly obvious incompatibilities that strike an outsider as grotesque. I often see couples who appear so deeply unsuited to each other, it's hard to imagine how they ever managed to get together in the first place—let alone live together for years and produce several children. None of the huge differences in style or values, or even a lack of common interests, have defeated them (partly because, as they often claim, 'we're so good for each other in bed'). Then it turns out they've reached a point of intractable difficulty over who will cook dinner on Thursdays when they both have to work late. Why don't they eat out on Thursdays, you want to ask, but the thing has escalated into such a passionate conflict, such a matter of hotly contested principle, that a rational solution would never be acceptable. Someone has to be seen to *give in*. It makes you wonder whether those deep incompatibilities were eating away at the marriage all along but were too big to confront, until they were eventually compressed into something small enough to focus on. Or perhaps there is such a thing as marriage fatigue that creeps up on people unawares, seeping into their systems, until some tiny dispute causes them to realise they've finally had enough of someone they once loved with utter devotion. (I've never had the chance to test that theory on myself: my own marriage didn't survive for long enough to get to that stage.)

It's clear from the silence in the house that the children are not at home. This is going to be a barbecue à trois. So, have the children been sent to Ruth's parents for the day, or the weekend, while Rich and Ruth have it out, whatever 'it' may be?

Ruth emerges from the house carrying a huge salad bowl and a bottle of dressing. She greets me warmly and smiles at Rich with a look of such unalloyed affection that I am momentarily rattled. I realise I'm jealous: I'd like someone to smile at me like that, in a way that Clare never did. But I'm being made aware of the improbability of my various speculations upon the state of this marriage. These two are clearly in tune; their secret harmonies are almost audible.

'Have you told Tom about our little problem?' Ruth enquires. Ah.

'Let's eat first, shall we?' Rich is intent on his cooking: nothing will be charred in this backyard. 'Time enough for Mrs Spenser after we've done justice to that bottle of red.'

Ruth turns to me with an ambiguous shrug.

'Poor thing,' says Rich. 'She's submitted plans to the council for a huge second-storey extension that is so absurd, so over the top, Ruth and I will have to oppose it. But we need your support: two letters of complaint are better than one. We might persuade Alex to weigh in, too.'

Oh.

'Frankly, Tom, I think the old lady might be losing her grip. I know Alzheimer's is overworked as an explanation for any odd behaviour in people over a certain age, but the signs aren't good in her case. Anyhow, let's enjoy lunch first and then we'll show you a copy of what she's proposing. You'll see at once it's outrageous.'

Rich looks edgily at his wife. 'Nuts,' he says, almost defiantly. 'The woman's gone nuts. This is what I mean about suburbia, Tom. This sort of thing couldn't happen—*couldn't happen*—when you're out on acres somewhere.'

I decide this isn't the moment to tell him about the goats in Megalong Valley or to remind him about a famous pig-farm controversy in the Hunter. When it comes to rural fantasies, Henry Lawson and Banjo Paterson have a lot to answer for. I can't understand why Rich hasn't bought a four-wheel drive.

EIGHT

'Poetry can save you from everything'

'Do you ever write poetry yourself? Do you ever read it? Come in. I want to show you something I wrote this morning.'

I follow Alex down the garden path of number seven and enter her house via the tiny front porch. She is in bare feet under a long black satin skirt and a floral tank-top that exposes her midriff. Her blonde ponytail bobs and sways behind her, brushing the smooth skin of her back and shoulders. Her baby is asleep in a bassinet in the hallway and Alex puckers her lips in a silent 'Shh!' as we tiptoe past.

She leads me into the kitchen and offers me a chair at a big pine table on which there's a bowl of fruit, a pile of unopened mail and a laptop. The kitchen flows into an airy sunroom that was once an open back verandah: like most houses in Winter Close, this one has been renovated and modified over the years. Chika and Alex have only been living here for about twelve months, but they've already spent a great deal of money on the place. The back garden has been extensively paved and landscaped and looks a picture—as does Alex herself, I can't help noticing, apparently unruffled by the absence of Chika or the circumstances of his sudden departure from the scene. (No one has heard anything; no one is asking questions.)

Alex hits the spacebar on her laptop and looks up at me, her chin resting on lightly clenched fists and her lips forming a tiny smile. 'So, do you?'

'Do I what?'

'Ever write poetry?'

'Everyone does, don't they, at some point in their lives? Love poems. Adolescent angst. I did when I was much younger, but not now. Not for years.'

'You should. You've no idea how therapeutic it can be. No one else ever has to see it—it can be completely private if you want it to be. I recommend it. And I think you need it, if you don't mind me saying so. Sometimes I think you look far too serious for your own good, as if you need a laugh. Something to lighten the load a bit. Am I right? Oh, are you offended?'

'No. Not at all. Well, a bit, I suppose. A bit. I don't like the idea of appearing to be so serious. Not grumpy, I hope? But I know what you're saying and I agree with you. Everybody needs an outlet, preferably creative. Poetry is good. Singing. Painting. That's the kind of the business I'm in, you know. Therapy. Counselling. Helping people to express themselves.'

'Oh, yes, I know that. Everyone knows that. I mean everyone in the street knows that. It's quite a little village, isn't it? We all know each other. We all watch over each other. Watching,

watching. Not so good, do you think, being too close to your neighbours? I need space, myself. I'd love to live somewhere in the country . . .'

'You should talk to Rich. He feels the same way. I think it's a dangerous fantasy myself. This is where we live, so let's live here. Why not? Surely it's not where you live but how you live that counts?'

'Oh, Mister Sobersides! You're much too rational for me. Too clever by half. You might be right, but I like to dream. People tell me I have a highly active imagination. I can see the very place— a little village somewhere, a vegie patch, chooks.'

'You could have a vegie patch here. This is like a little village here in the Close—you said so yourself.'

'You didn't believe me, though. Not from the look on your face. And I didn't mean it, anyway. One street isn't a village. I know that. I mean a lovely little country town—a row of shops, a School of Arts, wise old men on verandahs with pipes and rheumy eyes, a dusty drive to the nearest big centre. Oh, and a school for Jemma. A little one-teacher village school. What's the matter?'

'Nothing's the matter. I'm smiling with pleasure. It sounds very Kenneth Slessor-ish. Didn't he write a poem about an out-of-date poster promoting some long-forgotten entertainment, stuck up outside a School of Arts and "sprayed with the sarcasm of flies"?'

'Yes, but you've forgotten the nice bit: "left there, less from carelessness / than from a wish to seem polite." Don't you think that's lovely? Less from carelessness than from a wish to seem polite? Different values, see. A different pace of life altogether. "Verandahs baked with musky sleep / Mulberry faces dozing deep"?' Alex closes her eyes and purrs her approval.

'It's a lovely picture, Alex, I agree. Sure. You can see those Schools of Arts in country towns all over Australia. They're a poignant reminder of . . . something. Hot, slow afternoons? Or a time when country towns took themselves more seriously than they do today? But most of them have become bric-a-brac shops, or tea rooms, or . . . nothing at all. They were once a sign of hope and confidence, but what are they a sign of now? I hate to sound like a wet blanket, but I think the moment might have passed, unless you want to join the dole queue in some virtual ghost town. There are plenty of those. You can find quasi-rural bliss on the coast, north and south of here, but most of that is an extension of Sydney's suburbs. I doubt if that's where you'd find the town of your dreams, *SeaChange* notwithstanding. You'd need to head inland. But what about flies and drought and commodity prices? What about rural services collapsing all over the country? What about the mass exodus of young people to cities—all those families having to split up? You might be happy in some struggling little hamlet, under-populated and underresourced, but, frankly, I doubt it. You're not a country girl, are you? You might be happier right where you are, you know. We've got something akin to our own School of Arts up the road—the community hall. And what about the amphitheatre? Have you been to any productions there? The Crag has its own charm, you know. Every suburb has a heritage. You only have to look for it. And at least we have a bank. Would your village have a bank?'

'Why do men always have to try so hard to sound sensible and rational? You know exactly what I'm saying. You're just like Chika—except you're not in gaol, of course.'

'Is Chika . . .'

'On remand. Change the subject, please. I don't want to cry. Not when I'm about to read you my poem. Poetry can save you from everything, you know.'

The poem is on her laptop and Alex straightens her back and squares her shoulders as she reads.

Clearing fresh bebop juice, hang willow down
Raking fresh rainbow leaves, dew-dappled crown

She looks up. 'So?'

I look away.

'Don't be a wimp. If you don't get it, say so. I don't mind. I love it. It really, really sings to me. Really sings. It's exactly the tone I wanted to create, and that doesn't often happen. To me, it's got that real country feel. I can smell it, practically. The leaves, the dew, the *juice*? The only thing is, it might flow too easily. What do you think? Our teacher told us that Dylan Thomas used to write what he wanted to say, then randomly rearrange the words to make the reader work harder. Or to make himself appear smarter and more . . . what? Abstruse? Obscure? Maybe I should try that.' Alex allows the ghost of a frown to flit across her entirely unlined brow. 'So, what do you think?'

'Well, I . . . Bebop juice?'

'God, don't tell me you're a literalist. Can't you imagine bebop juice? Like, some crazy, complex thing—some wild potion that makes your head spin? Squeeze it from a bebop plant, if you must. God, there, I've practically killed it trying to explain it to you. Just let it sing to you.

'I wonder if maybe you think too much, Tom. It's possible, you know. You often look to me like a person who could think too much. Anyway, our creative writing teacher said we should put in one totally amazing, totally unexpected word every now and then, to totally arrest the reader. Mine was bebop.'

'You've done that all right. It worked for me. I was totally arrested. Definitely.'

'All my stuff's derivative, I know that. Bit of the old Gerard Manley H, bit of Slessor, sure, bit of Brian Ferry, probably. I play his stuff when I write, so it's bound to rub off. My poetry always rhymes, though. That's not good, but I can't help it. My teacher says I'll have to break the habit. Rhyming comes naturally to me, I'm afraid. I'm a bit with Robert Frost: "Writing free verse is like playing tennis with the net down." Do you play tennis, by the way?'

'Bit like writing poetry. I did, but I don't now.'

'You make yourself sound like a spent force. I think I might need to invest some time in you. You should take a leaf out of Brian's book.'

'Brian?'

'Brian. You know Brian. Lives at number one. Brian and . . . I don't know his wife's name. He's always putting poems in my letterbox.'

I receive this information like a blow. I don't know why, but it has an unpleasant, unsettling effect on me. 'Brian Stuthridge? A poet? Writes you poems?'

'Let's me see them. He doesn't write them *to* me. Give me a break. He showed up at the Leisure Centre a couple of times. That's how I met him actually, not that he said anything much and I couldn't understand him anyway. He's never spoken to me since. But he writes. *He writes.* You should try it, you know.'

'Perhaps I should.' I'm still struggling to comprehend the idea of Brian Stuthridge, tucked away in that house, refusing to engage with his neighbours, quietly sapping his wife's patience and destroying her hopes, and . . . writing *poetry?*

'I'll take that as a yes.'

'Take it as a maybe.'

'I think you need to commit. Less thinking about things, more commitment. That's my advice for this morning, Tom.'

'Is his stuff any good? Brian's?' I'm wondering if Mrs Stuthridge would feel better or worse if she knew she was married to a poet. Perhaps she'd be grateful to Alex for encouraging him, if that's what she does.

'Any good? Wrong, wrong, wrong. Wrong question. Don't be so judgmental. He's writing, isn't that enough? We're never allowed to say we like or dislike each other's work in my creative writing class. What would be the point of that? People are peeling off their skin and letting themselves spill onto the page and you want to know if it's any good? Get a grip, Tom. Anyway, listen to this new one of mine one more time and then I'll make you some coffee. Don't think. Let it, like, sweep you along. It'll take you with it if you let yourself go.'

It's impossible not to be enchanted by Alex and her earnestness, but I feel an urge to postpone the second reading. 'One other thing, Alex. Dew-dappled crown. It was "crown" you said, not "brown"? Dew-dappled crown? I was wondering . . .' I shouldn't have asked. Alex rolls her eyes and shuts the lid of her laptop. But she's still smiling.

'Poetry can only save you if you let it. See if coffee helps. I might put some bebop juice in it. You're a man in need of a kick.'

When will I ever learn? If Alex had shown me a new baby, would I have asked evasive questions about it, wondering if perhaps its eyes weren't a bit too close together, or too far apart; tentatively enquiring whether the ears were quite as symmetrical as they might be? No. So why would I risk offending her by asking *any* questions about her new poem. *Her* poem. Her *creation*. Her baby.

Perhaps I spend too much energy trying to avoid hypocrisy. What's wrong with a little hypocrisy? Why has it become the cardinal sin, all of a sudden? Is it any worse than being hurtful? The choice is simple: admire the poem insincerely—lie—or criticise the poem and hurt the poet. It's not much of a choice, especially when it's a poem created on the kitchen table of an engaging, troubled young mother whose husband is in prison awaiting trial.

'Alex,' I say, hoping it's not too late, 'I do admire your poem. I can see there's beauty in it. Your feelings are in it. I—I like it.'

'Lighten up, Tom. You don't get it at all and you don't realise that's okay. You're trapped in the idea that not getting it must be the same as not liking it. You'll learn the difference one day. But it's very sweet of you to say you like it. I'll take that as a compliment—not to the poem, but to me. I'll interpret that as meaning you've decided to take me seriously, after all. That's a start, isn't it?'

NINE

How could my own feelings fluctuate so wildly between enchantment and loathing?

I suppose I ought to say this: my devotion to my wife was not as uncritical at the time as I sometimes hear myself describing it in retrospect. When I said that our emotional filters distort our recollections of people who have rejected us (or those whom we have rejected), I made it sound as if those filters are always negative. But they can be positive too. I hear myself talking about Clare—how much I loved her, how boundless my devotion was, how heartless she was to leave me for that sleazy squadron leader—and I know I make myself sound more wounded, more noble, or possibly more pathetic, than I felt at the time.

The truth—or, at least, another twig in the bundle of contradictions that passes for truth—is that, when we were together, I would sometimes find myself sitting across the dining table from Clare, or lying beside her in bed, and feeling something so close to hatred that if I'd had to give it a name, that's the word

I would have chosen. But it wasn't hatred exactly. It was a curious mixture of things: loathing, fury, impatience, resentment, regret, even envy. Sometimes I felt as if it was an effort to restrain myself from actually reaching out and hitting her. Instead I would settle for silently, inwardly chanting 'you bitch, you bitch', over and over like a mantra of hate, as a way of safely channelling my feelings so they seemed to be both contained and expressed. Waves of such intense negativity would wash over me that I would wonder how I could ever have summoned up feelings of affection, let alone love.

Later—it might be moments or it might be days—the certainty of love would return, sometimes with a rush of bewildering passion, and I would ask her inane questions: 'Are you okay, Clare? Is everything all right? You haven't seemed yourself.' (In truth, she was being absolutely herself; the inconstancy was all mine.) Even while I was asking, I knew the real question was this: how could my own feelings fluctuate so wildly between enchantment and loathing? It was as though I was living with two different women— or was she living with two different men? If she sensed my treachery, she never let on. But perhaps that's why she went, in the end; perhaps she knew precisely how much hate coexisted with my love. If I'd ever had so much as a hint that she harboured such dark feelings about me as I did about her, I would certainly have left, squadron leader or no squadron leader.

Clare once asked me what I'd do if she left me. Without thinking, I said, 'Reorganise the pantry'. It was an unwise thing to say, despite being true. A more complete and generous answer would have acknowledged the prospect of searing, shattering grief.

Strangely enough, when she left, I did reorganise the pantry— that very evening—though that's not as heartless or insensitive as it sounds: she'd cleared out with half the tins and packets in the cupboard, so it was as much a matter of restocking in a hurry as introducing some order into the chaos that Clare contrived as a symbol of her longed-for spontaneity.

TEN

Rich looks like a man with more on his mind than student evaluations

'I think I'll have the trout and salmon, but you should try the quail.'

Rich Abel and I are having one of our occasional lunches together at Audrey's in North Sydney. As this one is taking place in late November the main item on the agenda is supposed to be the street party. Every year, Rich likes to plan things carefully, suggesting who should prepare what food, whose home should be the focal point for serving drinks and what kind of music should be played over whose sound system. The planning is largely irrelevant to the event itself: every year, it descends into enjoyable anarchy, though it's possible that Rich believes he has it under control. Perhaps it's enough for him to know that it wouldn't happen at all if he didn't nip at our heels. We're a bit like sheep in need of Rich's sheepdog-like approach, and perhaps it doesn't matter to him if we end up in the wrong pen.

As usual, Audrey's is full of advertising and PR types—mostly young, mostly male, bristling with mobiles and Palm Pilots and pagers, and shouting across tables at each other. The floor is paved with terracotta tiles and the walls are bagged bricks, painted white. There are no soft furnishings of any kind—not even tablecloths—so the noise is awful, but the food is worth it. Every time we come here, Rich explains the theory that leads people to raise their voices in a crowd, instead of the preferable strategy of speaking more softly so everyone can be heard without their throats being ravaged.

He always orders for both of us so he can extend his gustatory ambit beyond the boundaries of his own plate. His marauding fork darts out at regular intervals, making lightning raids on my food. I've raised the hygiene issue with him, but he waves it away. (What am I worrying about? Rich spits so much when he is in full cry that an alien fork poked into my quail is the least of my worries.)

'You wouldn't believe what's going on in universities. The bean counters have finally taken over. It's like a coup. The academics are in disarray. Get this—we're being asked to put numbers on the efficiency of each member of the department, me included. Numbers. There's a fucking formula, believe it or not. Number of students enrolling, students' grades, ratio of drop-outs to stayers. Plus, *plus*—here's the cream of the joke, only it isn't funny: student evaluations. Stu-dent e-val-u-a-tions! Get it? Our performance is being appraised by our own students, based on a questionnaire developed by some human resources geek who's still wet behind the ears. Those figures go into the black box along with all the other bumf and, hey presto, out comes your magic number. You're in or you're out. Your salary is increased or it isn't. You're a serious proposition—serious in their terms, that is—or you're not. You're a satisfactory human being, or you're not.'

'My clients vote with their feet. Same thing, in a way.'

'Same thing? *Same thing?* I can't believe you're saying that, Tom. Same thing? Whose side are you on?'

'I can see it's open to abuse, but—'

'Shut the fuck up, Tom. You don't know what the hell you're saying. This is not like your customers—clients, whatever—coming or going. You decide whether to stay in business, right? You do your own sums, right? No offence, but you're in business. You put yourself out there. I'm not in business. I'm a serious academic person and I live for my research. It's good research and I don't care whether the students or the bean counters or the fucking vice-chancellor think so.'

In seven years of being Rich's next-door neighbour, I've never heard him talk like this, never once seen him out of control.

'The other thing is, the bureaucrats don't listen. There was supposed to be consultation, but no one's seen any sign of it. Plenty of meetings, but they're for showing us the tablets they brought down from the mountain. No one listens to you. I'm no expert on all this stuff—I just want to get on with my research, frankly—but I can see where it's taking us. People are going to play the system: tell more jokes, butter up the students. Marketing—that's the name of the game. Market your courses! Smarten up your presentation skills! Turn the place into a charm school. Marketing my *arse.* You know the latest? Staff are applying to switch to online courses in droves. And why not? No face-to-face teaching—less sweat, for a start—and the students' ratings tend to be more favourable because they've got less to go on.'

Rich makes an angry lunge at my plate. According to Rich, Doctor Ruth never lets him swear at home; she'd faint if she heard this conversation.

'The bush beckons, Tom. I'm getting out of here, setting myself up on a little place. I won't have to tolerate any of this type of bullshit.'

For a well-educated man—a serious scientist—Rich's blind spot about rural living is extraordinary. Compared with the vagaries of the weather, his bean counters would be a pushover.

'I know what you're thinking. Out of the frying pan . . . *And* I know you think I overplay the village thing. But look, it's all about control, Tom. I want to be in control. I admit it. I'd settle quite happily for being a big fish in a little pond, believe it or not. I have no ambition to run the country, or even the university. I want to get on with my life in an environment that's shaped by me, and no one else. If I fail, I want to be the one doing the failing. Get it?'

I nod. There's nothing to be said on this subject that Rich and I haven't debated a dozen times over the side fence, though it occurs to me that the situation in Rich's department at the university, serious though it undoubtedly is, hardly justifies the full extent of his evident emotional disarray. Rich looks to me like a man with more on his mind than student evaluations. Even his ritual remarks about the rural life seem to have a new edge to them—bitterness, perhaps, or despair? I'm not sure.

Rich swoops on the remains of my vegetables and calls for the dessert menu. 'What about Mrs Spenser's extension?' I ask, more to change the subject than out of real interest. It's clear she'll get approval for her second storey, however outrageous Doctor Ruth might think the plans. I went along with her objections, as relayed to me by Rich, but my heart wasn't in it.

I can see there might be some discomfort in living, as the Abels soon will, in a bungalow wedged between two double-storey houses (neither of them vast or grand, by the way), but the edge has been taken off Ruth's objections by her own endless ruminations about extensions: 'Should we go up or out?' has been a recurring theme, according to Rich, and Ruth herself has outlined the options to me on several occasions across our side fence. If they are going to extend, they'd better get on with it: too many people seem to dither for so long that they create wonderful spaces for their children to enjoy at precisely the time when the children are thinking of moving out—or spending as much time as possible away from home. A friend once proudly took me on a tour of his extensions—itself a very Sydney thing to do. Panelled walls and a cathedral ceiling enclosed a vast and silent space that housed a ping-pong table *and* a billiard table, plus wall-projection TV and full wraparound sound . . . and not a teenager in sight. He called it the rumpus room without a hint of irony.

Rich shakes his head and takes a generous gulp from his glass of red. Sitting opposite him for an hour, I notice that his physical shape is not as good as it was. His face is puffy and sallow and his paunch more pronounced. He hasn't suggested golf for months.

'What can I say? Doctor Ruth can jump up and down all she likes, but a thing like this puts all that stuff into perspective.'

'A thing like—'

'The university. The assessments. Haven't you been paying attention? I thought you were the master of the listening art. Counsellor's stock in trade, am I right?'

'Sorry. Of course.'

'Five point seven.'

I raise my eyebrows.

'Five point seven, on a ten-point scale. Five point fucking seven.'

'Your assessment?'

'Five point seven. I've been in this particular job for nearly twelve years. Theoretically, I've got about twenty good years left in me. I've had a couple of modest breakthroughs in my research, some good reviews of my book, more journal articles than you could poke a stick at. Three of my graduate students have been offered plum posts overseas—prestigious stuff. Five point seven. Do you have any idea what that means?'

'I can see it's disappointing. It's unfair.'

Rich dismisses my attempt at sympathy with a curt wave of the hand.

'I'll tell you what it means. Five point seven is borderline. No salary increase, research funds frozen *and* I'm on probation. I'll say it slowly, Tom. I'm on probation. Can you believe that? A man in my position? Could be worse, I know—I could have been downgraded. That's happening, you know. Lecturers becoming tutors. The indignity of it is incredible. I've seen colleagues in tears.'

'What does Ruth think?'

'You think I'd tell Ruth? I'm a hero to Ruth, believe it or not. She loves being married to a scientist. She talks about my work to the kids. Shows them my book. Humbold already wants my job when he grows up. You think I'd tell her? I'll tell her if things change, if I need to look around. Any luck, we'll have gone bush before it gets to that.'

'You're serious.'

'You bet I'm serious. If there's one thing I can't stand—never could stand—it's not being in control of my own destiny. Five point seven. It's a bit like having one of your balls torn off.'

As we leave the restaurant and walk to Rich's car, he puts an arm around my shoulder, another thing he's never done. 'Thanks for supporting Ruth over the Spenser caper. The old lady won't love you for it, but these things pass. She'll get her approval. Anyway, she's still asking Ruth for free medical advice, so there you go. Oh, we didn't discuss the arrangements for the street party. I'll pop over one night. I'd like to get it properly organised this year. Last year, as I recall, things got a bit out of hand. You have to watch Upton—heart of gold, but a bugger when he's pissed.'

'I think that's Socrates,' I venture, recalling the philosophers' song from Monty Python's Flying Circus, but the reference is lost on Rich. He is devoted to US sitcoms and shows no interest at all in my old BBC tapes.

We reach Rich's car and he offers to drive me to my office, but I decline: I'll enjoy the ten-minute walk and, in Rich's present state of edginess and anger, I'd rather not be in a car with him at the wheel.

ELEVEN

'Why do people have to talk about the suburbs as if living there is an admission of social or cultural failure?'

'I'm worried about Rich.'

Maddy is used to my ruminations on the people who populate Winter Close. She seems to welcome them, as if she needs to be reassured that I have some regular human contact apart from my work. Her disapproval of Alex is undiminished, though, and she issues frequent warnings about the dangers of being manipulated by young women for sport. The fact that Alex is married seems to be the least of Maddy's concerns.

She's never met any of my neighbours, but says she feels as if she knows them as well as the actors in any TV soap. She shares my concern about Rich, though her theories about why he seems to have become increasingly edgy—and increasingly pudgy—are more lurid than mine.

'He's not a happy camper by the sound of what you're telling me. Ruth probably works longer hours than he does—men don't like that. They're supposed to be the serious breadwinners, slaving late into the night and dragging themselves home, exhausted but triumphant, to the waiting arms of the patient little woman. The cave man is never far below the surface—even in you, Tom.'

'You're in the wrong century, Maddy. Your daughters wouldn't stand for that kind of talk, and I don't think Ruth would either. She and Rich must have worked this stuff out years ago, wouldn't you think?'

'Listen, Tom, I wouldn't stand for that kind of talk myself, but look at me. Look what I've put up with. When did Harl ever lift a finger to cook a meal for me, even when he sank into that state of gracious semi-retirement called "consulting"? Don't think I haven't raised it with him, by the way. The fact that I slave away here doing a full-time job doesn't count: he's still the breadwinner. He bought the entire bakery, to be honest, and whose complaining about that? But my job is just "an interest". That's what he says to his friends: "Maddy's job is an interest for her, now the girls are grown up and gone". It sounds like the ultimate put-down. When I hear him saying it, I sometimes think I might hit him, right there in front of his friends, but I doubt if he'd realise why I'd done it. Even so, I still might hit him one day, quite hard, just for the heck of it.'

'I don't think there's a delicate way to put this, Maddy, and I know you're a thoroughly enlightened woman—liberated, clear-headed, wonderfully rational in many ways—'

'Get on with it, Thomas. I might hit you one day too.'

'I suspect Harley is a lost cause when it comes to gender issues. He belongs to the wrong generation. There's a huge difference between sixty and forty. You're a bit of a shock to Harley's system:

he probably can't imagine why you bother to work at all when you obviously don't need the money. But Rich wouldn't have expected to marry a professional woman and then have her sit at home in a frilly apron minding the children and grilling the chops.'

'Don't be too sure. Plenty of modern men melt at the sight of a frilly apron, or even at the thought of one—but let's not go into that. I'll tell you what Rich's real problem is. He's got an entertainment on the side, for sure. All the signs are there. He probably fantasises about a getaway, but his guilt will keep him right where he is. See if I'm wrong.'

'Anything's possible, I suppose. But the Abels look like a pretty tight-knit family to me. Rich adores those kids and Ruth is an astonishingly supportive wife. Frankly, I don't know where she gets the energy to do all the wife-and-mother things, plus run a medical practice.'

Even while I'm saying that, I'm recalling my own recent speculation about the state of the Abel marriage. I was wrong then but, as one of my colleagues is fond of saying, you never know what's going on in a marriage if you're not under the bed. And something is certainly eating Rich.

'Anyway, what about your lot? What news of the girls?'

Maddy's lips tighten and there's a long pause while she pours two cups of coffee. 'Don't ask. I'm sure you can imagine the scenario. Susie is back from London, back at work, head down, getting her scholarship application together for the master's course she wants to start next year—full-time, naturally, so that means two years with no income. Fi, needless to say, met a new man at the friend's book launch and has fallen helplessly in love. Now she wants to stay in London for a while . . . and guess what Daddy says.'

'Whatever will make her happy?'

'Exactly. "Whatever will make her happy." Can you believe it? Well, you obviously can.'

Maddy gazes out the window at a sudden downpour. Fleetingly unconscious of me, her face reveals a hint of sadness.

'Maybe you should make an appointment for him', I venture, only half joking. 'I'd quite like to go three rounds with Harley. "Whatever will make her happy!" How do people keep a straight face while they say that sort of stuff? Is Harley serious? Does he think about what he's saying? That must be one of the classic signs of a parent who's given up.'

'Tell me something I don't know. But Harl doesn't know it, or he won't face it. All that money has ruined his sense of perspective and it's rapidly ruining Fi's, although I think she was a lost cause from the beginning, between you and me. Anyway, there's no room for either of the girls in the new apartment, so they have to fend for themselves to some extent, even if Harl does foot too many of the bills.'

Not having a family of my own, I'm sometimes perplexed by Maddy's determination to keep her daughters at arm's length. I accept that parents and children have to fight a war of independence, and the children have to win, but I would have expected Maddy to enjoy the fact that her daughters are still so closely in touch with her. They were obviously shattered when Maddy and Harley decided to sell the family home in Wahroonga and move into an apartment: even though neither of the girls was living at home by then, they were both inclined to drop in for overnight stays and Fiona would move back in for weeks at a time whenever she was nursing the wounds of yet another failed romance. The symbolism of selling that home hurt the girls deeply.

But not Maddy. In the months since the move, Maddy has become devoted to life in the CBD, shedding the Wahroonga house like a dowdy old coat. She is so passionate about the joys and blessings of her new way of life, she can't believe she once loved the suburbs. Like a religious convert, she's trying to persuade me of the glories of city living.

'You should try this, Tom. A man in your situation, stuck out there in the suburbs . . .'

'Castlecrag isn't exactly the western plains, Maddy. I'm only fifteen minutes from the CBD. I like living there, believe it or not. I like the space. I like the neighbours. I like the peace.'

'No, you don't get it. You could be in a nice apartment—no garden to worry about, no dogs to crap on your lawn, no neighbours to annoy you *and* you would be right in the middle of everything. We walk to the Opera House, you know. We walk to the movies, we stroll around the gardens, we've got the best restaurants in Australia on our doorstep . . .'

'And you're stuck in an air-conditioned box, fifteen floors up. I'm sure it's wonderful for you and Harley, but it doesn't appeal to me, that's all. Why do people have to talk about the suburbs as if living there is an admission of social or cultural failure? Castlecrag is a suburb, yes, but suburbs aren't parasites that suck the life out of the thing you fondly imagine is the *real* city. Suburbs aren't festering pustules of humanity that sully the purity of this place called "the city", this place where the beautiful people hang out. They're real people out there in the suburbs, Maddy, and some of them are beautiful too. Don't talk about the suburbs as if they're a brackish breeding-ground for an inferior form of pond-life. There's as much fun, and as much tedium, to be experienced in the suburbs as anywhere else.'

'That could be your problem, Thomas.'

'What, living in a suburb?'

'No, the way you talk. You get too worked up. Too defensive. "Festering pustules that sully the purity of . . ." whatever you said. You do rather go over the top sometimes. Look at you: your face is quite flushed. I find it touching, in a way, but a lot of people would be disconcerted. You don't exactly come across as the King of Cool.'

'You're sounding like Alex, which won't please you. But I wasn't attacking the suburbs; you were. And you lived in one yourself until about ten minutes ago.'

'I was simply saying I thought you should give the city a go. Suburban life can be deadly. I'm not saying it has to be, and I'm not saying it is for you. I'm saying it can be. I'm suggesting you give the city a try. Rent something for six months. See how you like it. That's all. I'm not *accusing* anyone of anything.'

Maddy has joined the trendy chorus of people who believe that suburban equals sub-human. The suburbs get a bad rap, which is unfair to the teeming millions of Australians who live in them and who are constantly being told their lives would be richer if only they lived somewhere else. Move into the CBD. Get an inner-city terrace. Give up your garden. Better still, go bush. Get onto acres somewhere and grow something worthwhile: canola, maybe, or garlic, or grapes. Anything but the suburbs. People never seem to think of the suburbs as the best of both worlds; only the worst.

Let's not forget it's the suburbs where most poems are written, most cups of sugar borrowed, most flowers grown, most lightbulbs blown, most babies conceived, most hopes dashed, most passions roused, most suicides committed, most marriages celebrated. Suburbs are where most parents feel those joyous surges of parental pride, swelling like silken banners in the heart. Suburbs are where faith is most often tested by experience, and where the most painful of all lessons—that love's work is hard work—is usually learned. Suburbs are where the joy of sex is most often experienced and its disappointments most often faced, where most intimations of mortality are first detected, and where a bewildering sense of contentment—yearned for, yet unexpected—most often descends on people.

None of this is because suburbs are better or worse places to live than anywhere else: all these things happen in country towns, inner-city terraces, caravan parks, fishermen's huts and CBD apartment blocks. But the suburbs have the numbers.

I say none of this to Maddy. 'I'll give it some thought,' is all I say.

TWELVE

'Is O'Good really your name?'

Upton and Sexy O'Good live on the corner of our street with a pair of teenage boys who are the offspring of neither of them. No matter how you want to define a family, this is one. They have such a good time that the rest of us often smile as we pass number two: the place is so alive with laughter, music, yelling and thumping.

Sexy's name ought to seem ridiculous, it's so obviously contrived and in your face. But when you meet her, it works like any other name. (We call each other by an amazing array of names, come to think of it, many of them capable of meaning other things in other phonic contexts: Billy, Ray, John, Mark, Neil, Sue, Bob, Brooke, Phil.) Sexy's 'real' name is Mildred, she admits, but when she met Upton, he told her that wasn't a very sexy name for a young blonde, and one thing led to another. She tells this story as though it's the kind of thing that could happen to anyone.

Short, overweight, fiftyish, with greying blonde hair left entirely natural in colour and shape, Sexy is the social heart of the Close. Nothing is ever too much trouble, no one ever a nuisance. I see her wave to Brian across the street, year after year, though he's never once appeared to acknowledge her.

The boys are either adopted or fostered, but they've all been together since they moved into the Close and no one needs to know any details. (We're a street, Rich, not a village. Privacy is respected here, though I confess I'd love to know the entire O'Good story.)

'Is O'Good really your name?' I once asked Upton. He's the sort of person who would never take offence. 'I can't recall ever having heard of another O'Good.'

'Absolutely, young Tom. The name of my father before me, and my father's father before him. Before that, who knows?' Then he gave me a huge wink and roared with laughter, as if to seal us in a conspiracy of silence about our disreputable forebears. It was a very Sydney moment: you can't be too careful in a society originally run as a convict prison by soldiers who adopted rum as their currency.

'My father was a comedian so it suited him to a tee. That also explains why he insisted on calling me Upton, over the strenuous objections of my more sensitive mother. Still, it's done me no harm. My brother's called Compton, which doesn't quite come off, d'you think?'

Upton is a professional singer who drives a cab to help make ends meet. I've often seen him driving the cab, but I've never heard him give voice, except at our Christmas party when he's the undisputed leader of the carol-singing. Sexy works in an office in the city. She's tried to explain to me what she does, but it sounds as if she's not entirely sure herself. She claims the work is so indescribably boring that she literally can't describe it.

Upton and Sexy seem to have alliances with everyone. The Nguyens go to them for help whenever they have official forms to be filled in, or tradesmen to be called. Alex and Sexy are often to be seen in the middle of the road, locked in earnest conversation while Sexy nurses Alex's baby and makes a fuss of her. Upton and Joe play bowls together as a prelude to long drinking sessions that seem to disturb neither Enid nor Sexy. In fact, since Joe's illness, Sexy often spends her summer Saturday nights sitting with Enid on one or the other's front porch, waiting for their men to return from the bowling club.

Clare became fond of the O'Good boys, Colin and Robert (named by their natural parents, luckily for them, before the O'Goods got their hands on them). That was unusual: she was never interested in children, never wanted any of her own and found the Abel kids a constant irritation. She liked Sexy and Upton, as everyone does, but her closest bond was with the boys, especially as they moved into their late teens.

Towards the end, she would sometimes spend whole evenings at the O'Good house, helping the boys with homework or . . . I don't know what she did. Being a teacher, Clare was able to give them chunks of her time during school holidays, taking them shopping for clothes and even giving Colin driving practice in her car when the O'Good van was on the blink, as it often is.

I could hardly fathom any of this. It might have been that she was missing her own younger brothers, both of whom were working overseas and rarely visited Australia, or she might have found the O'Good boys a useful means of escape from me. I was insanely jealous—of their youth, their good looks, their energy, their freedom, their outspokenness . . . it was easy to see why she preferred them to me, when I compared my own increasingly depressed and despairing mood with their reckless charm.

Even at the time, I knew the correct response was to be glad she had befriended the boys, whose own lives must have been difficult and patchy before they found safe haven with Upton and Sexy. I knew that if I could only be pleased that would have made me more attractive to Clare and then she might have been more inclined to be with me, to respond . . .

I couldn't help imagining the worst. Trapped in the coils of my own anxiety, it was almost a comfort to tell myself stories that justified my descent into the black pit. When I was in a sufficiently black mood, I would become convinced that Clare had created a love nest in the O'Goods' back room. There she would let the boys take turns, teaching them everything she knew about the arts of passion, gradually transforming them into her sex slaves. As time wore on, she would become bored with one-to-one sessions and invite both boys to join her in threesomes of such lasciviousness, she would be unable to look me in the eye when she came home (that part was true). Upton and Sexy, meanwhile, would be in the dark. They would have no idea that Clare had turned their boys into her willing, submissive instruments of pleasure, and they would continue to welcome her into their home, assuming her motives were friendly and pure . . . until one night, when Colin, seized by jealousy and rage, would let slip that Clare was in bed with Robert in the back room and Sexy would hurry to investigate, finding a scene of such debauchery that she would never forgive Clare. Somehow the child welfare authorities would learn of this outrageous episode and Sexy would be forced to hand the boys back. They would be fostered out to a family who would tolerate them, but never love them as she had.

This would inevitably drive Clare back into my arms, seeking forgiveness and understanding. The tenderness of that reconciliation would make the preceding nightmare worthwhile. We would have to move: it would be impossible to continue trying to coexist with the O'Goods.

I still find myself looking over the O'Goods' fence sometimes, wondering whether all that time she spent with the boys was entirely innocent. But if Colin or Robert ever see me, they greet me with such open warmth that I'm forced to laugh at my own foolishness. I acknowledge that, at the time, it was impossible for me to be enthusiastic about Clare's relationship with them: my misery stifled the possibility of a normal reaction.

I take no pleasure in admitting that I feel more alive in the troughs than on the peaks. Clare knew that, and she was right to stay clear of me when the black fog descended. 'Always looking on the dark side,' she'd say. 'Always putting the bleakest possible interpretation on everything. Always looking for trouble. Always lifting the rock and disturbing the lowlife underneath.'

Is this an occupational hazard, or am I in the wrong job? No one comes into my consulting rooms dying to share their good news with me, except, occasionally, at the end of a long and painful series of sessions. Even then, people are inclined to cancel their final appointment rather than bothering to come, or even to phone to tell me they're feeling better. (Why pay someone for the privilege of telling them you're feeling okay? Friends will listen to good news for nothing.)

Even if I were not a counsellor, I think it would be hard to avoid the burden of other people's grief laid on us by the modern, media-saturated world. I wonder how much depression is aggravated—or even caused—by the relentless news of trouble, disaster, scandal, terror, death and destruction. My clients, my friends and my neighbours in Winter Close make constant demands on my reserves of sympathy and on my moral courage: am I expected to feel the same kind of connection with the victims of the terrorist attack on the twin towers of the World Trade Center in New York, or with refugees from Afghanistan, survivors of an earthquake in India, a flood in Bangladesh or a famine in the Horn of Africa . . . or with people whose lives are torn apart by the death of a child, or the rape of a teenage daughter, or the conviction of a son for armed robbery?

All those things are terrible. Other people's traffic accidents are terrible. Mass retrenchments of total strangers from large corporations are terrible. But if I try to feel my way into other people's trouble, am I shouldering an impossible emotional burden? Am I falling for the idea that things are far, far worse than they actually are? When I look at those shock-horror road-safety or anti-drug commercials on television, I wonder the same thing. They're so well made, so real, it's easy to feel as if I'm the one who's been bereaved.

Do any of us have the emotional reserves for so much involvement, so much sympathy, so much *reaction?* Wouldn't it be healthier to build a little wall to protect us from other people's disasters? Shouldn't we learn how to resist being drawn in, so we have something left for the stuff we have to handle, here and now, in the lives of the people we know?

As every new client walks through my door, I brace myself for another tragedy, more sadness, more mistakes, more mess. Perhaps I am in the wrong job. Clare thinks (or used to think) I am. What should I turn to at forty years of age? What should I become? A comedian, like Upton's father?

THIRTEEN

The flowers kept coming and coming

It would be impossible to dislike Joe and Enid Riley in number five. It's hard to imagine quite how they ended up in Winter Close, though we're all pleased to have them here. Joe was a trade union official of some kind before he retired to establish a lush suburban garden—the fulfilment of a dream Enid says he has nurtured for as long as she has known him. In spite of the sandy soil of Castlecrag—he could have achieved lushness more easily in many other places—the garden is a joy to Joe and a fine example to the whole street, though most of us fail to follow it.

It took a near-tragedy to draw Joe and Enid fully into the circle of our little community. They'd been living in the Close for two years, keeping to themselves and even declining to attend our Christmas parties, when Joe fell ill with a mysterious blood disorder, never fully understood or confidently diagnosed, even now.

We knew, via Alex, that Joe was unwell and that he'd had a few days in hospital for some inconclusive tests. Then the flowers started coming. At first, there were a couple of deliveries over a couple of days, but then there seemed to be a constant stream of florists' vans in the street and we began to realise something was dreadfully amiss.

Alex recruited Sexy O'Good for moral support and together they visited Enid and Joe.

The house was bedecked with flowers. As news of Joe's illness spread through the union movement, the flowers kept coming and coming. The flowers told us things we might not otherwise have realised: Joe Riley had been a figure of vast influence and stature; he was the kind of man people wouldn't forget quickly or ever stop loving. Enid arranged for some of the flowers to be sent to the local hospital and she gave some to Alex and Sexy to distribute to the neighbours, 'not that I know anyone here. It's not a friendly street, is it?'

Not friendly? Us? Alex and Sexy were shocked, as the rest of us were when they told us later. This street, *our* street, not friendly? We'd all introduced ourselves and been as friendly as we thought appropriate. But they seemed to prefer to keep to themselves and there was an issue of respect, an issue of propriety; we thought they *wanted* us to keep our distance. Approaching seventy, they were clearly older than most of the residents of the Close—Rich, Ruth and I are all around forty, Alex and Chika ten years younger than us and the Nguyens somewhere in between. Samantha and Jodie in number four are virtually kids. The O'Goods—Sexy fiftyish and Upton a few years older—are a bit closer to them in age, but only the Stuthridges and Mrs Spenser could be said to be about the Rileys' vintage.

Mrs Spenser, it turned out, was the problem. During one of her virulently anti-social episodes, she had marched up to Enid Riley's front door, warned her against 'the nasty element' in the street and urged her to stay right away from the Christmas party which was only 'a front for drugs' and bound to be raided by the police one year—probably that very year. (No wonder they didn't come.)

According to Enid, Joe had been inclined to rubbish Mrs Spenser's story, but Enid herself was more cautious and, over the next few weeks, she observed the rest of us quite closely. What she saw didn't impress her.

Through her eyes, we looked like a rather furtive bunch, mostly coming and going by car and keeping pretty much to ourselves. It was easy to believe, once you started looking for the signs, that drugs were 'an issue' in the street. Chika's brushes with the law didn't help and the appearance, from afar, of the eccentric O'Goods, combined with Sexy's name, created an impression of raffishness that, viewed in the light of Mrs Spenser's warning, disturbed Enid.

Her one attempt at a friendly overture was ill-conceived, though she couldn't have known that. Catching up to Mrs Stuthridge on the way home from the shops, she invited her and Brian, of all people in the street to pick, to come over on the following Saturday for afternoon tea. She had apparently judged the Stuthridges to be quiet and conservative, and similar in age to her and Joe. Compared with the rest of us, they had looked like a safe bet.

Mrs Stuthridge reacted to the invitation like someone caught in a spotlight and scurried into her house without giving a clear response. When Saturday afternoon came and she was still unsure of whether the Stuthridges would visit her or not, Enid walked down the street to where Brian was working in his garden. True to form, he slithered out of sight as soon as she approached and she wisely decided not to knock on the door. End of overture.

Once her relationship with Alex and Sexy began to thaw, she confided in them that she had written Rich and me off as arrogant yuppies, based on our long hours away at work, the fact that we both paid someone to mow our lawns and maintain our gardens and someone else to clear the leaves out of our gutters, my propensity to sit on my balcony and survey the scene (though I was sure I'd waved at Joe in his garden more than once), and Rich's smartly restored black VW. You never can tell what's in the eye of the beholder.

Enid had felt she could trust Alex but not Chika (correct call), that Mrs Spenser was somewhat eccentric (right again), and that Clare—this was only weeks before she left me for the squadron leader—was somehow disengaged (three out of three). Doctor Ruth and the children looked 'nice, but aloof' and the Nguyens were as much a mystery to the Rileys as the Rileys were to them: the language barrier made the Nguyens more reticent than they felt. To Enid, their respectful caution seemed evasive, even furtive.

So there was our lovely street looking decidedly unlovely. What seemed to us a close-knit little community, each of us watchful and caring but not intrusive, appeared to a poorly briefed newcomer as a threatening ghetto of unfriendly weirdos whose main characteristic was their standoffishness.

Joe's illness lasted for several weeks and, at Alex's urging, several of us began to visit, taking food, staying to chat, hoping to create the impression that we might be half-human, at least. As Joe regained his strength, our conversations became longer and more robust, and he began to concede that perhaps he had not landed himself and his beloved wife in an unpleasant little pocket of suburban smugness, disconnected from 'the real world'. We were interested in many of the same things he was interested in. Rich and I, in particular, turned out to be more left of centre than he was on most social issues. On law and order, censorship, refugees, I was a bit bleeding-heart for his taste, but even that was better than he had feared. (The stiffnecks are a tad further east, Rich told him.) He was suitably roused by Rich's account of the new approach to university funding and management, and he seemed to enjoy having something to fret about. Rich and I quickly established ourselves as the kind of neighbours he could talk to, but when Sexy started bringing Upton to see him, he knew he had found a firm friend.

FOURTEEN

'This is, like, more conventional than marriage'

Where will I start?

Tell me a little bit about yourself. Family, friends, what you're up to . . .

What is there to tell? I don't think I have many relatives, you know? Lots of friends, though. Not many relatives. But, hey, I'm not going, like, poor me. Plenty of people my age have lost their parents. Can I smoke in here? My father disappeared, apparently, soon as Mum fell pregnant. I've learnt all that like a history lesson. Like, it doesn't really mean anything? Like, you can go, 'My father disappeared soon as my mum fell pregnant,' but what is it supposed to mean? What am I supposed to feel? I don't feel anything much.

I have no idea what it would be like to have a father. I see other people's fathers—I saw other girls' fathers when I was a kid—but that's like saying you see other people's budgerigars?

Budgerigars?

(Client sobbing.)

This girl . . . her budgerigar was, like, a friend? Sat on her shoulder and everything. Like, chirping at her and everything? I always wanted one . . .

Do you want to say anything about your mother?

Not really, no. Her thing with men was, like, shit. I didn't want to know, you know? Like, when she died, I was nearly fifteen and the welfare never told me nothing. I had two foster families after that. They were great, mostly. I still see one of the mothers. She's lovely and everything? But I'd never tell her where I live? She'd tell the welfare. DOCS have stopped looking for me, I think. I hope. So it should be, like, whoopee! Free as a bird!

But it isn't like that? Is that what you're saying? You feel . . .

(Client sobbing.)

The man I'm seeing is married. I know that. He knows I know it. We never say nothing about it? He has this real middle-class wife. She has a child. Well, they have a child. Let's face it. They have a child. A baby. We never say nothing about her either. He talks as if it was nothing to do with him, as if his wife, like, did it all by herself? He wants me to live in the moment, you know? That's what he says, but . . .

(Client sobbing.)

But?

He goes, like, I'm like his little piece of heaven. Like, two or three times a week, his little piece of heaven. But, hey, not so great he wants me all the time? I don't go, like, stay with me, stay with me. Nothing like that. I try to get on with my life, but it's not that easy? When we're fucking, it's easy to forget whatever else is going on in his life, but the moment he's gone, I start going, 'Where is he, who's he with?' As if I don't know. It sounds such a—

Cliché?

What? No. Such a soapie. It's like I'm living in a soapie? Mind if I have another ciggy? Sorry about the ash on your nice table. This is, like, more conventional than marriage. It's all so predictable and everything? I never wanted to be this conventional, so why am I stuck with this shit? You think it will be excellent and romantic and thrilling, and it turns out to be dull, dull, dull. It's, like, a routine? It becomes, like, a drag. Like being married, I suppose, only worse? It's not, like, what bus will you catch tomorrow darling, or who'll get breakfast darling, or time to pick up the little darlings from netball darling. This is tougher? Like, really, really tough. There's all these rules. Really rigid. Where you can go. Where you can't be seen. What you must forget. What you must remember. His rules, not mine. I'm muggins, as usual. Mum always used to say that. It's easier at the moment, though. He's . . . away for a while. He still rings me up, though, and he's, like, how's my little piece of heaven? And I feel . . . I feel . . . like a little piece of shit.

(Client sobbing.)

I suppose you think it should be simple and straightforward for me. It's not fun any more, so, like, kill it? Drop it? Is that what you think?

I don't have an opinion. I'm only here to help you decide what's best for you to do. Whatever that is. Whatever that may be. Up to you.

(Long pause.)

Do you want to tell me what made you decide to come here?

It was my bad dreams that did it. There's this girl at work. She's lovely. Her mum came to see you and she said it was great—talking about everything, and everything? My friend is lovely, but you can't tell friends everything? Like, what if they go off you and start blabbing to everyone else about you? I couldn't tell her about my dream, but I told my doctor. He thought coming here was a good idea? So here I am. I can pay for these sessions. You don't have to worry about that. I've got a job and everything? I know what you're thinking, but, hey, I'm not . . . you know. Nothing like that. I get money from Tony, but I'm staying away from shag city. I've got a proper job in an office and everything?

. . . I'll tell you about my dream, if you like. I have it practically every night. Have I told you this before? I'm a bit confused. I've been taking stuff and I can't always remember who I told what to? Anyway, I'm racing around the house trying to lock something— a door—or else I'm trying to switch something off. But it's all too late and I know I'll never make it. Whatever I do, it's too late. The damage has been done and they're all bound to die. All my family,

my kids . . . and there's nothing . . . it's too . . . it was all my fault, you see. I left it too late. It wasn't deliberate. But I know it was up to me, and I failed. I let them down.

(Client sobbing.)

So I wake up, every single night, in a panic. Sometimes I'm out of bed, racing around in my sleep, trying to turn off this switch, or close this door, whatever. I have to save them all. It should be easy, but I can never manage to do it? I can't find what I'm looking for. And it's my problem, because I'm the one who left the door open, or turned the switch on in the first place. I have to fix it up, or they'll all die. I'm never quite sure how they will die, but it's like, inevitable? I know that. Every night I know it. My heart breaks every single night and I have to start again, every morning, telling myself, like, it's all okay and I haven't done nothing wrong and no one's been killed yet.

Are you taking anything to help you sleep more soundly?

The doctor said that would only mask it? He wanted me to come and see you first. He was, like, 'No good trying to stop the kettle boiling over by jamming the lid on tighter—we've got to turn the gas down.' You know?

How long have you been having this particular dream?

Weeks. Months, really. It's happened before, but this is the first time it's gone on for so long. I stay up as late as possible to make myself tired, but it makes no difference.

Tell me about your other friends. Apart from Tony.

I'm only calling him Tony; I don't want to say his real name. My other friends are . . . well, I'm friendly with the girls at work, like I said. All of them, really. They don't know what I'm up to, though. They know I've got more to spend than what I earn at work? Tony is excellent about money, I'll say that. I supply the other girls with eccy, but they don't ask questions. Why would they?

You mentioned you were taking stuff. Did you mean ecstasy?

What else? It's excellent. I'm not an addict or nothing, and I steer clear of crack and that. People say E is for losers but, hey, I'd never be without some eccy in my bag. It's not only the rush, it's the weight. Like, if I stopped using it, I'd put on heaps? I'm a lot slimmer than what I used to be. I'd never go dancing without it. Like, what would be the point?

FIFTEEN

A construction project in a well-established street like ours is like a creative act performed in public.

I can't get Alex and her poetry—and her bare midriff—out of my head. I see her most days, one way or another, and I keep promising her I'll put pen to paper, but that seems unlikely in my present frame of mind. Even if I did write something, it wouldn't be the kind of thing I'd care to show Alex.

It's clear to me that my new client is Chika's girlfriend. Everything fits, including the fact that he's in gaol at present, on remand. The ecstasy, the 'middle class' sledge, the wife and baby, the frenetic lifestyle. Such people are a dime a dozen, I suppose, but there's something . . . it's as if she brings a sense of Chika, an aura, into my office with her every time she comes. That's exactly the kind of thing life does to you. A huge warning bell appears, hanging above your head, and then, in case you hadn't noticed, it starts clanging in your ear. (Okay, okay, I get the message: *Chika exists.*)

My client is like a less refined version of Alex. They're uncannily similar in appearance, and they have many attitudes in common. If Chika liked the look of one, he'd certainly like the look of the other. (From the back, Alex could pass for an eighteen-year-old with that swaying ponytail and her slim hips, though she must be thirty. My new client *is* eighteen.)

Chika's case has been briefly reported in the newspapers though not on television, much to Alex's relief. He's being held on charges related to a large quantity of ecstasy tablets bound for the dance market. Chika is denying everything, claiming he's been set up by a friend—a *friend?*—who asked him to deliver 'a bag of stuff' to an address not far from here. In spite of his denials, Chika is being kept on remand. His record must be worse than we knew. Alex doesn't want to discuss it, and neither do I, I suppose. Better not to know. On every other topic, conversation between us runs remarkably smoothly.

I want to be supportive of Alex and Jemma—Alex's parents live interstate, but they've promised to come and stay with her over Christmas if Chika is still in prison. If he's back home they'll keep their distance, according to Alex. No love lost, I gather. But I don't want this to become more complicated than it already is; in particular, I don't know how much longer I can go on pretending there's a poem brewing inside me. When I have coffee with Alex at her kitchen table, she often puts her hand on mine while she's talking: I wish she wouldn't and I wish she would. Even if I didn't have any moral qualms, the thought of Chika would be a sufficient caution. This is a violent man. Alex says she worries for herself and the baby, yet never even hints at the possibility of leaving him.

Lying in bed this Sunday morning, ruminating about Alex and Chika, it's easy to love Winter Close. All I can see out of my window are the branches of trees against a clear blue sky. The air is full of familiar suburban sounds: birdsong; Enid Riley sweeping her front path (as she does, reassuringly, seven days a week); a distant mower; some enthusiast, up too early, hammering and sawing his way to DIY heaven; the muted screech of Rich ripping the green plastic wrapper off his fat Sunday paper; the hum of traffic on Eastern Valley Way as people head in their thousands for the northern beaches.

I can also hear Mrs Spenser scraping a slice of burnt toast out of her kitchen window, but that isn't unusual. I've sometimes thought of offering to show her how to ensure unburnt toast, though it's hard to see how to broach the subject without giving offence.

The silence from Mrs Spenser's building site is a pleasant sign that it's Sunday. The weekday sound of the builders' radio, starting at seven o'clock and turned up loud enough to be heard above the noise of their own work, is not always welcome, but the work itself is proceeding smoothly. The back half of her roof is off, several tarpaulins are strategically placed, like a masseur's towels, and the timber frame is taking shape.

If I prop myself up on one elbow, I can see where the new roofline will be: it won't affect my sunlight or my views, and I doubt that it will have much impact on the Abels' place either.

Rich and the children have shown keen interest in the construction process. The paling fence between them and Mrs Spenser has been temporarily removed to facilitate the builders' access, which makes the children feel as if the whole thing is happening in their own backyard. Humbold is scavenging timber offcuts, and the girls are impressed by the materials—timber, tiles, window frames, plasterboard, insulation batts, guttering and downpipes—neatly stacked and waiting their turn. Rich has discovered the many pleasures to be found in living beside a building site: the smell of sawn timber, the various demonstrations of tradesmen's skill, the progress that seems almost imperceptible in between sudden, dramatic leaps. The frame is up! The windows are in! The floor is down! I see him prowling around the site every afternoon when he comes home from the university, as though the project is his own.

I've also seen Doctor Ruth and Mrs Spenser chatting amicably several times since the work began. There are clearly no hard feelings, but there probably never were, on Mrs Spenser's side or even on Ruth's. It struck me at the time that the Abels' objections were lodged more as a matter of principle than as an attack on Mrs Spenser's specific intentions, Rich's dark references to Alzheimer's notwithstanding. It's remarkable how easily people manage to keep their feelings towards each other quite separate from the action they take in official contexts, like councils or courts. One of my clients told me the story of her bitter fight with her ex-husband in the Family Court over their children's custody and access arrangements, followed by a bout of passionate lovemaking in a city hotel where, on impulse, they booked a room and stayed for two nights while their children—the object of all the fuss—were cared for by neighbours.

Perhaps different contexts create independent sets of feelings—even quite contradictory feelings—that can be attached to the same person at the same time. I sense that Joe Riley is in precisely that situation in his attitude to the Nguyens: he strongly disapproves of the level of immigration from South-East Asia, but he has warm affection for the Nguyen family and is becoming something of a surrogate grandfather to the two girls. I see him walking them to the local park, though if he saw other Asian kids at the park, he'd be fretting to anyone who'd listen about the problem of ethnic imbalance in our migrant intake.

In fact, Rich and Ruth Abel were probably reacting to the half-formed idea that anyone wanting to put any extension on any house that happened to be next door to theirs must be nuts—not Mrs Spenser specifically; *anyone*. Neat separation, but it keeps wheels turning that might otherwise seize up. I'm relieved when I see people shaking their fists and talking about the *principle* of the thing: at the deepest level, it usually means they don't care too much about the thing itself.

Building works inevitably attract attention. The residents of Winter Close regard it as something of a treat, having such a major extension taking place in their midst. People in new subdivisions must become blasé about it, but a construction project in a well-established street like ours is like a creative act performed in public. In the same way as people tend to stand behind an artist, watching the application of a few brushstrokes and wondering whether the picture is meant to be a literal representation of the scene the artist appears to be addressing (to which it often bears so little resemblance that passers-by are tempted to ask, 'What are you painting?'), so the neighbours like to cruise past a construction site, checking progress and asking questions of the tradesmen: What's that going to be? Is that as high as it's going? Are you putting a window in that wall? What will you do if it rains before you get the roof on? Do you do odd jobs as well—I've got a laundry window that's stuck; it would only take a minute. Will you be finished by Christmas?

SIXTEEN

'The more we've talked, the less we've liked each other'

I'm on my balcony, watching the Abel and Nguyen children playing in the street. Though Humbold is the only boy among four girls, he doesn't appear to mind: the younger Nguyen girl, not much older than Ethel, mothers him as if he's even younger than he is.

They're playing some kind of ball game which appears to be beyond the younger children, but they are jumping around on the edge of it, keen to be part of the action. The ball frequently bounces onto the road, and, as Laura runs to retrieve it, she is becoming less and less vigilant about watching out for cars. Living in the Close creates a dangerous illusion for children: the road feels to them like their own private playground. There's an extra risk, because so few cars come into the street and the children assume that any car must belong to a resident who will be friendly and alert.

But we have service vans, council inspectors, delivery vehicles, cabs . . . plus our share of hoons from nearby suburbs who love to test their skill on the left-hander out of Eastern Valley Way, skid into the Close, do a quick circuit, then hurtle back out onto Eastern Valley Way, accelerating up the hill to Edinburgh Road.

I find myself becoming uneasy as the ball lands with increasing frequency on the road and the children seem too slow to return to the footpath. Then I see Robert O'Good backing the family van out of the driveway of number two and glancing at the children. He pulls into the kerb, leaves the engine running and the van door open. Sporting his shaved head, nose ring and lurid tatts, he walks over to the children. After a moment's discussion with Laura—her earnest, endearing face turned up to his—he shepherds them into the Nguyen's front garden and shuts the gate behind them, pausing for a moment to see them settled into their new spot.

As Robert gets back into the van, Joe Riley emerges from the gate of number five and saunters along the footpath, looking grey, bent, and older than his seventy-odd years. He waves to the children and stops outside the Nguyens' fence, clearly intending to keep his eye on the ball. I wish Rich were here to see all this.

I am overwhelmed by the realisation that I have always wanted children.

Has Clare had a child since she left me? It seems unlikely, but how would I know and why am I interested? (Why do I imagine I'm entitled even to ask the question?) We never resolved our attitude to children. You would think such things would be settled before people decided to marry, especially if you were into your thirties, as we both were, when you tied the knot. There was a vague assumption on my part that children would go with the territory but once things began to turn sour, about three years into the marriage, it was a subject we never mentioned. At least I had the sense not to press for children as a way of rescuing our failing relationship—or perhaps I didn't think of it.

Clare's theory, often recounted, was that women who bore children experienced such a deep sense of fulfilment that they never had the pressing urge, characteristic of many men, to create a legacy.

'Why do you think all the world's greatest composers and artists have been men?' she would ask, especially if dinner-party conversation was flagging and she was feeling reckless. 'It's because men can't have children—that's why they're so desperate to leave something behind; it's their bid for immortality. Mothers can afford to be more relaxed about all that: they know what they've done. They know their progeny will outlive them, and that's why they smile at each other the way you so often see them doing. It's like a secret society.'

'But men have children, too, Clare,' some poor sap was usually foolish enough to say. That was the signal for Clare's lecture on Richard Dawkins, the selfish gene, the need for men to spread their seed around, the lack of any male equivalent to the physical act of childbirth, etc, etc.

'Find me a father who feels fulfilled by his children the way a mother does—viscerally fulfilled—and I'll show you a man who would never even dream of straying from his mate. Never even dream of it. I'll also show you a man who wouldn't feel any need for monuments to himself. No flash cars. No corporate pyramid building. No framed certificates. No book in his head that he's determined to write one day. No obsession with his legacy. Ha.'

'So people like Bach and Mozart had it both ways—reams of kids *and* a musical legacy that will last forever?'

'No, no, you're missing my point. They had it one way and one way only. The music was their legacy and their fulfilment. At the deepest level, the children belonged to their wives. Men hate to hear that but it's true. Don't tell me you think Bach and Mozart were deeply contented family men who had to tear themselves away from the hearth to wring a few more wretched notes out of their reluctant imaginations. Come *on*. Music was their passion, like kids are the passion of most mothers. Try to get them talking animatedly about anything else when they're in the full flush of motherhood. Why should they? They've found the secret of contentment without lifting a pen, a chisel or a brush. They've opened their legs and fulfilled their destiny, easy as that. Meaning of life. You can intellectualise it all you like, but I can see it in their eyes and I can hear it in their cosy chat.'

I don't think anyone ever believed her—least of all any mothers who happened to be present, especially if they were wrestling with toddlers. You could see their jaws drop. (On the other hand, it was true that they rarely spoke with passion about anything but their children.)

Clare was clearly excluded from the 'cosy chat' of mothers' groups, but it was never entirely clear from her tone and manner whether Clare's Theory of Fulfilment Through Motherhood had been framed in a spirit of praise or contempt for mothers. It certainly had the capacity to stimulate male fantasies of predatory sex and domination over pre-revolutionary women—pregnant, barefoot, etc—so the married men at the table often found their wives' discomfort strangely satisfying.

Like any talk that drags deeply embedded cultural material to the surface, Clare's theorising outraged, challenged, intrigued and sometimes even distressed both men and women. Even if it was late enough in the evening for everyone to be mildly drunk, a sense of hostility towards Clare would usually emerge. Women (both those with and those without children) found her tone patronising; men, after they'd got over their initial amusement, had trouble reconciling Clare's airy dismissal of fatherhood with their own turn-of-the-century determination to be active, loving, responsible, devoted and *involved* parents. (Most of the men who came into our circle would have had at least one book on fatherhood and/or manhood prominently displayed on their bookshelves, even if unread.)

At some point, our guests—especially the women—would naturally want to ask Clare about her own position. You could sense them edging towards the question, wondering if it would be polite to ask, but I don't recall anyone ever being brave enough to go all the way. Clare could be an intimidating figure when she was in declamatory mode and she was the kind of person who was proud of keeping her theories completely detached from her personal situation. (Her pronouncements about the bad behaviour of men, for instance, bore little relation to anything I'd personally been up to, though I sensed, towards the end, that I was being asked to bear the burden of guilt for the sins of the fathers, the grandfathers, the uncles, the cousins, the blokes in her office and the unborn generations of male scoundrels still to come.) Whenever I asked her where she herself stood on the question of her own destiny—her legacy, her creativity—she'd say it was irrelevant. She was talking about the species, not herself.

I can't help wondering, even now, whether things would have been different if we'd had children. On the Clare theory, I should be feeling some urgency, by now, about the fact that I have neither creative nor corporate monuments to my name—forty already, and heading towards cultural oblivion. (At least Rich has published a book and Edith Riley once told me that Joe has his name on a plaque stuck up on a building somewhere.) But genetic oblivion feels more threatening to me, whatever Clare might say. I experience the lack of children as a large hole in my present and a shadow already cast over my future.

Over the years we were together, I tried to encourage Clare to talk about her attitude to having—or not having—children. But she always insisted on such rational analysis of the question that my desire to explore the idea would evaporate under the intense scrutiny of questions like: 'Why would you destroy the life we have now? Have you ever calculated what it would cost, over twenty years, for education alone? Don't you think there are more than enough children fighting for survival on the planet without us adding to their number?' And always the clincher: 'You want to convert everything into words, Tom. Why do we have to *discuss* everything? You think I kill the idea of children by the things I say, but I don't want to say anything. *You* kill the idea of children by bringing it up all the time.'

But it wasn't only children: I encouraged her to say more about everything—about *her*—than she wanted to say. She accused me of being unhealthily curious, which may be true, but it was more than that: talking came more naturally to me than to her. In fact, she once let slip that the more we talked, the less comfortable she felt with me.

'You don't get it, do you? We were blissfully in love when we scarcely knew each other. The first couple of years were good years for me because you weren't prodding and poking around in my psyche, trying to dig out some treasure that would enrich this peculiar thing you call "the relationship". Well, I'll tell you this for nothing: our relationship, whatever it is, was fine until you started trying to enrich it. Don't you realise that some of the most successful marriages in history have been arranged marriages, or marriages where two people lived together in relative harmony precisely because they *didn't* try for too much intimacy?

'They ate together when it suited them, talked politely about whatever they needed or wanted to talk about, made love to each other when they felt like it. If they had children, they shared the business of raising them, like responsible parents rather than youth workers or child guidance officers. They probably didn't flip if either of them had the odd stray fuck either, if it gave them some relief from the intensity of being always together and sent them home happy. And—*horrors!*—they might even have read the paper while they were eating their breakfast. They respected each other's privacy. Get it? *Privacy*. That's a word you should write in your little book, directly above the R word. Because without privacy, the whole idea of a relationship stinks. If you can't have some time and space to yourself, you'll go quietly mad. And if you can't have a bit of intimacy—closeness—with a few friends of your own, without turning each other's emotional pockets out every night, hunting for small change from the day's transactions, then you're sunk. Finished. You might as well live in a prison, or a lunatic asylum, as have the kind of relationship you seem to dream of.

'I loved you, Tom. I came into this marriage with high hopes and grand plans. I wanted you and I wanted the marriage. What I didn't want was to be thrown into some sort of concentration camp where the commandant—or the weasel who thinks he's in charge—tries to hack his way into my head and take a look around. Regularly. As if it's fun. Or necessary. Or healthy.

'Face it, Tom, the more we've talked, the less we've liked each other. A bit more silence would have been very golden indeed. Do you think you understand any of this? Do you think you can get your prejudiced, talk-addled brain around the idea that a relationship—ha! it's contagious—might actually be enhanced by saying *less*?'

My whole professional life has been based on what Freud called 'the talking cure'. But I'm no Freudian myself; Carl Rogers is my man, and I've seen the brilliant therapeutic effects of client-centred counselling. I've watched the blossoming of a new sense of clarity and the intense feelings of relief as people experience what it's like to be listened to with empathy and concern—people who've spent their whole lives searching for someone to take them seriously. So, when Clare said all that, I resented it as a direct attack not only on my work, but my entire belief system.

And now? Well, I've run that conversation through my head a thousand times. 'The more we've talked, the less we've liked each other.' I accept it was true for her. It might even have been true for me, I suppose. For Clare, being taken seriously did not mean being listened to all the time, because she didn't want to talk all the time. I interpreted her silences as barriers; she interpreted my appeal for constant talk as an intrusion.

The talking cure. You only need a cure if you're sick. You wouldn't take antibiotics if there were no infection. For normal people—whatever that means, but it does mean something in my line of work—there might be such a thing as *too much talking* and too much talking can cause trouble. So can too much silence, but I always knew that. I needed Clare to teach me that words can get in the way. Talk can sully and complicate. I can see how my desire for endless articulation might seem like an assault to someone who is more comfortable with a gentler pace, a quieter tone, a less demanding conversational agenda.

Looking at those children at play, and at Joe's benign figure watching over them, I wonder if I will ever have children and, if I do, whether I will be smart enough to learn Clare's lesson. I've had countless teenagers in my consulting rooms, yearning for parents to back off and give them more space. If I had to identify the most common complaint among the teenagers I see, it would not be their parents' neglect or lack of interest in them; it would be that parents push too hard, crowd too close and get *too* interested. Being taken seriously sometimes means . . . yes, Clare was right, damn her . . . it sometimes means being left in peace to work things out on your own.

Now I find myself wondering how many clients I've disappointed by assuming that taking them seriously can only mean getting them to talk to me. How many of them have been privately resenting my implied pressure on them to keep talking? How many have been praying for a break from all the talk—for a gentler, less verbal approach to their problems? Some of them might even have been married to people like me: according to Clare, I was a relentless, merciless communicator, with expectations that frightened her. There must be many people—people who might once have gone and sat in a silent church—who dream of an escape to a dimly lit room where a counsellor gives them permission to talk when they want, and to shut up when they don't—someone who'll let them say what they want to say, but only when they want to say it.

Here's a consoling thought to someone who's beginning to wonder if he's a neurotic talker: there are people living in Winter Close to whom I've never spoken at all. Brian Stuthridge, for one, but that's not for want of trying. (Brian, come to think of it, might be a classic case of someone who is frightened by the expectation that he should talk on cue. He looks like a man with other problems, but have I been making too much of his preference for non-engagement?) I've never spoken to Mr Nguyen, but only to Mrs, and then only at last year's street party, nor to either of their daughters, though I have waved as I passed them in the car. I've smiled at Samantha in number four, owner of Zorro, but I've never spoken to her, and I've never had any contact with her housemate, Jodie.

There you are, Clare: I've never spoken to seven out of the twenty-three other people who live in this street. I think I'll stop feeling guilty about that and wait for them to make the first move.

SEVENTEEN

Like all addicts, the last thing he'd want to hear is the shock in my voice

As it happens, it doesn't take long for one neighbour to come to me. The request from Mrs Stuthridge is alarming in its simplicity: 'Brian wants to see you.' She is standing on my doorstep in an apron and slippers.

'Now?'

'If possible, yes.'

I put on my jacket ('Don't you ever go anywhere without a jacket?' Clare often asked me) and walk with her across the Close to number one.

The front door is open and Mrs Stuthridge leads the way inside.

'He's upset, I think,' she says to me in the low voice people use when they're visiting the dying.

'Upset?'

'Come through and see for yourself. See if you can understand him.'

I am ushered into a dark space. Although the hall is short and opens almost immediately into a living room, heavy curtains are drawn across the windows. We cross the living room and pass into an equally sombre dining room. I notice I'm walking on tiptoe. In silent procession, we reach a closed door and Mrs Stuthridge knocks.

'He's in there,' she announces and withdraws, leaving me in the gloom.

Nothing happens. I have no idea where Mrs Stuthridge has gone and there's not so much as a rustle from behind the closed door. I can hear gusts of wind stirring leaves on the footpath outside, but nothing at all from inside the house: not the high whistle of a far-off television set, not even the hum of a refrigerator, the drip of a tap or the creak of a door. Nothing.

I cough. Still nothing. I tap tentatively on the door as Mrs Stuthridge had done. Silence.

A dog barks and I distract myself with a recollection of the encounter between Mrs Spenser and Samantha. Is that Zorro or Harold, or a bark from a more distant backyard? Impossible to tell from here. My eyes are becoming accustomed to the gloom though, and I can make out a framed photograph on the wall: a formal portrait of a young couple, both dressed in black, she sitting on a couch and he perched on its arm. I can imagine a musty studio, the photographer crouched under his black cloth, the wife telling the husband to sit up straight and the husband telling the wife to smile, or at least to try to soften her expression. (Clare refused any formal photography at our wedding. She was reluctant for us to be photographed together in any circumstances. I used to imagine it was a deep-seated mistrust of frozen moments that, knowing me, would be subjected to too much scrutiny in the future. It's true: I love gazing at photographs—or, rather, gazing *into* photographs—that seem to reveal things not always obvious at first glance. I usually begin by assuming that no situation is ever quite as idyllic as it can be made to appear in a photograph. But if you look and look, the truth is often in there somewhere.)

Without warning, the door to Brian's room swings wide open—exactly the opposite of the chink I might have expected. He stands back to allow me to enter the room.

For a moment, I'm overwhelmed by a sense of impenetrable chaos and confusion. The room is literally full of books and papers. They are crammed into shelves lining every wall; they are stacked in teetering piles on a large desk in the centre of the room and on a smaller table behind it; they are bursting out of cupboard doors, and spilling from drawers. The floor appears to be covered by loose sheets of paper, magazines and more books. As I step into this extraordinary space, I'm conscious of the rustle of paper underfoot, but there's nowhere else to tread. My first thought is that the place is a fire trap. My second is that I must be in the presence of a full-blown, out-of-control neurotic. This, surely, is Marshall McLuhan's 'typographic man' carried to new and desperate extremes: a man so wedded to the printed page that he has lost all sense of any other possible reality. Brian Stuthridge now appears before me as a quintessential media victim, but his is not a fashionable case of the disease; it's not video games or television soap operas or talkback radio or the Internet that have captured him, but good old print. He's fallen victim to bibliophilia. Gutenberg is the father of his downfall, not John Logie Baird or Bill Gates.

Brian is an addict. Must be. Dysfunctional, isolated from the external world, socially inept to the point of becoming a recluse, gripped by an obsessive need to maintain a reliable supply of the drug that has him in its clutches: yep, it all fits. An addict. Classic case.

Like all addicts, the last thing he'd want to hear is the shock in my voice, or the tedious repetition of the question that everyone must ask, involuntarily, when they see this room for the first time. Avoiding the torrent of print all around me, I nod towards the photograph hanging in the hallway: 'Your parents?'

From somewhere in the back of his throat, Brian makes a gutteral sound that could be disgust, or deprecation, or embarrassment. He shakes his head vigorously. 'Graghh. Nnn . . . *graghh*!'

'No? Mrs Stuthridge's?'

His face reddens. It might be fury. It might be a blush. He shakes his head again, and again the harsh sound issues forth—powerfully expressive of something, but I am at a loss to know what.

'Carrth nnn . . . carrth. Carrth?'

I'm certain it's a question. But what is he asking?

'Brian, your wife said you wanted to see me. Can I help you in some way? I'm Tom.' I extend my hand. 'We've never met. Not properly.'

Brian grips my offered hand firmly and looks directly into my eyes. He seems to be smiling with everything but his mouth: the expression on his face is benign, yet his lips are immobile. He continues to grip my hand in his, and to stare. This is the first time I have ever looked closely at him. He seems a good deal older than I had imagined and there's a distinct impression of frailty. He's well into his seventies, perhaps even older. (So perhaps I have been quite wrong in assuming he drives to work every day. Where else might he go? To a library? To second-hand bookshops? To a warehouse that feeds his habit?)

A mane of white hair falls over his ears and covers his collar, and his shoulders are slightly stooped. He's wearing a tartan dressing gown flapping open to reveal a soiled vest and an improbable pair of faded, ragged jeans. His feet are clad only in brown socks. His face is deeply lined and both front teeth are missing—one of the factors, according to his wife, that might have discouraged him from a face-to-face meeting with his old school friend. I had not imagined that the threatened encounter was to have been between two such old men.

There is no sense of hostility in his manner towards me, but it's nevertheless an uncomfortable moment and I wonder how on earth we are going to break through to some more useful contact. Again he tries to speak: 'Quwarrgh, mboy. Nnn . . . quarrgh, nnn graghh.'

I am sure I can detect 'mboy' in there. Perhaps we are starting to get somewhere.

'Look, Brian, I'm sorry about this, but I can't quite pick up what you're saying. Do you want to take it more slowly? Are you upset about something? Is something wrong? Can I help in some way?'

The thought crosses my mind that he might have suffered a mild stroke; that his wife might have been too alarmed or too frightened to know what to do. Yet she obviously has access to our local doctor: I've shared the waiting room with her more than once. At the same time, I've never heard Brian attempting speech before and there could be an impediment so great that, at moments of awkwardness like this, he becomes incoherent. If that's the case, things might become easier if I can only be patient.

I look around for some sign of Mrs Stuthridge, in the hope of securing her help as an interpreter, or at least receiving some reassurance from her that there's been no sudden change in his condition that might warrant medical attention. But the house beyond the doorway to this strange room yields nothing, and I'm reluctant to call out for fear of irritating or upsetting Brian. Eccentricity is no particular challenge, but I'm not yet convinced there isn't something more. Addicts, even to print, can be unpredictable in their furies.

'Can we sit down?' I enquire cautiously, trying not to slow and simplify my speech as if I'm talking to a child, a foreigner or a patient in a psychiatric ward.

Brian brightens, as if the idea had not occurred to him until now. He shuffles around to the other side of the huge desk, drops into a swivel chair and motions to me to sit in an upright wooden chair facing him across the desk. I have to remove a heap of books to do so, and I place them carefully on top of an existing pile of papers.

As soon as he is seated behind his desk, Brian assumes an air of authority and confidence I would not have believed possible if I had not seen it. The transformation is remarkable: he is clearly the master of this enclosed universe. Watching him carefully, I conclude that his addiction is focused not so much on the room as on the desk and the chair: this is where he feels powerful; this is where his insatiable need of the printed word can be made to appear legitimate; this is where he is able to convince himself that he is not the victim of an addiction at all—rather like the alcoholic who manages to convince himself that the first drink of the day has been forced on him by the pressure of social convention. ('It would be churlish to decline.')

But then he tries to speak and the composure falls away. 'Drreghh . . . nnn . . . drreafl.' He is struggling painfully, but he seems to be saying 'dreadful'.

I imitate: 'Dreadful?'

Again he brightens, nodding his head as vigorously as he had previously shaken it. He waves his arms around: the place is a dreadful mess, would be a fair translation of the gesture.

I smile. 'Would you like to write something down for me? Would that be easier?'

I see at once that I have offended him. He glowers at me, clearly determined to speak. (Yet Alex tells me he sends her poems and never shows the slightest sign of wanting to communicate in any other way.)

'Grrggh. Nnn . . . Grrthisll have. Nnn . . . Thisllhave, ah, go. *Go!*'

I stand to leave, instantly disappointed in myself for having failed so comprehensively to be of any use, yet relieved at the prospect of retreat. Brian also rises, but he is looking agitated and displeased. The face reddens again and he waves at the chaos surrounding us both. He makes a supreme effort to speak: 'This'll go. *Go.* Nnn . . . got to go!' He motions to me to sit.

He produces an envelope from a drawer in the desk, opens it and hands me a sheet of paper. It emerges that this is the note from his school friend.

B:

I was pleased to receive your latest, together with the final ms of The Geography of War: Thermopylae to Long Tan.

I've passed it on to George, as requested, and he's already sent it to their US affiliate—he reckons there's no one qualified to handle it locally. He is deeply impressed, and so am I.

Sorry I intruded, but I would have liked to see you again after so many years—shake your hand, etc. To be frank, I also wanted to see the place where such an astonishing piece of work was created. George thinks this will blow several entire theories out of the water and even rehabilitate Montesquieu. He's predicting the establishment of an entire discipline based on the historical consequences of geography and meteorology. Needless to say, he's hunting for a catchier title. Don't mind George. He also wants to know whether you've ever thought of studying the effects of diet on the outcome of the great battles of history. I think he's joking. (Actually, I suspect it's already been done.) Do keep in touch—I enjoy your letters, and I agree with you about the political scene. How have you managed to stay off the electoral roll? The hermit life has much to offer, but Barbara won't come at it—she still hankers after the limelight. (No, I don't get it either.)

As ever, Len

Brian is a scholar, not an addict. I am a fool. His incoherence is the perfect disguise.

I hand back the note, look at him and smile sheepishly, though he can't have known what was going on inside my head. 'Congratulations.'

'Thghrrks. Nnn . . . all grrhht go. T'go.' Again, he stretches his arms expansively.

'All to go? Your books and papers? You're planning a clean out?'

Brian almost smiles, clearly relieved the struggle is over.

'To a library? Or a university? What about your friend Len? Is he a publisher? Might he be able to help?'

He points directly at me, nodding.

'You want my help?'

He hands me another sheet of paper, this one containing the name and address of a well-known Melbourne historian.

'Shall I contact him on your behalf? I'd be pleased to do that. Should I mention your forthcoming book?' I *am* pleased to do it, though it's unclear why Brian has chosen me.

Brian shrugs. His whole demeanour has changed. As long as he is not attempting speech, he appears tranquil, content, fulfilled. Clearly, the book has been a life's work and it's a triumph for him. We both rise and move towards the door of his study.

I point to the framed photograph in the hallway. 'Might I enquire who they are? Your side of the family, or your wife's?'

With obvious irritation, Brian takes the picture off the wall, turns it over, and shows me the inscription on the back: Otto von Bismarck and Johanna von Puttkamer.

EIGHTEEN

'Are you one of those tragic types that actually feels better when you're down?'

'Johnny O'Keefe used to live round here. The Wild One, you know?' Alex asserts this with the confidence of a quizmaster who knows the contestant is way out of his depth.

I enjoy surprising her: 'Oh, I know who Johnny O'Keefe was. Australia's answer to Elvis, no less. And yes, I did know he lived in Castlecrag. So did Gwen Meredith, by the way.'

'Who?'

Jemma is asleep in her bassinet and Alex and I are sitting on her back verandah, sipping coffee from mugs decorated with Leunig cartoons. I'm not surprised she's never heard of Gwen Meredith; I wouldn't have been surprised if she'd never heard of Johnny O'Keefe.

'She wrote the ABC's longest running radio serials—first *The Lawsons* and then *Blue Hills*. It was nothing less than a life's work—thirty-two years of continuous scriptwriting. People were positively hooked on them apparently, before television. I never heard them myself—I must have been too young, or perhaps my parents weren't interested. But I'd be prepared to bet you'd have loved them. *Blue Hills* was based on the life of an extended family in rural Australia and people say it was one of the things that kept the rural fantasy alive for an entire generation of suburban housewives.'

'Are you calling me a suburban housewife?'

The words were out before I had realised what I was saying. 'What? No. I mean . . . in Gwen Meredith's day, that's what most women were. That's all. No offence.'

'Ah, Tom, you're a strange man sometimes. I was joking. Of course I'm a suburban housewife. What else am I?'

'Well, I guess you're . . . a dreamer, a poet, a mother, a . . . a wife. And any time you chose to, you could be . . . what was your job before the baby?'

Alex wrinkles her nose and shrugs. It's clear she was never a career woman. 'I worked from home for my father. Keeping the books, ordering stuff, paying the wages, making appointments. All the usual things to do with running a small business. Dad is an electrical contractor. I'd love to have another little job like that, part-time, but Chika doesn't believe in wives who work.'

'So you're prepared to go along with that? That and living in the suburbs?'

'Oh, Mister Cut-and-dried! Who said I was resigned to anything? Hang loose, Mother Goose. That's me. Keep your options open.'

'But you are married. You do have a child. And you're not about to move, not after you've done all these beautiful renovations.'

'Which century did you say you were living in, exactly? Oh dear, Tom, you need to think outside the square. You remind me of my father. Don't be offended, by the way—I love my daddy dearly. But he is rather inclined to think you can only be one thing at a time. Not me. Chika doesn't want me to *work*. That doesn't mean he doesn't want me to *live*. I'm all the things you said, and more. *And*, just in case you're in any doubt, I'm a suburban housewife as well. If I wanted to be, if I chose to be, I could be *nothing but* a suburban housewife. What would be wrong with that?'

I hold my hands up, palms outward, and say nothing. Sometimes I say nothing when I'm with Alex because I don't entirely trust myself to stay within the limits of what I take to be safe ground. Sometimes I say nothing because I'm frankly enchanted; speechless; bewildered by the intensity of my response to her. Sometimes I say nothing because I learned my feminism at the feet of Clare and I realise the world has moved on, even in these past few years, with remarkable speed. I sometimes wonder whether Clare now talks the same way Alex talks. Feminism used to be about being tough and independent—and a paid job was *de rigueur*. Now, Alex tells me, it's about choice, including the choice not to be independent. I enjoy the paradox.

Perhaps I don't need to be so careful, though. Alex's guiding principle seems to be that everything is okay; everything is cool, as long as it's said or done with good intent. Openness is the abiding virtue in Alex's book. She's convinced that I'm too judgmental in my attitudes, to everything from her poetry to the failure of my own marriage.

'You make Clare sound like a bully. What would she say about you? When people say there are two sides to every story, they hardly ever mean it. What they mean is there's a right and a wrong side to every story, and theirs is always the right one. Open yourself up, Tom. Hang loose. People are mostly doing their best. Give them the benefit of the doubt. And when it turns out you're wrong, when you hit the wall, go away and do something else. Find someone new. Give it your best shot, sure; stick with it while the vital signs are good. But if you hang on past your use-by date, there's always trouble. Capital T. It's never a good idea to push: people are either with you or they're not. You can't persuade them, and it's a big mistake to try. You end up being a pest and someone's sure to swat you, like Clare did. But face it, baby, she was getting on your nerves too. She'd passed her use-by too. You were ready to swat *her*. So why the long face all these years later? You carrying a torch, by any chance . . . eh, Mister Cut-and-dried? Or are you one of those tragic types that actually feels better when you're down? Nothing you like better than licking your wounds, going over old ground: Poor me, what a cad I was, what a failure I am, nobody loves me . . . is that it? I hope not. I don't think so. Anyway, God, you're the shrink. What am I saying?'

'A counsellor, Alex. A psychologist. Not a shrink. That's a psychiatrist. Different thing.'

'There you go again, Mister Cut-and-dried. That's a good name for you. You seem to have everything in a neat box. Who gives a . . . well, I was going to say who gives a shit about the difference, so I'll say it. Who gives a shit? Okay? You're in the people business right? Healing the sick, one way or another? You're supposed to be the expert on all this relationships stuff.'

There's a snuffly cry from the bassinet and Alex jumps out of her chair and goes inside. I hear her cooing and clucking. She begins humming a tune. Soon the baby is settled. 'Come and look,' Alex calls softly to me.

I join her, bending over the bassinet. As I gaze at Jemma, I feel Alex's hand slide up my back and curl over my shoulder. The moment is charged for me with sexual energy; for her it's a routinely affectionate gesture, with about the same significance as patting Mrs Spenser's dog. I *hope* it has no more significance than that for her; I hope there are no complications in our increasingly frequent meetings—every Saturday afternoon and one or two evenings during the week. To tell the whole truth, I hope even more desperately that there's every imaginable complication; that she is conflicted and confused; that she is struggling to keep her feelings towards me under control; that every touch, no matter how light, is a sign. Fortunately for my sanity the evidence supports the first hope more strongly than the second: why would I want to become involved with a woman more than ten years my junior with a new baby, a husband on remand and goodness knows what prospects?

Alex talks as if she both loves and fears Chika; harbours genuine affection for him and loathes the life he leads; worries about where all his money comes from and spends it cheerfully; respects him as the father of her child and believes he's set on a course of self-destruction that may well drag her and the baby into a lifetime of trouble.

We draw back from the bassinet and return to the verandah. 'I've been to see Brian Stuthridge,' I say, mainly to prolong the conversation. 'He's written a history of war that is apparently going to take the academic world by storm. Have you ever seen his study, by the way?' I feel a stab of guilt, as if I should have been more respectful of Brian's privacy.

Alex appears not to be listening. She is biting her lip and stifling a sob. I stand up and move towards her, and she launches herself out of the chair and throws herself against my chest, weeping. I hold her gently, murmuring reassurances.

This is about Chika. (What else would it be about?) Looking at the baby, summoning me to share the moment with her, Alex must have felt a sudden pang over the absence of Jemma's father. Gazing together at a new baby must be such a natural, intimate thing for parents to do; perhaps it would be easier to handle such a separation when there were no children at all and the remaining partner could be out and about, enjoying some unexpected independence. Even if the children were a little older, and the dynamics of family life more established and balanced, one partner's absence would not be so noticeable. (Some of my friends tell me that when they come home after a business trip, their wives make it clear that everything was running so smoothly in their absence, their return home is a bit of a disruption to the routine.)

The other thing for Alex, trembling against me, must be the uncertainty. She has been on her own for several weeks already. Now, with Christmas looming, there's no sign of a quick resolution. Depending on the outcome of Chika's trial, this separation could easily stretch into years. What kind of marriage would that be? What kind of plans could she make?

'Come and let me read you some of my new poems. Don't say a single word, okay? No dumb questions. No false compliments. Sit and listen. Be open.'

And so I am.

Later, seeing me to the door, Alex pauses. She's calm this time, but she places both hands against my chest and tips her head back to look up at me. 'The tragedy is, I think I could make you really, really happy,' she says, and kisses me lightly. Then she places a finger over my lips, smiles and pushes me out the door. 'Wild one,' she calls to my retreating back.

Back home, I check my e-mail. I have a friend in Melbourne who likes to send me pearls of ancient wisdom in response to whatever is going on in my life. True to form, he has offered a Confucian commentary on the account I sent him of my meeting with Brian Stuthridge:

> *The Master said: 'A scholar sets his heart on the Way; if he is ashamed of his shabby clothes and coarse food, he is not worth listening to.'*

NINETEEN

Ordinary streets for ordinary people

Living in Winter Close has one serious drawback. Every time we give our address to someone, we get the same response: 'No, we have to get through autumn yet.' Or: 'Yes, there's a definite nip in the air.' Or, most commonly: 'Is it?' People seem to feel some reaction is called for and they never let themselves down.

The name comes from a certain Alderman Winter, an irascible member of the Willoughby Municipal Council in the 1930s. Winter was a passionate advocate for the creation of a new housing estate consisting of 'ordinary' building blocks in 'ordinary' streets for 'ordinary' people. His attention had been drawn to a few acres of vacant land that lay to the east of Eastern Valley Way, on the border between Willoughby and Castlecrag, and the subdivision of this area had become his obsession.

Winter had been an outspoken opponent of US architect Walter Burley Griffin's plan for Castlecrag: the council's minutes record a series of colourful diatribes directed at 'self-aggrandising fascists who want to tell people what they can and can't build on their own land', 'the lunatic fringe of urban design', 'a bohemian rhapsody heading for bohemian tragedy' . . . all peppered with dark references to 'fairies at the bottom of the garden' and 'nefarious goings-on under cover of bushland'. He was particularly enraged by tales of poetry meetings held under the auspices of Burley Griffin and his wife, Marion Mahoney. Members of the Griffin–Mahoney circle were also wont to hold fancy-dress parties and to support the work of a local enterprise known as the Haven Scenic Theatre. All this was anathema to Winter and he could scarcely contain his rage at the thought of such activities taking place within the very municipality of which he was an alderman. 'Smokescreens, you mark my words,' he would say, though what they were meant to conceal was never specified: it's hard to imagine what could have been more scandalous, from Winter's point of view, than poetry readings.

In response to all this ponceyness, Winter was determined to put his plain stamp on the remaining parcel of land, so he bludgeoned the council's officers into creating a series of straight and parallel streets that protested, by their very existence, against Burley Griffin's seductive curves, circuits and crescents. He gave his streets plain names like William Street and Richmond Avenue. Within these plain streets, he insisted on the creation of conventional rectangular building blocks with a building code that ensured no one would build anything but achingly conventional bungalows. Winter dismissed Burley Griffin's dream of houses integral with the landscape as fanciful nonsense. (In fact, out of the fifty houses Burley Griffin planned for Castlecrag, a mere sixteen were built. Griffin and Mahoney left in 1936.)

When the planning of Winter's subdivision was almost complete, and only one of the new streets was still without a name, the council's officers, possibly making mischief, did something Alderman Winter could scarcely resist: they named the last street after him. The irony was that this one remaining street was a curved cul-de-sac, one of Winter's pet hates. What he made of 'Close', rather than Street, Road or Avenue, is not recorded, but the officials had their way. A rocky creek that ran past the end of the street (since converted into a covered drain) prevented a link to any other street, so Winter Close it became.

We have one advantage over the other streets in Winter's little domain. Perhaps because our street bore his name we had a paved footpath from the beginning; the others are still waiting for theirs, seventy years later.

Winter would have been delighted by the way things have turned out. The houses in our part of Castlecrag are as tediously homogeneous as he intended them to be and occasional attempts to modify the basic bungalow theme haven't worked. Grotesque add-ons—a Spanish arch borrowed from some hacienda, a couple of Greek columns or the mock-Tudor cladding of a fibro gable— look like aliens that were never likely to be assimilated.

There are quieter forms of resistance to the Winter aesthetic. Houses in strictly planned subdivisions like ours are a bit like the handwriting of people who all learned to write from the same teacher: the basic form is recognisable, but the drive for self-expression gradually asserts itself as personal flourishes are incorporated into the standard style.

Letterboxes are a favourite form of deviation from the norm. Mrs Spenser has a tin drum supported by a wavy chain in defiance of Winter's edict that letterboxes should be discreetly set into the compulsory brick front fence. The O'Goods have half-a brick lying on the ground, attached by a length of rope to the base of a nearby shrub: the postman is meant to place the letters under the brick so they won't blow away, and I suppose he does.

The longer you live in a place, the less the aesthetics matter. I see clients from all over Sydney whose loyalty to their local areas is often passionate: the concept of the stamping ground lies deep within us. A client from Mascot once expressed bewilderment at the thought of anyone choosing to live in the Eastern Suburbs or on the North Shore. She wasn't talking streetscape or money or convenience: she was expressing the powerful sense of identity that small, local communities confer on their members. Tucked into the nooks and crannies of any big city, it's these little communities— the mothers who hover at the school gate, the regulars at a pub or coffee bar, the joggers who nod to each other on their regular beat even if they don't have the wind to speak, the local shopkeepers, the neighbours walking their dogs and wheeling their bins in and out—that allow people to make sense of the idea of belonging to a place. Who could feel comfortable and secure trying to belong to something as vast and amorphous as 'Sydney'? The truth is, Sydney broke apart long ago. Part of the magic of the place is that everyone who clings to their own piece of it thinks they have hold of the real Sydney. 'Sydney's such a small town,' people say, as they carve out their lives in one of its many little compartments.

TWENTY

This has not been an auspicious first encounter with my neighbour

Sitting on my balcony at dusk, Christmas lights already winking from the windows of the Abels' and the Nguyens' and our street party only a week away, it would be easy to become sentimental about the Close. The curious collection of people who live here form the closest thing any of us has to a domestic herd.

Sometimes it bothers me that I have no family—then again, neither does my new eighteen-year-old client (Chika's mistress: I'm convinced of it) and neither does Brian Stuthridge (though he does have a wife, which is more than can be said for me). Being 'alone in the world' is a melodramatic way of putting it: many people survive perfectly well without a family context. As the birthrate plummets, many more will have to get used to the idea. Clare's grandmother was one of thirty-one cousins, but those days are gone.

But I doubt we'll become a nation of recluses. The more we live in ones and twos, the more our herd instinct will assert itself. Rich's longed-for village will become a widespread reality in suburbs like ours. If the extended family isn't going to be the herd we graze and mooch and moo with, we'll have to create our own substitutes. For some of my friends, it's the work group; for me, it's the Close. I can't easily imagine moving. Rich, Ruth and the three children, Enid and Joe, Sexy and Upton, the Nguyens, Alex and Jemma, Mrs Spenser, even the Stuthridges—these are my people now. I didn't say 'my friends'; I said 'my people'. Like families, you can't choose your neighbours.

My neighbours in number four, Samantha and Jodie, are the only renters in the street, as far as I'm aware, and my best attempts to set aside all the usual prejudices about renters have failed. There's no getting away from the fact that they don't look after the place. The garden is a mess. The lawn is rarely mown. The blinds at their front windows are torn, the curtains bedraggled. My bedroom looks into their backyard and that's an eyesore too. Discarded bits of gym equipment—an exercise bike, a mini-trampoline, weights—lie in a pile beside the garage and the vegetable garden established by the owners has been overrun by some kind of vine. Assorted boxes and cartons are left out in all weathers, crushed and whitening.

My reticence about talking to the two young women who rent the house has placed me in the position of not knowing my own next-door neighbours—the Sydney stereotype. It's easy to remain aloof, even without trying: although I walk to and from the bus stop, they go everywhere by car. (That's another irritating thing about them: they park one car in the drive—never in the garage—and the other stays in the street.) From my balcony I've waved to Samantha walking her dog, but that's about it.

Now, as darkness closes in, the other tenant, Jodie, is calling me. There's no particular urgency in her voice, but it's an unmistakable call for help.

I run downstairs and out into the garden, jumping the low fence that runs between us. Jodie is standing in her front garden—short, slim, fair and fresh-faced—wearing jeans and an oversized, mannish-looking shirt open over a singlet. Her feet are bare, her long hair piled and pinned on top of her head. I make the assessment that seems to have become habitual: no, even if I'd married young and had children straightaway, she's a bit too old to be my daughter.

'What can I do for you?' I say, conscious of our absurd status as total strangers, though neighbours. 'Is there a problem?'

'Hello,' she says warmly, 'I'm Jodie. You're Tom, is that right?' I nod, wishing I'd begun like that. 'This is going to sound totally pathetic, but there's a huge tarantula on our bathroom ceiling and I'm too much of a wimp to get rid of it. Sam usually attends to that kind of thing, but she's away. Would you mind? I'd hate it to disappear before we caught it, and then not know where it was lurking. I'm sure it's harmless, but it's a bit, you know . . . freaky?'

'Snakes might be a problem, but spiders I can handle. Lead on.'

Jodie stands aside to let me through and closes the front door behind us. The interior of the house is quite a different proposition from the exterior. All the floors in the living area are bare timber boards and the place is sparsely but stylishly furnished in the Scandinavian manner. Bright posters adorn the walls and everything looks remarkably neat and tidy. A computer sits on a pine desk in one corner of the living room, surrounded by stacks of manila folders, and a tall bookcase serves as a room divider between lounge and dining areas. The components of a stereo system are stacked on top of each other in another corner and the sounds of Enya are filling the space. It's the very model of a spartan interior.

Jodie reads my mind, unfortunately. 'You probably expected this to be a dump, judging from the outside. We're not very good neighbours are we? The truth is I'm used to living in apartments but Sam persuaded me to share this place with her while she finishes her doctorate. It was cheaper than anything else we could find in a hurry. But we're not gardeners, I'm afraid. I'm not used to having an outside as well as an inside. Well, I didn't have to tell you that, did I? Anyway, here's the bathroom.'

I poke my head around the door and there, sure enough, is a huntsman—huge, grey and hairy—clinging to the ceiling directly above the toilet.

'Do you have a broom? A plastic container would be useful too. Something with a lid.'

I stay in the bathroom, keeping an eye on the spider, while Jodie fetches a fluffy yellow nylon version of a feather duster (don't they own a proper broom?) and a large plastic bowl with a blue lid. My plan is to sweep the spider off the ceiling and into the bath, and then trap it inside the plastic bowl. What we then do will be up to Jodie: Clare would have insisted on 'restoring it to nature', but I suspect Jodie will want me to flush it down the toilet, quick smart.

The handle of the brush is disconcertingly short and the ceiling is quite high. I decide it would be prudent to stand on the lid of the toilet for my initial sweep. I take off my shoes, lower the lid and stand on it. Even on tiptoe, I can scarcely reach the ceiling and my movement has already disturbed the spider. Accompanied by a muffled shriek from Jodie, followed by an embarrassed giggle, the huntsman has crawled into the centre of the ceiling, directly above the edge of the bath. From the point of view of its ultimate destination, this is an improvement, but reaching the spider will now be more difficult. I might have to stand on the edge of the bath itself.

Although it will be a stretch, I decide to make one attempt from my vantage point on the toilet lid. I glance at Jodie: she has covered her face with her hands and is peeping out between her fingers. I rise onto tiptoe again, lean to my right, over the edge of the bath, reaching as far as I can without losing balance. It's clear that I will be able to reach the spider, but I'll have to flick it quite sharply to disengage it from the ceiling and send it into the bath. I consider going home for a ladder, but I'm reluctant to leave in case the spider scurries into another room and Jodie loses track of it. It could become a long night.

As I stretch out, carefully positioning the end of the brush for the right angle of flick, there's an almighty crack from the plastic toilet lid and one foot goes straight through, into the water in the bottom of the bowl. The sequence of events in the next few seconds is complex, and Jodie's shrieks add to the air of chaos, but it goes roughly like this: with my right calf jammed in the broken toilet lid and my foot still immersed in the water below, I lose my balance completely, but not before the spider, no doubt as confused as I am, jumps onto the end of the extended brush. It then rushes along the handle, across my hand and up my arm as I fall heavily to my right, across the rim of the bath, whacking my hip and hitting my head on the side of the bath. Too dazed to be concerned about the huntsman now crawling over my face and into my hair, I struggle to sort out where my limbs are and where they should be.

My right foot has been lifted out of the water in the toilet bowl, only to be jammed at the ankle by the jagged gash in the toilet lid. My right knee feels completely immobilised—twisted and painful. My left leg is free and undamaged, lying uselessly on top of my right. My right arm is pinned beneath me, my neck is twisted and, to judge from Jodie's sympathetic dabbing, there's a certain amount of blood seeping from a wound in my head where it came into violent contact with the bottom of the bath.

Frankly, I'm surprised to be conscious.

'Could you possibly free my foot?' I ask Jodie, hoping she turns out to be a practical kind of woman, in spite of her fear of spiders. I need not have worried: she's quickly on the job with a kitchen knife, hacking away at the remains of the plastic lid and easing my foot out through the rough hole she's created.

'Don't try to move. You've cut your head. I'll get a clean cloth to stop the bleeding. Is anything broken, do you think?'

I'm feeling too groggy to speak, but I grunt in a way that's meant to encourage rather than alarm her. I wouldn't be at all surprised if my right leg has sustained some serious damage and I'm worried about my neck. A dislocated shoulder seems possible too, but there's surprisingly little pain.

Jodie returns and presses a fresh cloth to my head. I assume the huntsman is no longer tangled in my hair, but I decide not to ask her to check: there's enough going on for now.

'Should I call an ambulance or a doctor? What do you think? Do you want me to try and move you out of there?'

I wave my free left arm to reassure her. An ambulance sounds like an overreaction. My right shoulder is beginning to throb quite painfully and my neck is sore, but I can move all my fingers and toes and my right knee, to my surprise, feels as if it is going to be able to function after all. But I need another moment or two to compose myself before I try anything too heroic.

There's a sudden crash in my ear and a triumphant shout from Jodie: 'Got him!' Drawing on hidden reserves of courage, she's trapped the spider inside the plastic bowl, pressing it against the side of the bath. 'Ooh, it's horrible. What will I do with it?'

Dizziness is overwhelming me; I shall have to leave the spider to Jodie. I hear her slide the lid under the bowl and snap the lid shut, but I can feel myself sinking under a wave of nausea. I need to get out of this position. Pressing my left foot against the rim of the toilet bowl, I ease myself further into the bath, with no apparent ill-effects. I manage to keep sliding until I'm lying on the bottom, with one foot resting on the edge of the bath. This has not been an auspicious first encounter with my neighbour.

When I come to, I'm still lying in the bath, but my head is supported by a pillow and there's a blanket over me. I feel comfortable, but disinclined to move. Jodie and Alex—*Alex?*—are both kneeling beside the bath.

'Where's Jemma?'

'Enid's looking after her. She's fine. But you . . . look at you!'

I flex both knees and, although the right one is excruciatingly painful, it works. I move my head gingerly from side to side: that all seems to work too, though my neck feels as if it might need some attention. My head throbs. Otherwise . . . okay.

'I'm fine, I think. Nothing broken.'

'I'll get you some tea,' Jodie says and disappears. Alex takes my hand in both of hers and gives it a squeeze. 'A bit unsteady on your feet, eh? Too much bebop juice? I knew you were a wild one.' The teasing intimacy in her tone is unmistakable and tears prick my eyes. She says nothing, but gently wipes them away. I'm not fully alert, still drifting a bit, feeling the need for sleep.

Jodie returns with some tea. I sip it gratefully, feeling simultaneously like a wounded hero and a total phoney. What made her decide to fetch Alex? How well do they know each other?

'Doctor Ruth is going to drop in on her way home from the surgery. Alex called her when she saw the state you were in.'

Bless you, Alex.

'Where's the spider?'

'Dead. Alex disposed of it for me.'

I feel as if I'm smiling. 'Sorry about your toilet lid.'

Doctor Ruth bustles in, toting her black bag and tut-tutting about the situation.

'Let me look at you.'

Before she says another word, she takes a foam collar from her bag and fastens it around my neck. Then she checks the wound on my head, runs her hands down my arms and legs and asks me to bend each knee in turn. She proceeds with what feels like a routine check-up, except that I'm lying in a bath and feeling even more foolish than I normally do when I visit a doctor to discuss symptoms that have miraculously disappeared on the short journey from waiting room to surgery. But these aches and pains are real.

'I think it's time to get you out of there and into a chair. Alex can help me.'

The journey to a chair is slow and difficult, but Ruth is strong and sure of herself and I am inspired—I think that's the word—by finding myself the exclusive focus of Alex's attentions. Finally, I lower myself into a canvas chair, feeling as if I've been restored to the real world. Jodie puts another mug of tea in my hand. Enya is still playing. Even in this enfeebled state, I realise it would seem churlish to ask Jodie to change the CD.

'I'd better pop in to see the children. Rich is held up, apparently. But don't try to go anywhere. I'll be back. I want to get something to support that knee and we might need to put your right arm in a sling for a day or two.'

I had assumed I would finally get around to meeting Jodie at the street party planned for the week before Christmas. If I'd bothered to anticipate what kind of meeting it might be, I would have imagined we'd say a polite hello and ask about each other's work—perhaps venturing as far as a tentative enquiry about our plans for Christmas Day and the holiday season, carefully avoiding any impression of prying into family or personal circumstances. Such conversational skirmishes are like a kind of reconnaissance—never aiming to hit any particular target, merely establishing what's there in case further engagement becomes either necessary or desirable. By convention, they are designed to discourage invasions of privacy (much less any surprise attacks on the psyche) and I hate their civilised restraint: I'd much rather go for the jugular, conversationally speaking.

Conventional wisdom says death is the last taboo in Western societies; in suburban culture, the last taboo is direct, confrontational, investigative conversation. We are more inhibited by our obsession with privacy—our own and each other's—than by any of the lurid sexual repressions that are supposed to cripple us. The so-called respect for privacy constrains our forays into each other's worlds to such an extent that most of the treasures on offer are never unearthed. (Friends hearing me talk about Winter Close often complain that the people who live in their streets are dull, which sounds to me like an admission of a tragic failure to connect. No human is dull, only defensive.)

But my contact with Jodie will never have an opportunity either to wither or to flourish: we'll be trapped, as in aspic, by our shared participation in a small but intense domestic drama. Our future conversation, however cursory and fleeting, is bound to be punctuated by jocular references to smashed toilet seats, menacing spiders, head wounds and blackouts. There'll be an implicit acknowledgment on both sides that our sudden and spurious intimacy was created out of nothing, and that, as is proper in such cases, we should stick to lighthearted, ritualistic repetition of the facts, embroidering them as we go. We'll accept as dangerous and delusional the presumption that there's some permanent bond between us because an accident threw us together: such presumptions raise hollow expectations, and we'll confirm our mutual understanding of that, at the right moment, by relaxed and confident eye contact.

TWENTY-ONE

'Loving him is like applying a daily ointment'

Doctor Ruth is a very different case from Jodie. She and I have had the framework of a relationship—nothing more—for years, maintained through cheerful waves over the fence and occasional matter-of-fact conversations about such things as the children's progress, Mrs Spenser's building application or, a few years ago, Clare's departure. (The breakdown of our marriage seemed dramatic to my neighbours because of its suddenness and the abruptness of Clare's goodbyes; they sympathised cautiously, but never probed.) But there's been no reason or opportunity to put any flesh on the bare bones of our connection. We've never talked to each other *about* each other. Ruth has been my neighbour's wife; I've always known her, as it were, via Rich.

In the aftermath of the accident in Jodie's bathroom, the tenor of our relationship has altered. Ruth has been to see me several times, each visit combining an assessment of my rate of recovery (quick) with some conversation over a drink (slow). It is as though layers of Ruth have been peeled back and someone quite different from Rich's portrait of the clinical 'Doctor Ruth' is emerging. I like her.

She is a less confident, less assertive and more engaging woman than I had imagined previously, based on Rich's descriptions and on my own cursory encounters with her. If someone is presented to you as being strong, accomplished and positive, you're unlikely to pick up any indications to the contrary in the tangential contacts of suburban life.

Still, I can see where 'strong, accomplished and positive' come from: Ruth is all those things, but they are softened by attractive hesitations and hints of disappointment. She is a frustrated opera singer, for a start, whose parents actively discouraged her early interest in music because they thought the hectic round of lessons, concerts, eisteddfods and travel would complicate their already busy lives. She somehow manages to squeeze private singing lessons into her schedule. (Do she and Upton ever sing together, I wonder; does Upton even know of her interest in singing?) Once she set her course for medicine—a choice that seems to have been more her father's than hers—her life was consumed by the combination of study and the care of her father: her mother died within a year or two of Ruth leaving school.

Up close, Ruth looks tired and worn. Her brown eyes are kind and concerned in their constant search for contact with mine, but they are troubled eyes as well. Though she smiles a great deal—a wide, open, generous smile, unambiguous in its message of goodwill—a cloud hangs over her like a veil of sadness. In repose, her face sags and her chin drops. Her back remains resolutely straight though, as if her father might have told her that anything can be faced if you keep your shoulders square. But it sometimes looks like a struggle.

Each of her visits ends with a long hug—affectionate, certainly, but expressing some need of support, some half-buried yearning for connection, as well.

It's hard not to be impressed by Ruth's loyalty to Rich, even though it quickly emerges that she longs to be taken more seriously by him. His self-absorption has disappointed her and she has been emotionally exhausted by his constant flirtation with the thought that life might be better if it were lived somewhere else.

'And the fuss he kicked up over poor Mrs Spenser's plans for a room in the roof was embarrassing. But that's Rich for you. Boots and all. You have to love his energy. I would be having a very dull life without Rich.'

'But I thought you were the main obstacle in the way of Mrs Spenser's plans?'

'Me? Good heavens, no. I helped her with the sketches. Rich was furious when he found out. Consorting with the enemy. I could never think of Mrs Spenser as an enemy. Could you?'

'Hardly.'

Obviously Rich has wanted me to believe that Ruth is less tolerant than she actually is and that he is more tolerant than he really is. Why? (Never ask why: that's the first rule of counselling. People might think they are expected to give a rational-sounding explanation for something that isn't rational at all. 'Is there anything else you'd like to say about that?' is much better: less threatening, less agenda-setting, less demanding.) For reasons known only to Rich himself he evidently wants to project the image of a person who wouldn't object to a perfectly reasonable building application by a neighbour, even though he is happy—even eager—to portray himself to me as being irascible, intolerant and feisty on other subjects.

At several points in our newly intense conversations, Ruth seems to reach a point where she is about to confide in me, but then she backs away. Now it is happening again.

'Rich and I . . . well, you know, things are never . . . You know about Rich and the university I assume.'

'Yes. It's tough. No wonder he's upset. I thought he seemed a bit reluctant to tell you all about it. I'm glad he did.'

'Oh, he's a baby. He's so transparent and so vulnerable. He tells me everything, even when he thinks he isn't going to. Sometimes he tries to protect me from whatever's worrying him, but it never works. Why should it? I love him. I want to support him, but I'm perfectly clear-eyed about him. He seems to harbour this idea that I have him on a pedestal and wouldn't be able to deal with some of the harsher realities about him or his job, or anything else. He's quite wrong, by the way. I could never love him if I couldn't reach him. It's his foibles that endear me to him as much as anything else, even though they drive me crazy—like his rural thing. I might wring his neck if he talks about moving to the country one more time. I often think of something a friend of my mother's once said of her husband of fifty years: I never once contemplated divorce; murder, often, but never divorce.

'I know where this pedestal thing comes from. He can't quite believe, or can't quite accept, that I'm committed to him. He was never loved in such an unconditional way when he was a child— I think his parents were always setting goals for him, egging him on, making him feel as if it was his achievements they loved, rather than Rich himself. He was a very bright boy, obviously, and he's a very clever man. But that's not what I love about him. I love the way his hair curls at the back of his neck as much as I love his mind. It's not about any of that, though, is it? It's never about specific things. You must understand that, surely, even if Rich doesn't.'

I am nodding and smiling, and perhaps I do understand, but my mind keeps flying to Clare: she, too, found it impossible to accept unqualified devotion. She seemed perplexed—even irritated—by any evidence that I was truly devoted to her. Our differences were never remotely connected to whether I loved her or not. I loved our differences, our disagreements; I loved her independence of thought; I even loved the passion of her challenges to some of my fondest beliefs. I didn't always enjoy it, but I was convinced, right up to the end, that the tension between us could be creative. I was wrong. My devotion was misplaced. But I don't think Ruth's is. Perhaps it's easier for a needy bloke like Rich—or like me—to live with a devoted partner. Clare found it too heavy a burden. She wanted to be loved with a light touch . . . the trouble was that I wanted both to give and to receive more than a light touch. Now, perhaps, I could settle for less. I'm not sure.

'I'll tell you a revealing little story about Rich.' Ruth has her hands clasped around her knees, lifting her feet off the ground and rocking back and forth in the chair. Her black hair is hanging loosely around her shoulders and she looks eager, like a student. 'His family lived modestly and austerely. They weren't poor by any means, but his parents made a religion out of abstemiousness. There was one regular treat though. His father used to bring home a box of chocolates every Friday night and present it to Rich's mother. It was always the same brand, always bought from the same shop in the city. The four of them—the parents and the two boys—would be allowed to eat one chocolate each and the box would be put away. After dinner each night of the week, the box would be produced again and, like a little ritual, they'd each have one. There was much debate, night after night, about who was choosing soft or hard centres, and whether people were properly acknowledging and accommodating each other's tastes and preferences. Then, on the next Friday night, the new box would be brought home and the cycle repeated.'

'Sounds quite sensible to me. You said it was a revealing story. Have I missed something?'

'It's not what his family did. It's how Rich reacted to it later. When we were first married, he used to bring home a box of chocolates every night and insist we worked our way through them in one go. I eventually had to put a stop to that, in the interests of both our waistlines, but it carried over into other areas of our lives. The chocolates were part of a bigger pattern. Rich's family would go to the same modest beach house for one week's summer holiday every year; that was the only holiday they ever had. When we were first married, Rich would sweep me off for frequent holidays— more than I ever wanted or needed—and never to the same place twice. It became an article of faith with him. It was like an obsession; like a rather childish kind of rebelliousness. He was quite conscious of what he was doing, but he couldn't stop doing it. Clothes, cars, eating out, theatre tickets . . . he wanted to live as extravagantly as we could possibly afford to and with us both working, that meant we could afford quite a lot.

'Then . . . the baby . . .'

Ruth falls silent. She is elsewhere. Her eyes are unfocused; her face becomes vacant, mask-like. I have no idea what she is trying to convey by any of this. Rich's antics sound like a pretty normal, if slightly immature, pattern of compensatory behaviour. Many deprived kids overdo things when they are let off the financial leash. They usually end up, as parents, being appalled by their children's willingness to follow their example of rampant materialism and, too late, start preaching about the virtues of their own more modest, more abstemious upbringings. Quite often parents become angry about the effects of their own lack of restraint and transfer that anger onto their children, criticising them for reflecting the very values the parents have transmitted. I'm constantly surprised by the number of clients I see who disapprove of their kids' values, yet have trouble detecting their own influence in shaping them. No wonder their kids are confused.

Ruth remains silent and so do I. Finally she speaks, quietly and haltingly.

'Laura is our second child, you know.'

'I didn't know. I'm sorry. Do you want to talk about what happened?'

'Rich has asked me never to discuss this with anyone outside the family, but I do want to talk about it, yes. But I don't want *you* to talk about it. Is that understood? I like you and I trust you, but I don't want to trust you with more than you're ready to absorb.'

'It stays in this room. But only if you're comfortable . . .'

'No, I'm not comfortable. I'll never be comfortable. But . . . sorry, that sounded a bit sharp. Still, this is your line of work in a way, isn't it? I don't suppose I ever would have gone to see someone in a more formal way. I should have, I realise. We both should have. But by the time I realised that, Rich was already into perfection and counselling didn't fit with his model of perfection. Anyway, I've been your emergency doctor, so you can be my spur-of-the-moment counsellor.'

'It doesn't have to be a quid pro quo, you know. I could be doing this as a friend.'

'Yes, I shouldn't have said that, but I think I need to justify this to myself. Rich would be furious, even now.'

'Only tell me what you want to tell me.'

'We knew there was something wrong, right from the start. But we had our dear little Jack for seven wonderful, blissful months. He was totally gorgeous, in a way that none of the others have been. Oh, they're all fabulous kids—you can see that—and we both love them to bits. But he was special, almost like an angel. He was born with a tumour in his brain—huge, malignant, inoperable and painless—and it was only ever going to be a matter of time.

'I couldn't get enough of that baby. I held him in my arms all day and I slept by his cot at night. I'd wake in a panic, night after night, and listen for his breathing. Rich became cranky and impatient with me. He found my devotion to the baby perplexing and even irritating. He was far more pragmatic about it all than I was: he wanted us to get on with our lives. I didn't want to do that at all. I wanted to freeze my life for as long as I had Jack—I didn't care how short or how long that might be. I wanted to be totally, completely, comprehensively Jack's mother.

'While I was neglecting Rich and giving myself up to Jack, the inevitable happened. Rich had an affair with a research assistant in his department. Oh, don't raise your eyebrows like that; I'm telling you this for completeness. I don't hold any grudges about it and, even then, I think I knew it was inevitable. In a curious way, it was a welcome relief from the pressure Rich was putting on me: as long as he was distracted by his paramour, he wasn't so resentful of my devotion to Jack, and there was no way I was going to be anything other than devoted.

'But the night Jack died, Rich was with his lover. He came home in the morning to find us both gone and a note from me telling him what had happened and where to find me. His reaction to all that was probably inevitable too. He cracked, basically.'

'Cracked?'

'Oh, he didn't rant and rave and go wild. No, it was quieter, more deliberate and yet, in a way, more debilitating than a simple outburst of the anger I knew he must be feeling—anger towards Jack for not being a healthy baby, towards me for being so helplessly besotted by a baby with such a brief span of life, towards the other woman for . . . I don't know: perhaps he was angry with her for letting him reveal his misery to her. Most of all, though, I think he was angry with himself for letting me down, for not being there when Jack passed away, for letting the hospital staff think what they thought when I appeared, distraught and spent, with a dead baby in my arms and no husband by my side.

'I think he was even angry at himself for having fathered a diseased baby, but let's not go there. There was a bit of that in me, too, however irrational it might sound . . .' Ruth's eyes are searching my face—for a reaction, or simply for a connection.

'The anger never came out as anger though. It gradually transformed itself into guilt and took up permanent residence in Rich's heart. Ever since, he's been trying to deal with it by being . . .

well, by being perfect. But his perfection takes a curious form: it's more extreme than the example of his parents that he used to mock so mercilessly. Believe it or not, ever since Jack's death, we've had one chocolate a *week*—we're constantly throwing out half-eaten boxes of stale chocolates. The children are allowed no other sweets, no soft drinks, no fast food—except when they're out with friends, when they gorge themselves. We have one beach holiday a year—in winter, mind you—in a rather tacky little shack at Austinmer that the children hate. They've probably told you about it. Any household expenditure is subject to the kind of scrutiny normally left to Senate select committees. To put it bluntly, Rich is as mean, as stitched-up and as rigid as they come. You can imagine the fuss whenever I've broached the subject of extensions to the house, or a new car. You probably think the old Vee Dub is a pose: I assure you it's not. It's an old car, that's all, and that's the way Rich likes it. Luckily the kids think it's cool and all their school friends envy them.

'This is Rich's idea of perfection: living poor to assuage his guilt. Any hint of criticism of him—even lighthearted stuff from the kids like you get in any family—cuts him so deeply I sometimes think he'll finally break down and let all the pent-up anger flow out like poison. But it doesn't happen. Or it hasn't happened so far.'

Ruth clearly wants me to say something and I decide to keep the focus on Rich for a bit longer: 'So the university evaluation thing was a more bitter blow than it might otherwise have been. I mean, if Rich is trying so hard to compensate for something—for Jack or whatever—being judged harshly by his own students . . .'

'Exactly. Mr Perfection—*Doctor* Perfection—suddenly finds himself exposed to criticism by his own students. For all I know, the students might have a point. It's hard to imagine that someone carrying Rich's anger around inside him would relate easily to today's crop of students. Rich doesn't exactly hang loose. His life seems to be all about closing off options.' Ruth permits herself a smile and leans back in her chair.

I'm reluctant to speak, but decide to try out an idea on her. 'I must admit I wondered whether his disenchantment with the university would spur him to make the final break and go bush. Is that possible?'

Ruth shakes her head. 'I honestly don't know about the rural thing. He goes on endlessly about it, but he's never taken any positive steps to do anything about it. We've never gone exploring country towns or ringing estate agents. He'll occasionally read out an ad from the *Herald* classifieds, but I don't think he's ever followed one up. I have a hunch it's a kind of Amish fantasy, minus the religion. I don't think his dream is about the communal life at all. I think it's about even more austerity, even more rigidity, even less fun than we have now. He talks about "the village" of his dreams, but everything he says about living in the country is more about isolation than connection. Yet I'm sure Rich is not a hermit at heart. It's all a mess—a huge bundle of conflicts and contradictions buried deep inside him. And it's so tied up with his guilt that he's going to keep the lid on it forever, if possible. Maybe it'll never come out. But he's a sitting duck for full-blown depression and I wouldn't wish that on him, or on me and the children, to be frank.

'So I keep loving him. And loving him. What else can I do? Maybe, one day, his wounds will heal. In the meantime, loving him is like applying a daily ointment. Needless to say, Jack is never mentioned by either of us. Right off the agenda. The children don't even know he existed, which I think is wrong, but I'm not prepared to fight Rich over that. They're bound to find out one day.'

TWENTY-TWO

'They only love me for my drugs'

EXTRACT FROM TRANSCRIPT OF CLIENT INTERVIEW

So, back again. You okay? What's with the neck brace and the sling and everything? You been in a car crash, or what?

A bit of a fall. Not as bad as it looks. I'll be right in a couple more days.

So, can I smoke? Nothing much to report. Job's good. Friends okay. Tony ... well, Tony's Tony, know what I mean? I don't know what to say. I've forgotten what happened last time. So anyway, how are you?

I'm fine. Absolutely. You might want to say something about those dreams you were having, or about Tony. Whatever's on your mind at present. No rush. We don't even have to talk if you'd prefer to sit and collect your thoughts for a moment.

Oh, yeah, well, the dreams. No real change there I'm afraid. There's a lot of panic in it? Sweating and everything? I'm still shit-scared to go to sleep, to tell you the truth. It's like, every single night? Every single time, I'm the, you know . . . the one who's done something awful and everyone's going to get killed. Like, it's always my fault?

Did you have the dreams before you started seeing Tony? We didn't talk about that last time. Can you remember having them at other times of your life, like at times of stress or worry?

No, this is something new. The doctor thought it could even be from too much eccy?

You didn't mention that last time. I think you said the doctor wanted you to see me before he prescribed something to help you sleep. Have you been back to see him?

Yeah, well. I went to a different doctor.

And?

And nothing. I went to a different doctor. I never go to the same doctor twice. Tony said not to. Anything wrong with that?

Nothing at all. That's up to you. So let's think about when the dreams started—when you started using ecstasy—when you started seeing Tony. Do you feel as if they're all linked in some way? Does it seem as if all those things have happened at about the same time?

Does it matter? Can't we get on with fixing the dreams?

I'm afraid we can't tackle the dreams on their own without thinking a bit about where they might have come from, what's causing the panic, what else is going on in your life that might need to be looked at.

Well, you're not going to be looking at Tony, that's for sure. He's still . . . away. He rings me though, like I told you.

Do you want to say where he is? He's been away for a while. Do you know when he's coming back?

Don't pry! How should I know? Probably the little wife knows. The little wife with the little baby. She probably knows. Fuck her. No, I don't know where he is. Just . . . away. Like, that's all he says? Away? Don't ask questions, he says, better not to ask. Fuck him too. He can be a real arsehole.

Do you know who his wife is? Do you know anything about her?

What is this?

Sorry. I was only wondering if you'd ever tried to put yourself in her shoes at all. Tried to imagine what she might be thinking.

This isn't like last time. Why are you asking me all this stuff? Are you taking the piss?

Not at all, I assure you. Let's start again. Try to think about when these dreams began. I think you said a few months ago. Was that around the time you and Tony starting going out together?

Going out together? Dream on. Going out? Fucking, mister. Fucking. That's all we do. I've never been out with Tony. Not once. Not to dinner. Not to a movie. Not even to the beach, and the beach is only two minutes from my flat. Not dancing, either. I met him at a dance, went to his flat, bingo.

His flat?

Yeah, his flat. You know, a flat? What are you, thick? He keeps a flat. Not the lovely house where little wifey lives, of course. A very nice flat, all the same. Well, I live there now. He pays for it and I'm available when he wants me? And I handle a little bit of E for him, for the girls at work and some other people and that. So . . . are you going to report me or what?

I'm not going to report you. I'm here to help you, if I possibly can. Let's talk about the dreams shall we?

(Client shouting.) Of course the fucking dreams only started when I started fucking Tony, you arsehole. What else do you think the fucking dreams might be about? I'm in trouble, you useless fucking prick. Don't you get it? I'm up to my fucking neck in Tony's shit and you think there might be some fucking connection between Tony and the bad dreams? You think you're a fucking genius. You're a fucking arsehole, what are you? Are you going to ask me to pay money for this?

If I can't help you at all, if you want to cut this short, I won't ask you for money. But let's see if we can make some progress together first, and then you can decide if you want to leave or stay.

(Client sobbing.)

Can I trust you? Tony's a real bad boy and I wouldn't be surprised if he's on remand. You guessed that, didn't you?

I'm not here to guess things. I'm here to help you if I can. If he was in prison, would that be a relief for you? You don't seem happy with the relationship as it has been. Is this a way out?

(Client shouting.) You don't get it at all, do you? Who the fuck else is going to give me a flat to live in, lots more money than I've ever had before and the promise of plenty more where that came from? If he goes down, I don't know what the fuck will become of me, but I'm sure as hell hanging on to what I've got for as long as I can. All my lovely fucking friends ... they only love me for my drugs, I know that. I'm not stupid. So what will happen if I can't supply them? Where the fuck is Tony anyway? When is he going to give me some more?

Last time, you seemed very unhappy about the price you had to pay—the emotional price—for your relationship with Tony. You seemed resentful, rather than grateful. Has that changed for you?

Do you like this job, you arsehole?

Yes, I like the job, but I don't like being spoken to like that.

Cope. Does it pay well?

Not bad. Not wonderful, but not bad. You could work out what I make. You know what you pay me.

Is everything about it perfect?

Not everything, no.

Are there some things you resent about it?

Well, sometimes, I guess. Maybe 'resent' is a bit strong, but it has its irritations, yes.

(Client shouting.) Nothing's perfect, you fucking moron. I bet I earn a lot more than you do, humping Tony's eccy to the girls, and yes, I pay a fucking price. What you call an emotional price, you pompous prick. My price is probably bigger than yours, but we both pay one. Difference is, you're up yourself and I'm not. I'll tell you another difference. I'll move on to something else when I want to. You'll still be stuck in this boring fucking room, listening to boring fucking people telling you their boring fucking lies. I don't know how you stand it. Do you ever take any risks at all? Like, do you ever stuff up totally?

Look, I'm not claiming to be anything special. I'm not claiming to have a perfect life. We're not here to talk about me. I'm here to help and if I can't help . . .

(Client sobbing.)

Help me. Please help me. I'm sorry for what I said. I'll pay you whatever you want. Just help me. I can't bear falling asleep one more single time if I can't get rid of those dreams. I couldn't stand one more night of it. What can I do?

I'm afraid there's no easy way of fixing the dreams. It's a lot more complicated than that. You already know that. Look, I don't usually express an opinion about things like this, but I think we'd better talk about how to get you right out of this situation and right away from Tony. It won't be easy, and it's up to you in the end. But if you want to make a fresh start and put all this behind you, we'll need to talk to a social worker, you might need to get back in touch with DOCS, you might need to contact the police. You'll need to see a doctor who can look after you for a few weeks and you might need a short spell in hospital to break the cycle of the dreams, maybe have your diet checked over, get your sleep pattern stabilised, but that will be up to the doctor. Then we should look at how we can get you out of that flat and into a different job. If this is as serious as it sounds, the police will probably want you to give evidence against Tony. By the sound of it, what you know could put him away for some time. So . . .

(Client sobbing.)

Please help me. Just help me with the dreams, okay. Tony would have me killed if I ratted on him.

Not if the police were protecting you. There are all sorts of ways of helping you if you want to be helped . . . if you want to be free of those nightmares. There are people who can help you find somewhere to live. You can move interstate, you can even change your name. This is one of those times when not having a family has its advantages. May I make a couple of phone calls for you? May I contact a social worker? I know a doctor who is used to dealing with this kind of thing—may I ring her? You don't have to deal with any of this on your own, you know. Take it quietly. Think about it for a few days if you like. There's no hurry.

(Client sobbing.)

Will I make those calls?

I don't know.

Do you want to come back tomorrow?

I don't want any more of those dreams. I'll go ... I don't know ...

(Client sobbing.)

Will I call that doctor for you? All the rest of it can wait till later, but I would like you to see that doctor.

That would be excellent.

TWENTY-THREE

I am a slow burner

'Hey, come over here, young Thomas. Show us your war wounds.'

Upton and Joe are sitting on the Rileys' front steps, enjoying the remains of an early summer evening. Walking is still a bit painful, but my right knee is strapped and, following Ruth's orders, I'm wearing the collar whenever it's practical. My right arm is still in a sling, too, so the total picture is probably a bit comical. Upton clearly finds it so, chortling unsympathetically as I limp across the road to the Rileys' front gate.

'Time we gave a bit of thought to the street party, isn't it? Rich was over here earlier, huffing and puffing. Told him to relax, which is like telling a dog to stop wagging its tail. That boy is even more uptight than usual. What's his problem?'

'He's got a fair bit on his mind. The university is going from bad to worse. The street party was all Rich's idea, don't forget. He's a bit proprietorial. Don't be too rough on him.'

'Well, I basically told him to piss off and leave it to Joe and me this year. He was none too pleased.'

Upton's tone is as hearty as ever, quite undimmed by the possibility that he's irritated Rich. 'I think he wants to draw up a street party manifest, filled out in triplicate and countersigned by Joe. Man's a bureaucrat at heart—never happier than when there's a bit of admin in the offing.' This strikes Upton as a hugely amusing analysis and he unleashes a peal of raucous laughter. Joe and I manage a smile. Upton is always looking for the joke, and he usually manages to find it. His trademark is helpless, red-faced laughter.

Perched on the steps of the Rileys' house, Joe and Upton make an incongruous pair. Joe is neat, slight, quiet and dignified; Upton is large and loud, his huge abdomen bulging over the belt of his bowling creams, and his red face and neck glowing in the fading light of early evening. Joe still has most of his hair, though it's greying at the temples; Upton, years younger, is almost bald, with long wisps of white hair sprouting from the sides of his head and hanging untidily over his ears. Though he can't be healthy, given his shape, he looks remarkably robust. Joe, by contrast, has aged noticeably since his illness: he looks pale—almost grey—and somehow shrivelled, though his face has retained its serenity and his smile is as ready as ever.

It's hard to imagine what they have in common, but their friendship is firm and their conversations often go late into the evening, their low murmurs punctuated by occasional roars of laughter from Upton.

'Righty-o, young Tom, so when exactly is the street party? Rich assumed we knew and I didn't like to disappoint him by confessing my ignorance. He might have confused it with lack of interest, which it certainly isn't. I've even been brushing up my carols. Shall I give you a verse of *God Rest Ye Merry*?'

'The Monday of the week before the week that Christmas Day falls in—that's Rich's formula. Christmas Day is next Sunday, tomorrow week, so the party's supposed to be Monday night, the nineteenth. Day after tomorrow.'

'See what I mean? "Rich's formula". Too bloody complicated for my liking. Anyway, what have you done to yourself?'

I describe my misadventure in Jodie's bathroom and Upton, true to form, finds this the year's most hilarious anecdote.

'What, your foot trapped in the loo? And all over a harmless bloody huntsman?' He's slapping his thigh and hooting with such ferocious glee, Enid and Sexy come to the front door to see what the commotion is in aid of. Upton runs through the story again, his version more lurid than the original, peppering his narrative with huge wheezing gales of laughter. Sexy rolls her eyes, Enid smiles, and the women retreat inside.

'I'll have a word with Rich about the party, Upton.' The sky is clouding over in the south, huge black clouds with a greenish tinge, massing like mountains. I can feel the temperature dropping. The best of the day has definitely gone. My knee is stiff and painful and I want to get back home to a comfortable chair. 'It'll be the usual—there'll be too much food, you and I will supply the drinks and one of your boys will organise the music. Is it ever any different? Rich getting agitated beforehand is part of the ritual. Everything will work out—it always does. Rich feels better if there's a detailed plan, but he never seems to mind when we ignore it on the night.'

'The Nguyen children are cooking something up as well. A musical item of some sort,' says Joe Riley, advocating like a grandfather.

'Not the violins! Anything but the violins!' Upton is holding his head in his hands, full of mock anguish, and Joe urges him to keep his voice down. He'd hate the kids' feelings to be hurt.

Back home, I sink into a chair. I wish Ruth would come and visit me. I wish I didn't feel embarrassed about walking over to Alex's place while Joe and Upton are still sitting outside. I wish I'd handled my new client better yesterday—been more authentic in my response to her, more determined to detach my feelings about Tony/Chika from my desire to help her. I feel a sudden urge to smack her face. Why do my most intense reactions always take so long to catch up with me? If counselling is a form of teaching— or learning—then I missed an opportunity to explain to her how people feel about having abuse hurled in their faces.

But, as Maddy keeps reminding me, nothing's changed. I am a slow burner. It took a full year for me to became properly angry about Clare's leaving. That was an extreme example of a general problem in our relationship. Often she'd look for a reaction from me to whatever she was saying—especially if she was attacking me, which she was, increasingly, towards the end. She'd want a fight, but nothing would come. I couldn't feel affronted, or hurt, or combative. Nothing.

Then, a day or two later, I'd feel a rush of reaction. But if I mentioned it then, when the moment had well and truly passed, Clare would look at me as if I'd woken from a deep sleep and missed the last reel of a movie.

My reactions to events are too slow, my imagination is too quick. It's not a comfortable combination.

None of this seems to affect the quality of my relationships with my neighbours though. Things are so much easier and safer when intimacy isn't an issue. I can think what I like, imagine what I like, miss countless opportunities to say what I wish I'd said and none of it matters. We move on, lightly and without the burden of *potential*. There's none of the residue that clogs relationships moving towards intimacy—or away from it, come to think of it. It's a relief to be able to chat without implying anything about the future, or the past; to do things for someone—take in their mail, put out their bins, feed their pets—without any sense of fixed obligations or commitments either way.

The contract between neighbours is based on *resistance* to intimacy, so a quite different kind of closeness becomes possible: easy, open, comfortable, but devoid of any ultimate responsibility or any glimpses into each other's souls. These are adjacent lives—sometimes even parallel lives—rather than shared lives. We compensate for our physical proximity by keeping our emotional distance. These are not like relationships between friends, or even between people who work closely together—I know Maddy better than I know Rich Abel, or Mrs Spenser, or Joe Riley. (And Alex? Not sure.) Perhaps the thing suburban life offers us is the possibility of living the life of a herd without the bonds of a tribe: proximity, familiarity, trust, support . . . but not intimacy. When we cross that line, we cease to be neighbours and become something else.

PART TWO

Weather Report

ONE

There is nothing to be done

By eight o'clock, the cloud cover has thickened, darkened and lowered. Powerful gusts of wind are disturbing the trees and banging doors shut all around the Close, but they are interspersed with periods of total calm. Once or twice, I wander out onto my balcony to watch flashes of lightning in the distant south, beyond the city, and to listen to the rumble of thunder. The wind feels like one of Sydney's classic southerly busters brewing, though it's a bit early in the season and it wasn't as if this was a day of such sweltering humidity that we were longing for the relief of a storm. That's February's story, not December's. The looming electrical activity seems different from those familiar and often welcome storms, though it's hard to say why. It seems to be building more slowly, more deliberately, as if waiting for some particular moment to strike.

A greenish tinge in the clouds at dusk had generated a spark of anxiety. Sydneysiders live with a heightened consciousness of the havoc that can fall from the sky. We're accustomed to hail, even quite large hail, but two storms have reshaped our view of the risk, even for those of us who live in parts of Sydney not directly affected by the full force of either of them. In 1991, a storm swept through the upper North Shore with such violence that the tree canopy was effectively destroyed. (In media discussion of the storm, we learned that the experts call established trees 'sky furniture'. Around Turramurra and Wahroonga, it looked as if the removalists had been in and cleaned the place out.) It took weeks to clear the streets of debris, and months to repair the houses. But the archetypal Sydney hailstorm was in April 1999 when a so-called 'supercell' hit the city and eastern suburbs. It developed near Nowra on the south coast, travelled north to Helensburgh, then cut a swathe of unprecedented destruction through eastern Sydney. Hailstones up to eleven centimetres in diameter struck the city and suburbs. The onslaught—the worst since white settlement in 1778—effectively destroyed thousands of cars, and even damaged commercial aircraft. Tens of thousands of homes suffered serious roof damage and many were practically demolished.

In the aftermath, many Sydneysiders took refuge in the view that such freak occurrences are so rare that, having experienced one, we are unlikely to witness another in our lifetime. But others saw the supercell—quite unlike a conventional thunderstorm in its structure, intensity and longevity—as a sign of changing weather patterns, possibly attributable to climate change wrought by global warming: they believe we're in for more of the same, or worse. Other people take the view that since meteorological records for Australia only go back two hundred years, there might be long-term cycles we don't yet know about.

But theories don't help when it happens.

By nine o'clock, the gusts of wind have strengthened and become more prolonged. Alex has been on the phone, checking that I'm home. She sounds like a nervous child and I contemplate going over to her place, but something makes me hesitate: perhaps I don't want to look as if I'm overreacting. Mrs Spenser's Harold is barking in an edgy staccato and I can hear the Abels firmly shutting all their windows.

I step out onto the balcony again. There's a spectacular lightshow in the southern sky, but the storm is inexorably closing on us and a sudden thunderclap, of such intensity as to make me jump, sounds loud enough to have been directly overhead. A few large spots of rain spatter my face, and I retreat indoors, leaving the curtains open so I can see out. The intensity of the wind quickly rises to a howl, at a pitch that makes it impossible to hear anything else. Even my favourite sound—rain on the roof—will be masked by this wind, unless we are to have a truly torrential downpour.

Standing at the window, I'm enjoying the prospect of another of nature's displays of raw power. Even as a child, I've never feared storms, or driving wind, or heavy seas. There aren't many occasions in our lives so devoid of ambiguity. Caught in a storm, we know what to do. There are no moral issues, unless they are to do with the need to protect or rescue others. The simplicity of the situation appeals to me, even though in virtually all other parts of my life, I thrive on complexity. But storms aren't about nuance or subtlety, and that's a kind of relief: they take us over, forcing us to react.

This one is no exception, by the sound of it. The wind's howl has risen to a roar and the thunder is like a continuous growl. Flashes of sheet lightning are now so frequent, the breaks between them look like erratic interruptions to power supply. Such intense activity is usually brief: I'm expecting it to move on and rain to begin falling in earnest, but there is no sign of any slackening; both thunder and wind seem to be increasing. The combination is impressive.

Close by, I hear a sound more mechanical than natural. It's like a series of rumbles, or the thumping feet of some giant possum on a roof. Looking out through the gloom, I can see what look like roof tiles landing in the street, slashing through the trees, and hurling themselves against hard surfaces on the other side of the road. They have probably been ripped from Mrs Spenser's partly dismantled roof.

I don my coat and dash for the front door, but as soon as I am outside, it's clear that progress is impossible. The wind is so strong it threatens to lift me clean off my feet and ram me against the house. I drop to a crawl, my damaged knee pleading with me to desist and creep back inside. Shutting the front door against the force of the wind takes all my strength and I hobble through the house, closing the windows so the wind will have nowhere to go if I have to open the door again. I consult the list of phone numbers Rich always distributes before the street party and pick up the phone to call Mrs Spenser. The line is engaged and I'm hoping this means Rich is already in touch with her, or that Mrs Spenser is calling someone for help. The tiles—if that's what they are—are still clattering and smashing their way along the street.

It's too dark outside to see anything clearly, even when lightning floods the sky, but I can hear sounds that suggest the bits and pieces of gym equipment in Samantha and Jodie's backyard are being lifted and hurled against various surfaces, including the wall of my house.

It's anyone's guess where such things might finally come to rest. The wind is so powerful that even my heavily laden garbage bins—and no doubt everyone else's—are being flipped and flung about, their contents spewing everywhere. I can hear bottles being smashed.

I try Mrs Spenser's phone again, but this time the line is dead. I dial Alex's number: silence. I dial my own number to see if I get the engaged signal. Still nothing. While there's no cause for immediate concern, and the wind is no worse, I am worried about Mrs Spenser. If her roof has gone, she'll need help. I should make a more serious attempt to get across to her house—or even into the Abels', where we might together be able to assess the situation from some closer vantage point.

Against all my instincts, I open the front door again and am deafened by a roar so frightening it could be an express train off its rails coming straight up the Close. As I stand there, amazed, it becomes even louder. I can't imagine what it might be, until I begin to hear heavy clunking sounds on the roof and then see great balls of ice, hailstones as large as cricket balls and larger, crashing onto the front lawn. Going out in this is out of the question: I'd be brained by a flying iceball, or a stray roof tile, or collected by my own garbage bin and recycled into goodness knows what. The noise is indescribable and, in spite of my history of wanting to experience such natural power off the leash, I feel a prickle of fear. I close the door with great difficulty and retreat to my study. The force of the wind seems to be increasing.

The size of the hail and the intensity of the wind make it inevitable that windows will be smashed and roofs penetrated. Some of the iceballs seem to be travelling almost parallel to the ground.

Within minutes, one of my own windows goes—it sounds like the bedroom—with a huge crash, followed by the sound of the storm surging into the open space. I run upstairs, my knee urging me to slow down, but can't think of anything to do to stop the rush of wind and rain coming through the jagged gash. A huge hailstone is lying on the carpet and I toss it back out through the gap, like some loathsome fish I never wanted to catch in the first place. I grab a pillow and stuff it into the hole in the glass with no real conviction.

Still the thunder pounds like an artillery battery and the lightning offers surreal glimpses of mayhem in the street. The roar of the hail has even smothered the howl of the wind.

The mobile phone! I grab it and dial Mrs Spenser's number again, but there's no response—all our landlines are dead and I have no idea whether she has a mobile. But Rich does. I dial his number, hear the ringing tone, and pray that it won't switch over to voicemail.

'Abel.'

'Rich! Tom. I'm worried about Mrs Spenser. I think her tiles might have been blown away. Can you check? Do you know if she's okay?'

'Abel.'

The phone is crackling alarmingly and Rich hasn't heard a word I've said. I run upstairs again and look out my bedroom window, taking care to stand back from the glass: I don't want an iceball or a shower of glass in the face. Looking across the roof of the Abels' house it's practically impossible to see what's happened to Mrs Spenser's place. Flashes of lightning reveal the stark frame of her extension, still standing, but I can't tell from here whether the main roof is intact.

We are being carpet bombed by hail: I can hear it on my roof, every salvo shaking the house, and I can't understand why it isn't coming straight through. But there is nothing to be done: it will or it won't.

There's a crack outside—an explosion—and I rush to the window in time to see one of the tall gums on the nature strip outside the Rileys' crashing onto the road, taking a smaller wattle with it. While I watch, the Abels' Volkswagen, incredibly, crawls out of their driveway, squeezes through a narrow gap between the fallen tree and the kerb and inches down the Close, like a tank picking its way through a battlefield. Where can Rich be going? What can he be thinking of? He must be mad! He'll be at much greater risk in a moving car than staying put: if the hail doesn't wreck his car, a falling tree will. He should be putting his children under the dining-room table till further notice and staying right there with them. Are they all in the car with him, or has he left Ruth and the children at home? I feel an intense fury—a certainty that Rich is making a run for some safe haven, leaving the rest of us to cope with the mess the storm is bound to leave in its wake.

But there's no time for speculation. The storm demands all my attention and all my energy. Even listening to it is exhausting.

TWO

I can't save the world

By ten o'clock the hail has stopped. The thunder and lightning have moved off to the northeast and we've had a sustained downpour of the heaviest rain I've ever known. It has fallen on us as if it were being tipped from some vast cauldron in the sky. My front garden is awash. If rain continues to tumble down at this rate, Winter Close will become a lake.

Then, improbably, the hail starts again—a second wave of terror—almost immediately punching its way through my roof in three places. The sound of the tiles shattering is unmistakable, though I've never heard it before. I can imagine great patches of dampness already spreading across the ceiling as the rain pours in. At any minute the pressure will cause the ceiling to give way, dumping water, ice and debris into all the upstairs rooms. Eventually the flood will run down the stairs, spreading filth throughout the house. I am remarkably clear, almost calm, in my anticipation of all this. I see it as inevitable. No spreading of sheets, blankets, tarpaulins or towels will make a jot of difference. The house is about to be wrecked. The storm has lost whatever charm, whatever power it had to impress me. Now I'm consumed by cold hatred of it. I want it over.

There's a sudden wrenching, grinding sound, quite different from the crack and crash of falling trees, that sounds as if it's coming from Mrs Spenser's building works. I limp upstairs again, scarcely caring about the catastrophe brewing in the ceiling, and look out the bedroom window. There's less lightning now, but still enough to reveal the framework of Mrs Spenser's extension teetering and disintegrating like a ship breaking up in heavy seas. The whole thing finally sinks out of sight.

Trees are coming down all around me, but the crack of their exploding trunks and breaking branches is no longer shocking or even surprising. I am in the grip of the storm now, as much a part of it as the trees and the ice; I've long since abandoned the privileged position of spectator. The lights flicker, go out, come back on again and then fail completely. Total darkness seems no more threatening than anything else that's going on; perhaps it's marginally better not to be able to see—my imagination couldn't dream up anything as bad as the fury raging outside. I decide not to bother hunting for a candle or torch.

The roar and thump of the hail gradually abate; giant iceballs are being replaced by more conventional hailstones, big enough to pit the bodywork of a car but not big enough to write the whole thing off. After a lull of a minute or two, the wind still moaning madly, another torrential downpour begins. Through the watery maelstrom, I hear a scream. A full-blooded, uninhibited, movie-style scream. It could be coming from anywhere, and it could mean anything, but I want to go to Alex. It's not a matter of heroics: I've lost interest in my own house and I want to go to Alex. Mrs Spenser might be in all kinds of difficulty. Joe and Enid might have lost their roof. The Nguyens might be paralysed by fear. Water might be pouring into Brian Stuthridge's study, converting his research into papier mâché. All that is possible. Probable, even. But I can't save the world. I might, though, be able to comfort one frightened young woman with a tiny baby. I'm going to Alex.

I put my coat on yet again, wrap a scarf around my neck brace, jam an old gardening hat on my head and open the front door. There's still enough of a gale blowing to whip the door out of my grasp as soon as I release the catch: in the darkness, I can't control it and it bangs open against the inside wall. For a moment I consider leaving it where it is—what could be worse than what's already happened?—but decide that would only be inviting yet more trouble. There's another tussle between me and the wind for control of the door unitl I finally wrestle it shut.

Outside, in the pitch black of the unlit street, I'm feeling more uneasy than I had expected to. The storm is crashing and banging around my head and there are still branches snapping, and whole trees falling, up and down the Close. Though I have lived in this street for eight years, and know the place like the back of my hand, I'm suddenly a stranger here. Far away flashes of lightning give an eerie back-lit menace to the clouds, still roiling and swirling overhead, but provide no illumination on the ground. I'm feeling my way, groping and shuffling like a blind beggar. I look towards where I think the Eastern Valley Way hill should be, but there is nothing there to reassure me: no headlights, no streetlights, no houselights. I imagine this must be what underwater disorientation feels like. Were it not for the fact that I can breathe, I could be drowning.

Before I've even cleared my own front gate my overcoat has become sodden. (Unfortunately, Clare's rejection of plastic raincoats is one of the few prejudices of hers that I've clung to.) I drag my feet through ankle-deep water and at every step I encounter the hard and jagged edges of objects that don't belong in my front yard, fallen branches and squishy lumps of material that could be anything from bags of garbage to dead possums. The wind is whipping at my scarf and coat, having already swept my hat away the moment I left the protection of my front porch.

My plan had been to cross the road in a direct line from my front gate to Alex's, but that now seems impossible. To have any chance of making it I'll have to stick to the footpath and hang on to the Abels' and Mrs Spenser's front fences for safety and guidance. It's a distance of barely fifty paces but, in these conditions, it might as well be miles.

It's hard to tell which trees are still standing and which have gone. A pittosporum in the Abels' garden has bent so far over their front fence it could snap at any moment. I have to edge around it, step by cautious step, almost out to the kerb, in order to get past. In spite of the path being awash, and the pain from my knee, I decide I'm more secure on all fours. But when I drop to the ground the amount of debris on the footpath, and the effort of trying to crawl through swirling water, soon forces me back onto my feet and I proceed in a tentative crouch. I'm soaked to the skin and my saturated coat is now a dead weight on me.

Gradually I drag myself along the Abels' fence until I reach Mrs Spenser's front gate. Building materials lie all around me and I can hear, above the wind, the sound of a tarpaulin flapping and ripping like a sail torn from the mast of an ocean racer. I can't tell whether her original roof is still on and I have no idea where she is, how she is, or if she needs help. There's no sound from Harold, which could mean anything.

I hear that scream again. It could be coming from Alex or from the Rileys', though neither Alex nor Enid seems the screaming type. I decide to press on. If Mrs Spenser is inside her house, perhaps she's okay. Someone else clearly isn't.

Overhead, the power lines are making a whipping sound. I don't want to be where I am if one of them snaps and falls into the lake that's formed. Spurred on by simple fear, I stumble the last few metres to Alex's gate, crawl across her front lawn and deposit myself, dripping like a seal, on her doormat. I have enough energy left to rattle her flyscreen door, though there's little chance she'd hear it above the racket still raging all around us.

Then I see a flickering light through the glass in her front door and Alex is opening it and dragging me inside. She wraps her arms around me and murmurs her gratitude and concern. I can see no sign of water inside the house, apart from the puddle I've created.

'I think I've been really, really lucky. A couple of panes of glass have smashed in the back verandah windows. That's it, as far as I know. And would you believe Jemma's asleep! But someone's in dreadful trouble. Have you heard the screaming?'

'Where do you think it is coming from?'

'I don't think it's close enough to be Enid, though how could you tell in all this? I haven't been able to make contact with her or Joe. The phones are out. You knew that, I suppose.'

'I tried to ring.'

'Shouldn't we do something about the scream? I'm horribly afraid it's Violet.'

'Violet?'

'Violet Nguyen. The children are bound to be terrified and Peter has been away all week. He isn't due back until Monday. Could you . . .'

'I'll go straightaway. I might as well take this coat off though. It's only slowing me down.'

'Can I get you one of Chika's?'

Even under these circumstances, this strikes me as inappropriate. 'No, there's no point. Nothing helps.'

'Do you want a drink?'

'Water, water everywhere . . .' I can't believe I've said something so lame.

'Poetry can save you from—'

'I know. You told me.' In that moment, through the miasma of dampness, pain, exhaustion and anxiety, I catch a glimpse of how ineffably tedious prolonged exposure to Alex could become. I don't honestly know if I could bear the grinding banality of such exchanges. On the other hand, heaven has always seemed a peculiarly unattractive prospect too, what with its eternal radiance, its lack of shadows to lurk in, the relentless cheerfulness of everyone. Surely you'd long for someone—God?—to throw a tantrum or at least have an off day. As a concept, heaven, like Alex, seems to lack subtlety.

My penchant for nuance, ambiguity and irony more or less guarantees that neither heaven nor Alex will loom large in my destiny. The more immediate challenge is to trace the screams to their source.

'I'll come back as soon as I can.'

'Here's a torch. It's got new batteries in it—good luck rather than good management, I assure you.'

Outside, things seem to have eased somewhat. The rain is still steady, but it's no longer torrential; the wind is blustery and powerful but not quite as furious as before. The ground is still like a rice paddy though, and obstacles are everywhere. I try not to think about the power lines. Perhaps that danger has passed.

I creep gingerly out of Alex's front gate and into the Rileys'. I need something to hang onto for support and I'm grateful for all these front fences that survived the seventies' fashion for open, unfenced front gardens. I make my way unsteadily up the Rileys' path, climb the steps where Upton was so recently amused, and ring their doorbell. There is no response, but from somewhere around the back comes a sound like a muffled version of the scream, more like keening now.

With practically no energy left, I shuffle, stagger, crawl and slide down the side path of the Rileys' house until I reach their back garden. I sweep the beam of Alex's torch from side to side. Beside an opening in the paling fence that separates their two backyards, Enid Riley and Violet Nguyen are crouched over the body of Joe, crushed beneath the huge trunk of a fallen tree.

The women look up, frightened, and I shout my name above the howl of the wind as I move towards them. They are both soaked through: they've been trying unsuccessfully to lift the fallen trunk off Joe and their hands are torn and bleeding.

'Come inside. None of us can move that. Not even the three of us.'

'Was coming to see if children are safe. Was wonderful man.'

'He was indeed. Come inside, please. Enid?'

Slowly Enid stands and straightens her back. She looks at me, rain streaming down both our faces. 'He thought he might make it to Christmas. That's all he was expecting. He was fading fast and he knew it. Another couple of weeks, that's all he wanted.' She turns and looks at her husband's broken body. 'Well, you didn't quite make it, Joey. Not quite.' She falls to her knees again, leaning over the broken body of her husband. Violet and I move away and wait.

When Enid joins us it's impossible to distinguish between the rain and the tears on her face. 'He would have done anything for those kids, you know.'

'I believe it. Come inside. Do you have a tarpaulin, or a ground sheet, or something I could . . .'

'There's an old army blanket in the shed. Use that. Should we ring someone? A doctor? Could Ruth come over? What about an ambulance? Vehicles mightn't even be able to get into the street. What will they do?' Grief sometimes fuels such intense concern with the practical details.

'Come into my house, Enid,' Violet says. 'I must go to children. You must come too.'

'I'll get the blanket. We'll sort everything out in the morning.'

Using Alex's torch, I find the blanket in the shed. I bend over Joe and as if grasping for a formality to mark this moment, I check that there is no pulse. I throw the blanket over the body and pause.

The wind has finally dropped and the thunder has become a distant rumble, but the rain persists. Taking my leave with a silent nod, I stumble home through the rain to get my mobile phone, flashing the torch around me as I walk. The scene is too terrible to take in; it can all wait till daylight. I collect the phone from the table in the hallway, without pausing to explore the state of my house, and pick my way through the debris, back to Alex. She is waiting for me at her front door.

THREE

None of this seems real

I awake to the sounds of Alex and Jemma cooing at each other and, for a blissful moment, I dream I belong here. Chika is locked up for life, Alex and I are together, Jemma has a baby brother and I've given up pretending I'm ever going to write poetry: I'm leaving that strictly to Alex. At any moment she will come back to bed and the children will snuggle between us, squirming and giggling.

Alex appears with her baby on her hip and a cup of tea for me. My knee is killing me, but this bed is warm and comfortable.

'The power's back on but the phone isn't. Your clothes are in the drier. They'll be ready in a few more minutes. It's . . . it's spooky out there. At least the rain has finally stopped. I think it poured all night. There's still not much light, but you can see what a horrible mess it all is.' Alex hesitates, reluctant to confront the awful question: 'And Joe . . . will they be able to . . .'

'There'll be a crew here as soon as possible. I left all the details with them last night. The SES and the ambulance people will attend to Joe, but I'd better get moving. Enid wants me to find Ruth and I'd better check on Mrs Spenser.'

Alex lays her baby carefully in the middle of the bed and sits on the edge. She takes my hand in both of hers, leans toward me and brushes my lips with hers. It's not exactly a kiss.

'I'll get your clothes. Come on, Jem.'

Alex insists on making me a second cup of tea and a piece of toast, and then I venture into the street.

Winter Close has all but disappeared, replaced by a scene of devastation. The road is crisscrossed with fallen trees. Jodie's car is lying on its side. (We'll have more to talk about than spiders after all.) Garbage bins, crates, boxes . . . every imaginable kind of junk is strewn all over the street. There's even a mattress lying where it was flung by the storm. Mrs Spenser's house has no roof at all—not only has the new work disappeared, but most of the original tiles have gone and the exposed timber frame of the old roof is badly knocked about. Her house no longer looks half-built; it now appears to be in the process of demolition. The three holes punched in my roof tiles are smaller and neater than I'd imagined. The metal roof over the Abels' front porch has been torn off and, from here, it looks as if the O'Goods have lost half their tiles and most of their windows. The Rileys' place appears intact, apart from a few broken tiles, but what consolation will that be to Enid?

In the pale light of a cloudy dawn I pick my way carefully through the debris and along the path to Mrs Spenser's gate. From there I see the two dogs—hers and Samantha's—strangely posed: Harold is lying down and Zorro is standing above him, stock-still, as if on guard. As I approach, I see that Harold is barely alive, skewered through the neck by a metal shaft, detached, no doubt, from the nearby pile of builders' rubble.

The front door is open. I call Mrs Spenser's name, but it's not her voice that answers. Through the gloom, I see a human version of the dogs' tableau: Mrs Spenser is lying on the floor of the hallway, covered by a blanket, and Samantha is kneeling beside her, administering water and talking to her in a soft voice. There's a jagged hole in the ceiling above them and a pile of debris on the floor. None of this seems real.

'She needs a doctor urgently, but there's no one home at the Abels'. Are they away?'

'I'm here.' Samantha and I both turn to see Ruth, black bag in hand, crossing the threshold. She looks exhausted. 'Let me see her, Sam. I saw two ambulance officers going into the Rileys', Tom. Could you ask them to come over here as soon as they can?'

'Joe's dead, I'm afraid. Did you know that? A tree fell on him. They can't even take him away until the SES lift the tree off him. It's a monster. I'll go over straightaway.'

Mrs Spenser, badly shaken but not critically injured, is eventually carried on a stretcher out of the Close and two hundred metres along Eastern Valley Way over fallen trees, flattened fences and assorted flotsam before she can be put into an ambulance. Two television crews and a newspaper photographer record her progress. An SES team are already at work in their orange overalls, with ladders, chainsaws, shovels, front-end loaders, skips and trucks, tackling the gargantuan job of clearing the street. According to the radio, the same scene is being played all through a narrow strip of suburbs running from Mosman and Manly in the south to Palm

Beach in the north. The hail didn't reach much further west than here, though the strong winds have done plenty of superficial damage across a wider area.

Joe has been released from his death trap, his body laid out in the shed until a spare vehicle can be found that isn't busy ferrying the injured to hospital. Enid is staying with Violet Nguyen. Alex has visited them. I am wandering around, vaguely hoping to be asked to do something helpful, while fighting a huge reluctance to enter my own home. I'm using Alex's place as my base today and that seems to be accepted between us.

I feel disconnected from the hive of activity in the street. I can't imagine why these men are here, voluntarily, doing what Upton and Rich and I should be doing. Why don't they want my help? Is someone making them tea? Where have they come from? What do their families think they are doing on a Sunday, off in some unknown street helping total strangers repair the fabric of their lives? I see them as if through a prism, distorted by my own bewilderment. I am inexplicably resentful of their efforts, even of their presence. The intensity of last night has found its counterpoint in an absolute failure to connect with what is going on, or even to care much. I'm floating, watching all this as if it's happening somewhere else, to someone else, and it will end like a play—with a twist, or a joke, or a death.

But then I remember we've already had our death.

I see Sexy O'Good going into the Nguyens and I wave half-heartedly to her. I presume that's where Ruth is too. (The women are all together; the men haven't even spoken to each other.) I haven't sighted Ruth since she attended to Mrs Spenser. I would like to speak to her, find out what happened last night, where on earth they went and where Rich is now. But mainly I'd like to see her; to connect. Alex is being kind, but she's busy with the baby and I think I've made her feel uncomfortable. I was supposed to be supporting her, but I think she has detected a neediness in me that doesn't please her. It doesn't please me either, and I'm not sure why it has chosen this moment to come to the surface.

FOUR

Perhaps the ravaging and repair of Winter Close is some great artwork on which we are all unconsciously engaged

I can't postpone the moment forever. It's already mid-afternoon, and the street is rapidly taking on the appearance of a lumberjacks' camp. Sawn logs are neatly stacked on the side of the road; most of the debris has been swept and shovelled into skips; our wheelie bins are back roughly where they belong; Mrs Spenser's tarpaulins have been replaced and any bits of salvageable building material have been stacked beside the house; Jodie's car is back on its wheels, looking remarkably intact except for some broken glass. A truck has arrived with a supply of blue tarpaulins ready to be stretched over roofs that are no longer weatherproof. The Close is quickly assessed and two of the tarps are unloaded before the truck races away to get other unroofed houses wrapped before nightfall.

Four men are assigned to the job of covering the O'Goods' roof with the two tarps roped together, and the boys, Colin and Robert, come out to lend a hand if allowed or required. Still no sign of

Upton, nor of either of the Stuthridges. At least their roof looks okay. How could the O'Goods' house have been so comprehensively trashed, while the one directly across the road looks virtually unscathed? (I know I should call on the Stuthridges, but my mind won't stay focused on the idea for long enough to make me act. I prefer drifting, observing, trying to look involved in all this wonderful work going on in my street, though I haven't so much as lifted a shovel.)

Small squares of blue fabric have been taped over the holes in damaged roofs, including mine, and one man is moving from house to house, tacking plywood over broken windows. The O'Goods' place is starting to look as if it's being wrapped and packed, ready for dispatch. I'm reminded of Christo, the artist who swathes whole buildings in vast sheets of plastic: perhaps the ravaging and repair of Winter Close is some great artwork on which we are all unconsciously engaged. That idea appeals to me.

But I can't postpone the moment forever: I walk towards number six, resolved to go home. The SES team have raked most of the rubbish off the front garden and lawn and, although everything is still very soggy, the surface water has drained away. I try to connect what I see with my experience of it in the middle of the night, but both cognitions are so disconnected from the way Winter Close has always been that I can't bring them into any sensible relationship with each other. Life has become a series of random flashes. (Why is everyone so calm? Why is everyone else coping so well with all this? Where's the famous bonhomie that's supposed to emerge at times like this, bonding us and nurturing our sense of community? It seems to have had the opposite effect on Winter Close. Where *is* everyone?)

I open the front door, bracing myself for the mayhem and chaos within. I stand and look for a moment. All is as it was when I left: the floor is still wet around the front door, but nothing else seems to have been damaged, let alone destroyed. I wander through the hall, across the living room and into the kitchen: fine, normal, clean, tidy. (Tidier than when Clare was in charge, if it's not too uncharitable to say so.) No sign of tempest or whirlwind or a malevolent universe having wreaked its dark will on my house.

Upstairs, the pillow is still jammed in the broken window. (How improbable is that?) The three damp patches on the ceiling are still there and, yes, one small section of ceiling has collapsed under the weight of water that had pooled in a corner above the bath. Above the bath! So the bathroom is a mess of plaster and other bits and pieces, but the promised flood never came. Or if it came, it filled the bath and drained away. I want to laugh. This can't be true: this is more surreal than anything else I've seen all day. I'm still lying in Alex's bed, surely, dreaming about a quirky little miracle that has saved my house from devastation.

The phone rings. We're back on the air apparently. I go into the bedroom to pick it up and a woman's voice enquires if everything is all right. I don't recognise the voice at once, though I know I should. I assure the caller I'm fine, and thank her for asking. My mental wheels are spinning, trying to get traction on the identity of whoever this is.

'You sound a bit strange. Are you sure you're all right? You do know who I am, don't you?'

It's Clare.

I don't want to talk to her.

Not now. Possibly not ever. But certainly not now.

'How did you know about the storm?'

'How do you think? The news has been full of it all day. Winter Close was even mentioned by name. I was sorry to hear about old Joe Riley.'

Old Joe Riley? Where does such familiarity come from? This feels like an invasion of the privacy of the whole street. Who does she think she is, ringing up like this and expressing her sorrow about a man who had only just moved in when she left me? What does she know of Joe Riley?

'Where are you?' As if I care.

'What do you mean, where am I? Where do you think I am?'

'How should I know? You've moved around a bit.'

'I still live in Byron. I thought you knew that. I live alone at present, if that's what you're fishing for. But I happen to be in Sydney for a couple of weeks. I'm going to spend Christmas here. Both the boys will be here.'

'The boys?' I'm completely out of my depth. I don't want to be having this conversation at all. Why couldn't the phone still be out of order?

'My brothers.'

'Ah. Your brothers. Of course. How are they?'

'Tom, I rang to see how you are. Were you hurt? Is everything all right? Is the house okay? You sound . . . I don't know, sort of dreamy. You haven't been hit on the head or anything, have you? The news said lots of trees came down.'

'It was a long night, if you want to know. A bad night. Joe Riley was crushed by a tree in his back garden trying to get into his neighbours' house to check on the children. Their father was away. I couldn't do anything for him, or his wife. Mrs Spenser's in hospital, her dog is dead, something very odd is going on with Rich, all the women are supporting Joe's wife beautifully, Brian Stuthridge might be dead too, for all I know. Alex has been, um, terrific, but you don't know Alex. Alex and Chika? No, after your time. The O'Goods' house is a bit of a wreck. Still, there are teams of men—hundreds of them; well, not that many—and they've been at it all day cleaning up and doing running repairs. Wonderful to behold, actually, their skill and their energy. I lack both right now . . . No, I'm fine, but I think I might lie down. And yes, I did recently hit my head, since you ask, but not last night. That was another story altogether. Thank you for asking.'

We both hang up and I'm conscious of a touch of incoherence on my side of the conversation. I can't quite work out what's wrong with me, though I doubt if I've ever felt this tired and disorientated before, and Clare ringing, out of the blue, is an unwelcome shock. We haven't spoken for more than two years and we'd more or less agreed to leave each other alone. But it was kind of her to enquire, I suppose, and this was an unusual situation: it's not every day your ex-husband's street—your own ex-street—is featured on the news as the centre of a natural disaster. It was churlish of me not to be more grateful, more responsive. I'm the one who was always calling for a more civilised approach after all. I handled that call poorly. On the other hand, Clare had the advantage of surprise on her side so it was easier for her to maintain her equilibrium.

I lie on my bed, feeling as if I've been robbed of my own space. Having rung once, Clare is quite capable of ringing again. Out of interest. Out of curiosity. Even out of a desire to keep me on edge. But out of sympathy? I have trouble assigning positive human motives like compassion or concern to Clare. I realise I'm being unfair and unreasonable, especially after all this time; but when I look right into it, I don't want a civilised relationship with Clare any more. I don't want any kind of relationship with her. She is an ancient reference point reminding me of how I used to feel. I don't want to feel like that now; I don't want my heart slipping backwards into any emotional quicksand. I don't even want to feel irritated by Clare. Most of all, I do not want to feel sorry for myself, and the thought of Clare—any thought of Clare—is the one thing that can still do it.

The phone rings again and I look at it for a long time, weighing the pros and cons of a second conversation with Clare so close on the heels of the first. She used to specialise in ringing straight back with afterthoughts.

'Hello?'

'It's Maddy.'

I don't want to weep, but the relief is overwhelming, and no call has ever been more welcome. Dear Maddy.

'Are you all right, Tom? I've been trying to ring all day. Harl and I were going to get in the car and come over if you didn't answer this time.'

'I'm fine. Well, not fine, exactly, but okay. It hasn't been much fun, but I'll come to work tomorrow. Let's see how we go. It's been quite a night here, I must say.'

'Are you sure you're all right? Would you like us to come over?'

'No, thank you. I think I only need a good night's sleep. I'll see you in the morning.'

FIVE

'I sometimes feel as if I'm in it, but not of it'

The front page of Monday's *Telegraph* features graphic pictures of unroofed houses and uprooted trees under the banner headline: SYDNEY COPS IT AGAIN. Inside, the plaintive question WHAT DID WE DO TO DESERVE THIS? is splashed across the top of a double-page spread with more pictures and stories about the storm. Winter Close receives several mentions, including a picture of Jodie's car and a misleading report, supported by another photograph, implying that Mrs Spenser's house was intact one minute and in ruins the next.

'This'll convince your Melbourne friend that Sydney is a good place to stay away from,' Maddy says, looking over my shoulder.

My nine o'clock appointment was cancelled because the client's house was damaged in the storm and Maddy called my ten o'clock and postponed him for a week. So now we're sitting together in my office, drinking coffee, waiting for my eleven o'clock to show up. Maddy has cross-examined me about the impact of the storm, responded with genuine sadness to the news of Joe Riley's death, briskly dismissed my references to Alex's support, raised her eyebrows—and kept them raised for several minutes—while I described Rich's Saturday night flit and Ruth's mysterious Sunday morning return, and endorsed my plan to take the afternoon off and visit Mrs Spenser in the hospital. She has also been trying to persuade me to stay overnight with her and Harley in their new apartment. I know this offer is made out of genuine concern, but it's also a ploy to stimulate my interest in the idea of renting a city apartment as a pathway to my personal renaissance. I'm pretending to think about it, but I don't fancy a night on a fold-out couch in Harley's 'study', where the shelves are lined with videotapes of famous Rugby matches and a complete set of Seinfeld episodes.

My Melbourne friend is a notorious Sydney-sceptic who loves bagging the place. His latest e-mail was a quote from Confucius, attached to a news item about a corruption scandal involving a Sydney property developer: *A gentleman seeks virtue; a small man seeks land. A gentleman seeks justice; a small man seeks favours.* And, yes, by such criteria you'd have to say that Sydney, like any thrusting city, is heavily populated with small men, especially at the big end of town.

'He doesn't need horror stories about our weather to convince him this is a tough town. He claims our convict origins are all-too-clearly visible through great cracks in our veneer of sophistication. Melbourne will never get over the shock of having been eclipsed by Sydney as the commercial hub of Australia.'

'Do ordinary people care about such things?'

'It's more a matter of bewilderment than simple jealousy. They console themselves—or my friend does—with the thought that Melbourne is still the intellectual capital of the nation. Politics, theology, philosophy, history . . . Melbourne thrives on all that, while Sydney gets on with doing another deal. I think he has a point.'

Sydney *is* a tough town—more ruthless, more arrogant than Melbourne, always on the make, more litigious than the rest of the country. We're the can-do champions of the world. (Look at the 2000 Olympics: best ever. *Best ever!*) In a word-association test, no one would make the mistake of connecting 'charming' to Sydney and 'brash' to Melbourne. Sydneysiders are more individualistic, more dog-eat-dog, less tribal than Melburnians (yet, paradoxically, Sydney's drivers are more cooperative, more conscious of traffic flow). We might seem open and expansive on the surface, but we're wary of intimacy and slow to invite people into our homes. We lunch together quite often, but not nearly as often as we promise to. The dollar is mighty here, our materialism scarcely challenged by the more subtle values of a place like Melbourne: even small-talk tends to be about real estate—purchase thereof, extensions thereto and views therefrom. Everybody has a renovation story.

'I see some church leader is already lecturing us about the Sodom and Gomorrah implications of the storm,' Maddy remarks as she takes the paper from me. 'Do people believe—I mean *really* believe—that God controls the weather and uses it to hand out rewards and punishments? I mean, does *anybody* believe that any more?'

'This is Sydney, Maddy, hotbed of the Biblical literalists. If you believe the world was created in six days, why would you have trouble seeing plagues, famines, fires and floods as evidence of divine intervention in human affairs? The ancient Greeks have got nothing on the fundamentalists. Some religious leader telling us the storm was God's punishment for our wicked ways—our unbridled hedonism, our materialism, whatever . . . why not? We *know* we're a mob of hedonists, and the storm did hit us hard, so why wouldn't they try to milk the connection?'

Religious fundamentalism thrives in Sydney. You get the impression that Sydney's Catholics and Anglicans have hewed their dogma out of theological granite: right is right, wrong is wrong, true is true, false is false . . . no quarter asked or given. The virgin birth: literally true! Physical resurrection: literally true! Salvation by faith in Jesus Christ alone: absolutely! Women priests? Get out of here! Homosexuality? An abomination! Compromise is a dirty word and so is symbolism. Even moderation is suspect. Black is black, baby, and never confuse it with grey.

I try to explain all this to Maddy, but she's glazing over.

'I'm sorry, Tom. I'm only a poor little atheist from Adelaide. Religion isn't my thing. I did go to a church school, mind you, but we weren't taught the spooky kind of stuff you're talking about. I don't remember everything being so cut and dried.'

'I should hope not. Fire and brimstone is hardly Adelaide's style. Sydney's fundamentalists make sense if you think of them as a natural reaction to the relentlessly secular history of the place— plus our convict past. Unlike your highly civilised home town, Maddy, we started out as a penal colony and that makes a huge difference to the culture—just ask my little Melbourne mate. We've basically been agin the establishment, especially the religious establishment, ever since. The adversarial climate suits fundamentalism down to the ground. No wonder Anglicans are more diligent churchgoers in Sydney than elsewhere: they have to be constantly girding their loins to cope with life in Sin City.'

'Sometimes you sound as if you agree with your Melbourne friend. You get all misty-eyed about Winter Close, but you talk about Sydney as if you don't like it much.'

Not like it much? Like any modern city, Sydney is a finely balanced mixture of things to love and things to hate. Many people who live here—especially the fortunate few with harbour views—think it's the most beautiful city in the world, and many tourists agree with them, though Japanese honeymooners have been known to complain there isn't enough to spend their money on. A former Australian prime minister once remarked that if you live anywhere but Sydney, you're just camping. Needless to say, that didn't endear him to the residents of everywhere else, most of whom can scarcely think of a reason to visit Sydney, let alone live here: The crime! The violence! The drugs! The smog! The traffic! The crowds! The pace! The *pressure!*

But all of that is easy to overlook in a city that's such a loutish, fun-loving, handsome devil of a place. 'No, Maddy, I don't hate it, though I do sometimes feel as if I'm in it, but not of it.'

'I sometimes wonder if that isn't the story of your life.'

SIX

'She dressed like a tart,
I always thought'

Mrs Spenser is in a four-bed ward at Royal North Shore Hospital awaiting some tests. There's a sturdy geranium in a pot on her bedside table, brought by Samantha under Mrs Spenser's instructions, I'd guess, and no other decoration. A magazine on the table is open at a travel quiz: 'Win a trip for two to Turkey'. Some things haven't changed.

Her head is bandaged and she looks frail and old. But she raises a smile when I walk in and those darting eyes are as bright as ever.

'I've got plenty of money, you know. Don't think I haven't.' Her opening gambit is a surprise, but the exaggerated stage whisper in which she delivers it is even more unsettling. 'Don't tell anyone around here though. I'm not one of them private patients, you know. I wouldn't fall for that crap. No way. But I've got more than a million in the bank. *More than a million*. No one here knows that. I'm only telling you, so you'll know. Don't you say nothin'. They'll rip you off in a place like this if they know you've got capital behind you. Oh yes, indeedy. Rip you off, soon as look at you. Thank *Christ* for Medicare, that's what I say. Anyway, not a word about the money, all right?'

The heads of the whole ward, including two nurses on their rounds, swivel as one to stare at the old woman in the bed by the window who has more than a million in the bank.

'Harold's dead, you know. Speared through the throat. Not a nice way to go. But they're giving him a good send-off. Sam promised me that much.'

With this latest revelation, the concentration of our audience becomes even more intense. I lean towards Mrs Spenser, in case she thinks she has to shout to be heard.

'Pull the place down. That's what I think I'll do. Not worth a cracker without a roof. No Harold. No roof. Pull it down. Start again. A million dollars says I can do what I like. But listen.'

I lean even closer. I *am* listening.

'Don't tell a soul. Between us, okay?'

'Mrs Spenser, I think you might be speaking a little more loudly than you need to. There are other people in the ward, you know. I think we might be disturbing them. Distracting them.' I murmur—almost whisper—this advice, hoping to set an example.

Mrs Spenser looks startled and jerks her head from side to side, suddenly aware of her companions' pop-eyed attention to her.

'Who are they?'

'Well,' I take this slowly, 'you hurt your head in the storm, and you've been brought to the hospital, and these—'

'Don't talk to me as if I'm an idiot, Tom. I know I was hit on the head. I know all about the storm. I know exactly where I am. All right? Now, who are these people?'

I'm not certain I've grasped the full import of the question, but I make another stab at answering it.

'They're in the hospital for various reasons . . . they're patients too, same as you. Or nurses. A couple of them are nurses.'

Mrs Spenser half-closes her eyes. Her mouth tightens.

'Get their names, you idiot. I want to know who they are. They've been eavesdropping, you know. Don't think I'm going to change my will because of them. I don't want any special treatment here just because I'm rich. Take their names. See if any of them work for the council.'

'The council? I don't think any of them would work for the council. The nurses work here, and . . .' I take a quick look at the other three women in the ward, all in their eighties by the look of them. '. . . I think these other ladies are all retired. I'm sure there's no need to be concerned.'

'If I'm to start again from the ground up, I'll have to nobble that nice young man in the council again. Rich Abel tried to stop my extensions, you know, but I found someone who soon put a stop to all that. Every man has his price, Tom. I'm no fool. We'll stitch him up again, no worries. Money talks. Have you noticed that?'

You could hear a pin drop in the ward. A television set that had been playing quietly above one of the beds has been muted. The nurses are not even pretending to be busy.

'So when is that bitch Clare coming back? Ever? Want my personal opinion? You're better off out of it. Little go-getter. She dressed like a tart, I always thought. Skirts too high, necklines too low. Clothes too tight everywhere they shouldn't have been. People think I don't notice. I notice, all right. Am I wrong? Wasn't she a bit of a tart? Didn't she run off with someone?'

'Well, I—'

'Find yourself another woman. Street's full of 'em. That little Jodie what's-her-name. Nice piece. Her and Sam might be lezzies, you know. Have you thought of that? Can't be too careful. Good woman, Sam is. Nice type. Understands dogs. Always a good sign. Lot of people don't, as you would know, man in your line of work. Some people prefer cats, but I wouldn't trust 'em as far as I could kick 'em. The cats *or* the people. What about that Alex? I see you hanging around her place more than is healthy. You cracking onto her, or what? Is her boyfriend really in the nick? That's what they tell me. Drugs, apparently. Funny old street, isn't it? Hey, where are you going?'

'I just popped in to say hello. It's good to see you looking so much better.'

'Yes, well keep that money business to yourself.'

I feel five pairs of eyes on me as I hurry from the ward; the sixth has already returned to the travel quiz. I rather hope she wins the trip to Turkey.

SEVEN

'Let the magic happen'

The character of the Close has changed. There are no tall trees left and even the low shrubs are looking sparse. The blue tarpaulins on the roofs of the O'Good and Spenser houses dominate the streetscape. I feel as if we're only camping here.

Brian Stuthridge refuses to come to the door, though I've called twice. His wife assures me that all is well: no rain came in and Brian's papers are intact. I ask her to relay the message that I've heard from the Melbourne historian and his department is interested in taking any material Brian wants to give them. They'd also like to see a copy of *The Geography of War*. Mrs Stuthridge looks puzzled by this message, and I wish I'd put it in a note. She has a nasty mark on the side of her face—a welt, not quite a bruise— and I wonder if she sustained some injury in the storm. She doesn't mention it, and neither do I.

Across the road, Upton is as solemn as any man who has lost a close friend, especially one acquired so recently and unexpectedly; but he can see the funny side of my (lightly edited) account of the visit to Mrs Spenser in hospital. Upton is determined the street party should go ahead, Rich or no Rich. We decide to aim for Friday night and I volunteer to ask around.

I'm grateful for a reason to call on Ruth. She seems to have been avoiding everyone but Enid these past two days. There is no sign of her children, or of Rich.

When she answers her front door, Ruth greets me with the hug that has become a ritual between us. She shows me into her lounge room and offers me a chair. It is the first time this has happened. All our previous conversations as neighbours have taken place out of doors or, once or twice, standing in her hallway or kitchen. In almost ten years of having lived next door, I can't remember ever having sat down in the Abels' house, even to talk to Rich. But, in the space of these past few days, Ruth and I have discussed more momentous matters than I've ever discussed with Rich, so this feels like an easy, comfortable moment between us.

Ruth offers coffee and I decline. She looks distracted, like a woman with something other than coffee on her mind, though her eyes are questing for contact, as they so often are.

'Okay, Tom, off with your shoes and socks. I'm prescribing a foot massage. You look awful, if you don't mind me expressing a professional opinion. Are you getting any sleep at all?'

A dozen questions rush into my mind: where are Rich and the children for a start? How does Ruth come to be here on her own? *Is* she on her own? Has she been at work? Where had she sprung from when she appeared in Mrs Spenser's hallway on Sunday morning? But I remain silent and submit to her suggestion, taking off my shoes and socks and stretching out on the couch. I feel a little self-conscious and hope this won't tickle.

Ruth puts on a CD of Yo Yo Ma playing Bach, turns off the overhead light and leaves the room, returning a moment later with a bottle of something and a towel which she places under my feet.

'Brace yourself for the smell. It's rather heavily perfumed moisturiser. The girls love it.'

I smile, close my eyes and wait.

The sound of Ruth squeezing the lotion into her hands and rubbing them together is brisk and businesslike. She takes one of my feet firmly in both hands and begins to massage it. It doesn't tickle in the slightest. Within moments, I have entered a trance-like state of comfort and security. I know Ruth is doing this partly out of professional concern for the state I'm in, and partly out of simple friendship, but coming at a time of such emotional fragility, it feels like the most loving thing that's ever happened to me.

Though it's only my feet that are being treated, a sense of contentment begins to suffuse my entire body. I can feel a knot in my stomach untying, my shoulders loosening, my jaws unclenching and my scalp tingling pleasantly. I want to talk, but I don't want to risk diminishing the intensity of this pleasure.

After giving each foot, each toe, her undivided attention, Ruth places the palms of her hands against the soles of both feet and lets them rest there, gently, for what seems like a very long time. I might have drifted in and out of sleep. Eventually, I feel Ruth wiping my feet with the towel and putting my socks back on. I'm reluctant to open my eyes. (Was it only yesterday morning I was fantasising about life with Alex?)

When I finally surface, Ruth is sitting in a chair on the other side of the room, watching me intently. She frowns and smiles, almost simultaneously. 'Okay?'

'Can I do that for you?' It seems like the natural question to ask—the obvious offer to make.

'Another time, certainly. That would be nice. Our feet love a bit of attention, don't they? They work so hard for us and we give them so little in return. Lie there for a while and let the magic happen. It will be my turn next time.'

I drift off again, woken by the sound of Ruth putting a tray on the coffee table and placing two cups in their saucers.

'Camomile. Another prescription.'

She pours two cups of pale tea from a cheerful blue and white pot, brings one to me and settles back into her chair with the other. I prop myself up on a cushion, feeling shamelessly indulged.

'You've been very discreet, not asking about Rich and the children. They're at my mother's. Well, the children are. Goodness knows where Rich is. In the country somewhere finding his dream home . . . his dream life. Maybe his dream partner, for all I know.'

I sit up, astonished.

'I've spent all these years worrying about Rich, attending to Rich, listening to Rich, reacting to Rich. I don't think I realised until Saturday night how thoroughly weary I've become of this whole Rich thing. I could keep the lid on my frustration as long as life stuck to its routines and the entrances and exits all followed the script—well, mostly. But the storm finished me, I'm afraid. I'm all used up as far as Rich is concerned. I have nothing left to give him. I still care what happens to him—he is the father of my children, after all. But I'm afraid it's nothing to do with me any more. I feel as if I no longer have a role in that particular saga.

'He insisted on driving us out of here when it was obvious that people were going to be in trouble. At first I refused point blank. Even when he woke the children and told them each to pack a bag, I resisted. They were absolutely terrified, as much by Rich's fury as by the storm. I pleaded with him to stay and be ready to help—especially for poor old Mrs Spenser's sake—and not to put the children at risk. But he absolutely insisted. I was sure a tree would fall on the car, or we'd be swept off the road, but somehow we made it. It was the ride from hell, I can tell you. The children were beside themselves—especially Humbold. Even they could see that Rich was crazy. I have no idea where he thought he would take us, but once we got clear of the worst of it I persuaded him to drop the children and me at my mother's house. After that, he took off. I haven't heard from him yet.'

Ruth is calm as she tells me all this. There's a lightness in her voice that suggests resignation to the point of relief.

'I'll tell you something else, Tom, something that means far more to me than the question of what Rich might decide to do. In the last forty-eight hours I've realised that I've been living with full-on guilt for years, and it's nothing to do with the death of my dear little Jack. I've long since dealt with that. I did everything I could for that baby and I have no regrets at all about behaving the way I did, even if Rich thought it was over the top. No, this is the opposite: it's about *not* being the right kind of mother for the three I have now. I've not been the mother I want to be, because I've been so intent on being the mother I *thought* I wanted to be, or the mother I thought I *should* be . . . and, mad though it may sound, the mother *Rich* thought I should be. After all I went through over Jack, I guess I took a different line when Laura was born: I didn't want any more of that frightful conflict with Rich. I became a certain kind of mother, at least partly as insurance against any negative reaction from Rich. There I go again: it's always been about Rich, one way or another. The only time I was true to myself—over Jack—I had six months of hell in my marriage.

'But Rich is not the only factor. I had a grand plan of my own, as well: I wanted to be a mother who could hold her head up and show her children—especially her daughters—what it means to be a fully liberated woman. Things might have been different if Laura had turned out to be another boy. But there's no point going there.'

Ruth sips her tea and sets the cup down distractedly, completely missing its saucer. 'This is the sort of stuff you must hear from women every day but it's real, I can tell you. For all these years, I've genuinely believed the children would benefit from having a mother who was also fully functioning as a professional woman. I bought the idea that I would be a better mother if I was finding personal fulfilment in my life outside the home. I wanted my children to be proud of me for being more than just a mother. I took them to the surgery and showed them what I do all day; I kept telling Laura and Ethel they could be whatever they wanted to be: they could have children and still be much more than a mother—*just like me*. I even told them—can you believe this?—that being a mother made me a better doctor and being a doctor made me a better mother.

'Goodness knows what they thought I was talking about. Ethel's only seven, God help her. Luckily, even Laura is too young to have a finely tuned bullshit detector. It is bullshit; I know it is. Oh, don't look too stunned—I'm not about to give it all up and stay at home all day. I couldn't, even if I wanted to. But some of the women who know me best have tried to tell me, over the years, that I wouldn't be able to do justice to three jobs all at once—wife, mother, doctor. Well, they were right. Maybe a different kind of husband would have made it possible, but Rich isn't that kind of husband and, anyhow, I don't want to play the blame game. Maybe a certain kind of woman could make it work, but I'm not that kind of woman. I'm me, and this is my life we're talking about. I've made a huge blunder all by myself. Now I've woken up. Not too late, fortunately.'

I'm reluctant to speak, so I take a sip of tea and look over the rim of my cup at Ruth. There are tears in her eyes, but she smiles at me.

'Shall I go on?'

'Please.'

'I've told myself all the usual lies. I *have* to work because we need the money. The children will benefit from the stimulation of childcare. The relationship between them and their grandmother will be enriched by spending so much time together—good for them and good for her.'

'Lies? All those things could well be absolutely true.'

'I think they probably are true. I think they probably are. They certainly are for many women. Perhaps I should have said "facts", not "lies". But some facts act like lies because they conceal the truth. And those facts concealed the truth *about me*, so they were like lies for me. The truth they concealed is that I can't stand being the kind of mother who's so busy at work that she never knows, from day to day, whether she'll make it home for dinner on time. I hate the thought that while I'm comforting some patient who's distressed, my own children might be distressed about something I'm not even aware of and I'm not there to comfort *them*. Or, even if they couldn't put it into words, they might be distressed because they know I'm absent. This is not about big things, Tom; it's about tiny little things. It's about being around on the off-chance you might be needed, or because your kids like to know you're around. If I can't admit that to myself, then all the things I say in praise of being a working mother—even if they are true in some cosmic sense—might as well be lies. They're not the main point at all. They might be true for thousands of other women, but not for me I'm afraid.'

The effect of the foot massage is still with me. I'm hearing Ruth's story with interest and concern, but with a kind of detachment. Knowing I'll sound like the stereotypical male, I ask the obvious question anyway: 'So what are you going to do about all this?'

'I'm lucky, I know, because I *can* do something about it. I'm sure plenty of women come to precisely this conclusion, but then realise they have no choice. They really do need the money. Well, I need the money too, but not this much money. Rich earns reasonable money, and I'm sure that, come what may, he'll help out with the kids' expenses. I've paid my own way all along, so that's nothing new. But I can stop work at two o'clock every day if I want to and be here when the children get home from school, or pick them up, or—I don't know—be around for them.'

Ruth jumps up and goes into the kitchen, returning with a brightly coloured painting obviously done by one of the children.

'Ethel brought this home from school last month. A picture of Mummy at work. Stethoscope around Mummy's neck, patient lying on the table, the full thing. It's quite good, don't you think? But you know what? It nearly broke my heart. I *love* being a doctor. I *love* it. And, truth be told, I love my kids knowing I'm a doctor. But I'm *too much* doctor and not enough mother. Frankly—though most of my feminist friends would lynch me if they heard me say it—I would have been rather pleased if Ethel's painting had been of me reading a bedtime story, or running the bath or—horrors!—bending over a hot stove. But that isn't what she drew for the perfectly good reason that that isn't what she sees me doing. I can't remember the last time I read them a story in the relaxed way I dream of doing it . . . or cooked a decent meal that wasn't thrown together in a hurry.

'And here's another thing. This isn't original, I know, but it's true. When the children were younger, I often used to drop them off at pre-school childcare, or at my mother's, with a sense of relief because I knew my paid job was a whole lot easier than the unremitting slog of being a full-time mother. Being a doctor is the easy part, Tom.'

Ruth runs a hand through her hair, sighs, and, for a moment, looks completely defeated. If she is intent on spending more time with her children, and if Rich and she have reached a final parting of the ways, the timing could hardly be worse for either of them. Rich is still wrestling with the possibility of his work at the university coming to an end—or at least being marginalised. Is he about to be marginalised as a father as well? If he is determined to move to the country and Ruth is determined not to, what role will the children's interests play in either decision? (And who will decide what might be in the children's best interests?) Will Rich arrange to spend regular chunks of time with them, perhaps taking them to a new home in some yearned-for village for weekends or school holidays? Would that mean the children would have less time to spend with Ruth just as she begins reorganising her life so she can spend more time with them?

I have a tendency to jump ahead, I know, and to tackle other people's problems inside my head, even before they've had a chance to formulate them for themselves. But this seems such a familiar ritual of unravelling families, I doubt if I'll be able to find anything reassuring to say to Ruth . . . or to Rich. They might both get what they both now want—different versions of 'freedom'—and they might both decide, one day, that they paid too high a price for it. I couldn't count the number of clients who have looked back wistfully on conditions they once regarded as intolerable.

'I hate to say this, Ruth, but I know lots of mothers who say they've dropped back to part-time work so they can be home for their kids, only to find the kids pleading to go to after-school care because it's cool. People speak of "after-care" as though kids are like cars or computers in need of regular check-ups. But some form of childcare is so common now that going home to mum is considered boring. The kids who do go straight home are the odd ones out.'

'I know all that. I hear the same thing at the surgery. But this is about me and my priorities and I'm quite clear. I don't want to be silly about it, but I also don't want to be a full doctor and only half a mother. I'd much rather be a full mother and only half a doctor. My guilt is real, not imaginary. I know that, when I strip away all the arguments, I've been selfish about this and I don't like knowing that about myself. I'd go so far as to say I'd rather be at home, accessible to the kids, perhaps even feeling a bit stupid, than at work feeling professional and smug . . . and absent. It's not an either/or, I know that. I'll keep working, but I'm going to radically alter the balance.'

Ruth looks at me in that searching way she has: not seeking approval, but only recognition, connection.

'And now, on reflection, I think I *would* like you to give my feet a bit of a rub. Why not?'

EIGHT

'You need to make the second most important discovery of all'

I'm uneasy about seeing Alex again, and when she answers her door, I launch too quickly into my enquiry about the timing of the street party.

'How would you feel about having our Christmas party on Friday night? Ruth doubts whether Rich will be back from his trip to the country, but Upton thinks we should go ahead without him. I'm inclined to agree. Joe's funeral is on Thursday, so we could still squeeze the party in before Christmas Eve. What do you think?'

'I think you're being rather cold and distant. Rather formal. You're coming on like Mr Administration. You slept here on Saturday night, remember? Then you hung around like wet washing all day Sunday and I haven't seen you since. I thought you might have drunk yourself into oblivion, but then I saw you skulking into Ruth's place last night. No doubt about you—Chika goes away for a while and you're dropping in night after night like you're my best friend. Then Rich takes off and Ruth gets the treatment. I'd better warn Mrs Stuthridge in case anything happens to poor old Brian. Beware! The Winter Close letch! Tom the heavy hitter!'

Alex's tone doesn't match her words. Neither do her actions. We're standing on her doorstep and she pulls me across the threshold and gives me a long and enthusiastic hug.

'Come and look at this.'

I fear this is going to be another poetry reading, and I follow her into the sunroom with my antennae twitching. There'll be no more dumb questions out of me, no more cautious attempts to appear helpful or constructive. I'll leave all that to her tutor. If I can't bring myself to shower her work with unstinting praise, my silence can speak for itself.

But it isn't a poem. Alex is creating a magnificent wreath, using flowers cut from her own garden woven into a wire frame already lush with camellia leaves.

'For Enid. I'm going to do one for Violet and the children too. Something brighter. Peter still isn't home, you know. He had to stay in Hong Kong for some more meetings—that's international companies for you. They pay you a fortune and extract every last drop of blood from you. Ask Violet what she thinks about all that. Anyway, he won't be back until just before Christmas. He might make it in time for the party, if we do have it on Friday, but there's no way he'll be here for Joe's funeral. So . . . what do you think?'

'Absolutely beautiful. I didn't know you did this kind of thing. That's quite magnificent. Is it for the funeral?'

'It's for Enid, dummy. Not for the funeral. For Enid. Even when the flowers die off, the leaves will last for a while and it will be nice for Christmas. She's amazing, you know. Really, really amazing. She knew this was coming and she seems to have prepared herself for it. I love brave people. I'm not very brave myself. I'm going to my parents' place for Christmas. They offered to come here, but I think it would be awful—you know, with Chika away and everything.'

'So there's no news?'

'He seems fine, though he prefers me not to visit him. We communicate by phone mainly. It could be weeks; it could be months. Irregardless of what happens, he doesn't think they'll let him out for Christmas. Just as well, probably.'

'You mean "regardless".' It was out before I could stop myself.

'What?'

'You said "irregardless". There's no such word. You can have "regardless" or you can have "irrespective", but you can't have "irregardless". Sorry, I shouldn't have mentioned it.'

'What about bebop juice, you *idiot*? That's not a "word" either.' Alex holds up two fingers of each hand, bending and unbending them in the approved fashion, to indicate that 'word' is in inverted commas. I'm relieved she's only exasperated. She doesn't even seem to be particularly irritated: my correction merely boosts her already rising confidence that the inadequate one here is me, not her.

I move on. 'Did you say it might be as well if they *don't* let Chika out for Christmas. I'm not sure I understand.'

'You know Chika. Well, I suppose you don't know him very well. The thing is, he'd do something silly and only make things worse for himself. He's so . . . defiant. I love him and everything, but . . . sometimes he can be really, really stupid. He's a good boy at heart, but he's got some bad friends . . . he always seems to be getting into trouble, as if he means to, which I'm sure he doesn't. I don't think he cares what happens to him, which would be quite a nice way to live if you had the right kind of friends. Anyway, there's nothing I can do. Jem and I are fine, and Mum and Dad are supportive—as long as Chika isn't around. They keep hoping everything will fall through with him and me, which it won't. Like I said: I love him. Simple as that. Who can explain any of this stuff. Can you?'

'Me least of all. I'm quite good at helping other people pick up the pieces, but—well, you know my situation.'

'No, Mr Wonderful, I *don't* know your situation, actually. You know how it looks to me? It looks as if you're a rather pathetic, sex-starved, middle-aged male who can't quite bring himself to make a fresh start, so you keep hanging on, hanging on, in this boring little street, hoping something will turn up. You're using us like a kind of surrogate family. I have the feeling we all mean a bit too much to you. Am I right?'

I hate these conversations. I try to match Alex's flippant tone but it never quite works for me. The trouble is, I can't help examining myself in the light of some of the things she says, and that's an uncomfortable process. This time Alex goes on before I can compose a suitable reply.

'Chika is the perfect excuse for you, isn't he? Even if you wanted to take me to bed, you'd be scared of Chika finding out. By the way, I'm not available, in case you're ever wondering. Just because I flirt with you and hug you and offer you a warm bed on a stormy night doesn't mean I'm hot for you. I like you, Tom. You know that. But I think you should be more honest with yourself. I wish you'd sort of straighten up, somehow. You seem all hunched over, as if you're hiding. I don't mean hunched over exactly. What do I mean? Closed. Stitched up. Everything's held too tightly. Why don't you let go a bit?'

'I thought I came over here on Saturday night to help you, not for you to help me. I wasn't hunting for a warm bed. I have a perfectly good bed at home.'

I rise to leave, feeling offended, and feeling stupid for feeling offended.

'Oh, come on. Sit down again. Why are you always aiming for the right effect? Don't be so prim. All right, you came over to help me and I appreciated it. But I can recognise a man in need when I see one. You're a nice man, a reasonably good-looking man. Quite sexy in a way, if I half-close my eyes. Only joking. You're not my type, as it happens, though I think I could put a smile on your face if I was looking for a project. But don't take everything so *seriously*. People are allowed to say what they think. And they're allowed to think something different tomorrow. The world won't end if I tell you what I think your problem is. I wouldn't bother if I didn't care about you. You might even be my best friend, right at this moment, so it's just as well I don't fancy you. Sex never goes well with deep and meaningfuls in my experience.'

'I'm afraid it's exactly the opposite with me—in theory, at least.'

'Tom, you need a fling. You need some sassy broad who flatly refuses to discuss the meaning of life with you, but can't keep her hands off your body. You need a truly wonderful fuck. You need to make the second most important discovery of all: that sex is meant to be . . . f-f-fun. Remember? *Fun*?'

'What's the *most* important discovery?'

Alex rolls her eyes. 'I don't believe it. Did you really have to ask me that? You're hopeless, Tom. *Hopeless!* You always go for the fine print. Didn't you notice the headline? SEX IS MEANT TO BE FUN! Did you miss that? Did you hear me mention fun and sex in the same sentence? Did you hear me recommend a cure for your current painful condition? Did you really have to ask, "What's the *most* important discovery?" Did you really? You're *hopeless!* What did you think I'd say? That reincarnation is the go? Or bathwater runs the other way round in the plugholes of the northern hemisphere? Or unconditional love is a myth? Or pale lipstick and short hair make you look younger? God, Tom, you're hopeless. Be thankful I told you the second most important discovery. Isn't that enough to be going on with? Find some guru up a mountain to tell you the rest. Now, come here and let me give you a big fat hug. Come on. And yes, I'll come to the street party on Friday on one condition.'

'Which is?' I dread hearing it. This will be a demand for eight lines of unrhymed iambic pentameter, perhaps on a Christmas theme. Alex won't rest until she has received my first attempt at a poem written under her enthusiastic tutelage: she even has an empty manila folder lying in wait with my name emblazoned on the front in multicoloured crayon.

'That you'll drop your guard. Say what you think. Act your age. You're only fortysomething, aren't you—not eighty? Hang loose. Be yourself. Be real.'

'How will you know?'

'I haven't been wrong so far, have I? You're lucky to have a neighbour like me.'

Now, the promised hug: Alex puts one hand behind my thigh and gently pulls it towards her, while her other hand rests against the back of my head. I feel her groin pressing into me and her tongue lightly brushing my lips. Yes, if she were looking for a project, I think she probably could put a smile on my face, though I'd never be able to believe a word she said.

NINE

Nature must take its course

Only two of my dreams have ever felt as if they had premonitory power. Most seem like a drainpipe for the day's spent emotions, flushing out the poisons of the mind. Sometimes they embroider feelings that were only transient or peripheral at the time, pushing some fleeting experience of malevolence to its remorselessly dark conclusion for instance, or elevating a moment's unimportant lust into bliss. But two dreams have felt like visitations rather than mere reprocessing—as if they were messages addressed to me from my future.

The first, three years ago, was brief and brutal:

Clare, arms folded across her chest, floats above a mansion being stripped of its contents. A diaphanous skirt blows about her thighs and she receives, with evident relish, the intimate upward glances of the removalists. Instead of loading the furniture into a van, they hurl it into an abyss. There's laughter in the air; I sense that everyone knows what's going on except me.

Clare was gone to her squadron leader within the week.

This is the second dream:

I am trapped in a crowded street—in a shopping centre, perhaps, or near a beach or a sporting venue of some kind. In spite of the pressure of the crowd, people are animated and cheerful. Strangers are talking easily to each other, the way Sydneysiders did during the Olympic Games when people were so relaxed and friendly they wished afterwards that they had been able to capture that spirit and bottle it.

But I am not part of the crowd. I am out of place and out of time. The buoyant mood unsettles me. I am certain these people are heading for trouble. They don't understand what will happen to them. (Or will it only happen to me?) The crowd surges forward, forward, giving themselves up to their own momentum, unwilling to think about what they're doing. Any minute, any minute . . .

They are all men, only men, yet I sense a woman's presence nearby, a woman's breath. She—whoever she is—is waiting for me to drag myself up a steep embankment, away from this human torrent, into her place of safety. She is expecting me to go to her. The crowd rushes on. Though I'm not part of it, I'm powerless to stop myself being swept up in its momentum. I try to call out, perhaps to Alex, perhaps to Ruth, perhaps even to Clare, but the murmur of the crowd grows into a roar and I must cover my ears to protect myself from its ferocity. The noise is so intense, it smothers any hope of making myself heard. I can feeling myself being carried past the point—whatever it is, wherever it is—where she might be able to rescue me. (Or must I rescue her?)

The mood of the crowd changes, turning dark and urgent. The men are racing now, rushing forwards as if striving for a prize they know they can never win. I am certain they are wrong to press towards this goal—misguided, foolish—but I have no way of warning them. I don't count; I'm not part of them; I'm not present to them.

Now they have fallen silent: I can only hear the padding of their relentless feet on the pavement. They are like predatory animals following the scent of their quarry, mindlessly drawn on, drawn on.

The men part, to make way for the snake. I always knew the snake would be there. The men are unconcerned, surging, racing past it as it writhes and slithers, waiting for me, only for me. As I watch, mesmerised, it raises its huge head in recognition. Am I to be bitten, or constricted in its powerful coils? Though I am being pushed from all sides, buffeted by the silent, surging mob, I come no closer to the snake. It begins to perform for me, shedding its skin in an elaborate ritual of renewal. I am gripped by terror and fascination. I want to escape, yet I want to draw closer and be drenched by the horror, the beauty of this weird dance. I am possessed by the desire to become the snake, to participate in this renewal, to shed my old skin too. But I am too terrified to move. I want to run, but I can't. I want to hide, but I can't. Nature must take its course. I must stay where I am. I must see it through.

The men surge past me now and are gone, swallowed up in the shadows of their own intensity. There is only the snake. Only the snake and me. The old adversaries. The bright promise of that new skin—gleaming, glowing, glistening. Against all my instincts, I reach out to touch it, my desire overpowering my fear. But the snake has become a rippling stream of water, welling up from a spring of deep darkness—fresh, pure, clear.

Now the stream rises before me, up and up—it is a celestial waterfall—and I see a vast dome of stained glass, ineffably beautiful, spreading above me like the vault of heaven. At its centre is the figure of a woman and I am suffused by the power of her love, her warmth, her peace. That same diaphanous skirt, floating out from the image in the glass, absorbs me in its folds. Is it Clare, pretending, teasing? No, there will be no lewd peeping. I call, yearning, to Ruth and she answers me with a soft touch.

TEN

Remember Rosemary

Not so fast, Tom. (I'm facing myself in the shaving mirror—always a vulnerable moment where my alter ego is concerned. We sometimes have these conversations, he and I.)

Your tendency to jump to conclusions, to propose lurid interpretations based on the flimsiest evidence, has got you into trouble more than once. Aren't you being a tad premature in assuming that dream was premonitory? Don't you know the difference between premonition and fantasy? Wasn't it only a day or two ago that you were dreaming of Alex and the children all snuggled up with you in a big warm bed? Get a grip: you're lonely, you've been destabilised by the unwelcome reappearance of Clare, and you're in danger of becoming a bit desperate. 'I call to Ruth and she answers me with a soft touch.' Christ, Tom. You're the soft touch.

— Well, it *was* a powerful dream and I'd be crazy to ignore it. I was right about the removalist dream, wasn't I?

— It makes a good story, but you knew, deep in your guts, that Clare was going, months before she went. You were miserable; she was miserable. Alex was right: you'd both passed your use-by date and it was time to call it a day. The dream only confirmed an idea that was already fully formed in your head. I don't call that premonitory.

— But this latest dream . . . I've never felt anything so intense. And what about the snake? Surely that's a sexual message of some sort.

— Make of it what you will. It's your dream to interpret any way you like. So what if it is a sexual message? You're in a state of perpetual yearning: who's surprised if you're regularly aroused by women who seem prepared to be kind and affectionate to you? But don't forget that, when it comes to dreams, most of the classic interpretations treat snakes as a symbol of change, not sex. We fear them in dreams, not because they'll bite us, but because they stand for upheavals and renewals we might not feel ready to handle.

— Well, I don't think I'd be reluctant to handle the kind of change the dream hinted at. Ruth is a wonderful woman. That episode with the foot massage was an experience of deep communion between us.

— That's how it felt to you, and maybe, just maybe, that's how it felt for her too. So what? Who doesn't love a foot massage? But for someone whose life is tinged with longing, a bit of sensual pleasure, even a bit of care of the soul, can easily be mistaken for 'deep communion' and then the boundaries get fuzzy and, in no time at all, you're thinking 'passion'. Go easy, that's all I'm saying.

Ruth might turn out to be the love of your life. She might turn out to be the close friend you crave. She might become your soulmate. Or she might turn out to be nothing more than a thoroughly pleasant next-door neighbour. She does have a husband, by the way. She might talk as if Rich is dead and gone already, but he isn't, you know. He could turn up at any minute, and he'll be a continuing presence in her life for as long as their children are around and needing them. That could be for another twenty years, if they're lucky, or thirty if their kids turn out to be true to their generation. Ask Maddy. The New Clingers stay at home with their parents till their mid-twenties, then keep coming back at regular intervals, in between travel, partnerings, jobs and disasters, acting like dependent children well into their thirties.

— So you think the snake might be about my fear of getting involved with Ruth?

— It's possible. Does it make sense to you? It's your dream, as I keep saying. I'm alerting you to a few of the possibilities beyond the one you obviously want to believe in, that's all.

— But I don't think I've let my fantasies run away with me in that department. I don't want some kind of showdown with Rich. Rich is my friend, too. And let's face it, I'm still getting to know Ruth.

— Facing it is exactly what I'm proposing. I think you're in danger of getting carried away. 'Premonitory' dreams? You're using the wrong adjective: 'wet' might be closer to the mark. Alex obviously thinks you're on the make, and she's smart enough to warn you off—as if you needed warning with Chika in the background ready to pounce. Ruth might want to get closer to you for all I know, but don't rush it. Remember Rosemary.

— How could I forget her? The memory is almost as humiliating as the event. In another era, Rosemary would have sued me for breach of promise. By the way, I never dreamed about her.

— You didn't need to. The whole thing was like a living nightmare. Remember her mother? She thought you might be after her at first. But when she realised it was Rosemary you had your eye on, she managed to overcome her disappointment and throw herself into the role of mother-in-law-to-be with such verve it was painful to watch.

— You flatter me.

— No, Tom, you might as well get used to the fact that, at the age of forty, the span of possible partners increases dramatically, up and down the age scale. Older women don't have any trouble at all imagining you might be lusting after them. On the other hand, you are also quite capable of evoking a motherly response, certainly in Maddy, and perhaps even in Alex. Cups of tea, drying your clothes, little homilies on your moral formation, urgings to make something more of your life, encouragement to write poetry: these things are a million miles from swishing about in diaphanous skirts. And let's not get too carried away with the foot massage caper either: Ruth probably massages her children's feet too.

— I don't wish to know that.

— Rosemary, by contrast, was *not* maternal in her response to you. Rosemary was more like a grotesque appendage requiring surgical removal. Do I have to remind you about that weekend in Melbourne?

— Look, Rosemary was a very nice woman, but I finally woke up to the fact that if she was gossiping about all her friends to me, she was probably gossiping about me to all her friends. I found, in the end, I couldn't trust her. Nothing rang true.

— Except her impatience to get you into her bed. That rang true. And her bizarre views on politics and the social order.

— Okay, I was a slow learner. Now, can we move on from Rosemary? This is all rather painful.

— Her case was instructive, that's all I'm saying. When you're in a certain mood—vulnerable, wounded—your imagination works overtime and you can easily lose your grip on the harsher realities of life. 'Wounded and vulnerable' is a good summary of how you seem to be at the moment, and I wouldn't want you to rush into another entanglement that could plunge you into yet another pit of embarrassment and remorse.

— Overactive imagination, eh? At least I see things in full living colour. Isn't it better to get carried away with my passions than to lead a grey and careful life? I think I'd even prefer to suffer the occasional Rosemary-style humiliation than never let my heart speak for itself.

— You know what I think the problem is here? I think there's an uncomfortable gap between what's going on inside your head and what everybody else sees. That doesn't make you a hypocrite, necessarily, but it does raise some important questions. Let's be blunt: you sometimes seem disturbingly passive in matters of the heart. You like to see yourself as a man swept by irresistible passions, but you don't seem to realise that that always puts you on the receiving end. By the way, Alex would be amazed to hear you talking about all this colour and movement in your life: she's always going on about how you think too much. You need to let go more, according to Alex.

— Now I'm confused. Are you saying I *should* let myself go a bit more? That I should let my feelings show? So how should I approach the Ruth thing?

— Tom, listen to me: there isn't a 'Ruth thing'. Not yet. Maybe not ever. That's the whole point. And Rosemary was a classic example of letting your heart—loosely defined—speak for itself. Brains have a role to play too, you know. You're supposed to keep your mind engaged, even when your gonads are calling the shots. In the case of Rosemary, you pulled back from the brink in the nick of time because you finally woke up to the fact that it would be a disaster, even though you and Rosemary were nuts about each other. You realised it would be unwise to commit yourself to a gossip, a liar, a cheat and a manipulator, no matter how terrific she looked in a pair of stretch jeans . . . or a diaphanous skirt, to return to your latest obsession. There's a role for out-and-out erotica in your life, Tom, but it's safer on the printed page, where you can close the book when you want to. Women are people—a tricky point, but worth remembering when you're in this kind of mood— and people want to be taken seriously, first and foremost. You never treated Rosemary like a person, because you couldn't get your mind off her body. Yet every time she opened her mouth, you cringed. She wanted to have boatloads of asylum seekers pushed back out to sea; she wanted the death penalty reintroduced; she hated movies with subtitles; she thought classical music went on for too long (she was amazed to find that not all music comes in three-minute chunks); she drank too much. Yet you kept telling her how desperately you loved her, when you actually couldn't stand her.

— Let's move on, shall we? The best thing to be said about Rosemary is that she sensed what was happening and ran for her life. Clever girl.

— Spot of revisionism there. I thought the official version was that *you* pulled back at the last minute.

— Yes, well, these things are never clear-cut. In fact, I'll always be grateful to Rosemary for knowing when to vanish.

— Okay, but don't get swept up in a wave of fervour and go ringing her up to *tell* her how grateful you are. Not ever. (See, I knew you were thinking of doing precisely that. What could it possibly achieve except a suggestion that 'we should get together sometime', and then what?) Next time you want a bit of porn in your life, get hold of a book or a video. Don't drag some poor woman into it.

— I admit there's a lot of tension in me over all this. Not over Rosemary. Certainly not over Rosemary. But the whole business of living in the expectation that the woman of my dreams is just around the corner. I know it's pathetic, but I do look at every woman, *every* woman—well, every vaguely eligible woman—as a person I could conceivably fall in love with. I do weigh them up.

— You're interpreting the 'live-every-day-as-if-it's-your-last' thing a bit too literally, a bit too sexually—which is hardly surprising, given the frustrations of your present circumstances. Yes, live as if your life depends on it, if you know what I mean, but don't forget everyone else has the right to do the same. If you go blundering into women's hearts, misreading the signs, over-interpreting to billy-o, it will end in tears every time. What if those women are also trying to live each day as if it's *their* last—being nice to you, being sensitive, being sympathetic, taking you seriously—and you react as if you think they're giving you the come-on? You could tarnish something that was meant to be innocent and uncomplicated, like treating a simple gift as if it's a contractual obligation. Living in a spirit of eager anticipation is one thing, but constantly expecting to stumble into passion, love and lust, all rolled into one . . . it's too much, Tom.

— But I don't think anyone else knows that. I control it. Women wouldn't notice.

— Rosemary certainly did, though that was an unusual case, I admit, even for you. Alex has a pretty good idea of the chasm between your head and your heart, but when she accuses you of being faint-hearted—with Chika in the offing—she doesn't know the half of it. With Alex, you've been half-flirting with the idea that she's a prospect when you both know she isn't. You're lucky she's amused rather than offended. If you think Ruth is a serious prospect, don't act as if she's one. Keep reminding yourself that she is what's known as 'thy neighbour's wife'. Remember the tenth commandment? Thou shalt not covet thy neighbour's house, view, power tools, sprinkler system, hard drive, Porsche or wife. That was the gist of it. It's an impressive list, and wives are right up there with all the other possessions—ox and ass, maidservant and manservant, you name it.

— Very funny. That was when wives were like chattels. But these days my neighbour's wife is a fully-fledged person with a mind—and a heart—of her own.

— And a husband, let's not forget. That's the thing about the old rules and regulations: when there's a dirty great list of what you can't do, the conscience is stifled. Strict and complex laws have always bred a thriving loophole industry. But in these enlightened times, you're supposed to cart your own moral compass around with you. Because so few things are prohibited these days—even adultery isn't illegal—you need to be doubly sensitive to the needs and rights of other people. And other people's wives. And other people's husbands. And other people's *children*, by the way: there's a not very subtle hint of yearning in the way you talk about other people's children—especially Ruth's and Rich's, and most especially Laura.

— Whatever happened to 'falling in love'? Such things still happen, you know.

— You're already in love with the idea of falling in love. Isn't that enough to be going on with?

— Anyway, she's asked me over for dinner. The children are still away. I regard that as an encouraging sign.

— Tom, you're incorrigible. What do you mean by 'an encouraging sign'?

— I mean . . . well, I think she's interested.

— Hold it right there. She's asked you over for dinner. You're developing a friendship with the woman. She's your next-door neighbour. She's in a state of emotional turmoil . . .

— Not at all, surprising though that may seem. She's perfectly calm about Rich's departure, if that's what you're referring to. It's the end of a long journey for her and she's arrived at the destination with a sense of relief.

— Tom, you're supposed to be a counsellor. *No one* is calm about the departure of a spouse after—how many?—ten, twelve years of marriage. No one. Ruth is in a vulnerable state. She needs company, support, attention, distraction, light relief. She's seeing a lot of Alex and Enid, but they're both pretty darned needy themselves, in their different ways. You're supposed to be the rock here. The brick. The reliable neighbour who gives her your precious time. A listening ear. Surely you're not going to race off on one of your famous tangents at a time like this.

Tom, listen. This is practically a professional assignment. Ruth herself said as much. Don't talk about 'encouraging signs', for God's sake. The way things are, you can be a good neighbour to Ruth. Mess this up, and not only will you lose her as a friend; you won't even have her as a neighbour. She'll cross the street to avoid you. You know the rules. This is the suburbs, Tom. No intimacy between neighbours, remember? Maybe between kids, but you're meant to be one of the grown-ups. Ruth isn't the girl next door—and even blokes who end up marrying the girl next door usually go away and come back before they realise what was on their doorstep all along. They have to stop being neighbours for a while. Being neighbours is a great barrier to intimacy—or should be, if the neighbourhood is going to work. In your case, the neighbour thing is too important, too precious, to be mixed up with your fantasy life.

— And if it happens? In spite of me being cool and neighbourly, what if Ruth sends me signals too strong to ignore?

— For once in your life, try to see it her way. Even those signals, if she did send them, would be confused. She'd be saying she's needy, which is right. But there would also be a subtext: 'Don't take advantage of me, Tom, just stick by me and help me through this.' Three kids, remember. And a husband who's gone off the rails. Possibly.

— How do you mean 'possibly'? Ruth is clear about this. He's gone.

— Maybe he has. Maybe he'll be back. Maybe that's wishful thinking on Ruth's part. Maybe that's her way of rationalising what's happened, or her way of defending herself against a very deep hurt. For all you know, Rich might be here, large as life, on Friday night. The street party is all his idea, remember. What's to stop him showing up?

— Yes, but . . .

— But nothing. But *nothing*. Go and have dinner with her, by all means, but don't take that dream with you. Put it in the deep freeze, if you like. Save it up for a few months, at least. But don't carry it with you into Ruth's place, into Ruth's fragile life. Don't act like a robot programmed by its own mad idea of a premonition. *Courage, mon frère!* You think it takes courage to keep yourself open to romance; you think that's like living on the edge, but you're wrong. It takes more courage to keep your head down and get on with the job—in this case, the job of being a good neighbour. Capital G. Capital N. Living on the edge—*really* living on the edge—is never about self-indulgence. It's about enquiry, investigation, examination, assessment. Living on the edge is hard work, noble work. Life on the edge is tough and uncompromising; it's no place for sentimentalists. Love comes sometimes, sure, even to those on the edge, but not when you stand on a street corner whistling for it, as if it's a lost dog.

— You're taking all the fun out of this.

— You want fun? Remember Rosemary. And don't cut yourself shaving: that's a new blade you're using.

ELEVEN

'If you report Tony to anyone, you're dead meat'

EXTRACT FROM TRANSCRIPT OF CLIENT INTERVIEW

So, yeah. So, how are you? I see the bandages have gone, so that has to be a plus, I guess?

Thanks for asking. Yes, I'm fine. But you—you seem more cheerful. How have things been going? Did you manage to see that doctor I put you on to?

Oh, yeah, o'course. She's lovely and everything, but I never went back or anything. Like, Tony always says it's a bad idea to, you know, keep going to the same one.

You went, though . . . and how did you find her?

Oh, she was excellent? Yeah. I might even go back to her if I need anything like that again. I don't know what Tony would think though.

When you say 'if I need anything like that again' . . .

Sleeping tablets and everything. If I take the stuff she gave me, I don't have the dreams. It's magic, actually, as long as I don't have any eccy at the same time? If you have them both together . . . hey, whoosh! Bad. Like, you can trash yourself mixing some of this stuff, you know. Anyway, yeah, she was good. Gave me all the warnings and everything? So. Here I am. Yeah.

Tony? Anything you want to say about Tony?

Tony?

You don't have to say anything about him. We're here to talk about whatever you want. We can sit here for a while. Take it quietly, collect your thoughts, same as before . . .

No, Tony's great. Yeah. No, I was just trying to, you know, remember where we got up to? You know, like, with Tony, everything's a blur. Like, that's just how he is? Like, a million miles an hour? That's Tony.
(Client lights a cigarette and takes a series of huge puffs, blowing the smoke towards me in a well-directed stream.)
So, no, Tony's great. Yeah. What else?

Whatever you like. Whatever you want to say.

(Client shrugs and goes on smoking.)

Last time, you seemed to think Tony was ... I think you said 'a real bad boy'. You seemed worried about what he might do to you if you reported his dealing.

I'd never do that. You'd better not either. If you report Tony to anyone, you're dead meat. I mean it. I'd do the job myself if I had to. I'd know what to do, know what I mean?

I won't be reporting Tony to anyone. Tony isn't my client. I don't even know Tony's real name.

Oh, yeah, o'course. I forgot that.

I want to be sure you're getting on all right. I was worried about you last time. So, you went to see the doctor. You liked her.

Oh, yeah, she was great. Lovely. Yeah I went to see her all right. Gave me stuff to help me sleep? Yeah, I already told you. No, she was lovely. A lovely lady. You know her?

Just professionally. I sometimes recommend her to people, like I did to you.

Yeah, right. No, she was lovely. Oh ... sorry I shouted at you last time. That wasn't fair.

No problem. So, anything else?

Work's great, yeah. Friends. Everything. Tony's great.

So, Tony's around?

What'd I tell you last time?

You were worried. I see in my notes you were feeling a little bit fed up with how life with Tony was turning out. His wife, and the child, and not seeing him much.

Notes? You got notes? You better tear them up, for a start. Like, Tony finds out you got notes and we're all in trouble. Tony's a good boy, really, but he does get mad as hell if he thinks people are trying to get at him in any way. You know, like, get at him? Like, criticise him, or laugh at him, or any of that shit? Hates it.

No, my notes are secure. And, as I say, they haven't even got Tony's real name in them.

Oh. Yeah. You said that. Yeah, I forgot. Can I have a cigarette? I'm right out.

Sorry, I don't keep any here. Would you like some water?

Typical. I want a ciggy and you offer me water. What is it with you this time? Like, you're edgy as hell. You worried or anything? You should see a counsellor.
(Client laughs.)
 No, Tony's great. Yeah, he's going to stay with me now. That's the end of the little wife and the little baby. Kaput. That's what Tony says. Kaput. He can't stand all that suburban shit. You know, like, she forced him into it? Got pregnant and everything? Tony's mad as hell. He'll pay up though. He's good about money. No one could ever say he wasn't. Know what I mean?

So, Tony's out and about?

Out and about? How do you mean 'out'?

You mentioned last time he was on remand.

Shit. Did I say that? I shouldn't have said that. Cross that bit out, okay?

It doesn't matter. It doesn't make any difference.

It sure as hell would make a difference to Tony. Look, mister, I probably said all kinds of shit. Like, it was the dreams and everything? Now I've got this stuff for the dreams and I'm fine. Tony's fine. Yeah.

But you made this appointment. I thought there might be something you wanted to say. Something to sort out. That's my job, you know, to listen to you and help you see things a bit more clearly—if you're worried, or confused about anything. So . . . was there anything?

I can't remember exactly. I think . . . yeah . . . I know: I'm here to clear the air? That's what Tony said: clear the air? He wants you to eat your fucking words, you arsehole. You were trying to set Tony up. Yeah, I remember everything now. Listen, you lay right off Tony, all right? Right off him. Tony's great. He's with me now and I'm looking after him. We even went to a movie together. Dancing and everything. He's, like, living with me properly? He said it all came to him while he was, you know . . . away? He doesn't want any more kids though. No way. Been there, done that, bought the T-shirt, Tony reckons. Never again. No way known. Suits me.

TWELVE

Am I just a heat-seeking missile?

What do I represent, exactly, as I approach the front door of number eight, a bottle of St Henri Shiraz in one hand and a florist's posy—irritatingly branded with a sticker on the cellophane wrapping—in the other?

Am I Cupid's eager arrow, aimed at Ruth's heart, pulled against a taught bowstring and ready to fly at the first flicker of encouragement? Or an artillery gun, aimed at the Abels' hearth, threatening to blow the whole place apart and finish the job Rich appears to have started? Or am I something even more stupefyingly predictable: a heat-seeking missile?

Or none of the above. Perhaps I'm what I appear to be: a next-door neighbour responding to a dinner invitation at a time of personal trauma for all of us, but especially for Ruth. I'm supposed to be a person who's mature and responsible and *caring* enough to keep his own rogue feelings in check and be prepared to listen. (You're a friend of Ruth's *and* Rich's, remember. *Remember?*)

The truth is less tidy than any of that. A dozen feelings, none of them particularly noble, compete for my attention. I feel excited, nervous, and full of foolishness. I feel as if, in spite of a lifetime's protestations, I might be devoid of any coherent ethical framework—as if my moral machinery has not so much broken down as never been assembled the right way round. I don't know what I'm doing, or why I'm doing it, even though, if pressed, I could give Ruth, or Alex, or even Rich, a plausible explanation. What I would say to them might even be true, though I doubt I'd believe it myself. It would be one of those things I sometimes say when I'm being swept along on a wave of piety or self-righteousness, buoyed by my need to justify myself or perhaps to fill a moral vacuum with sound.

I also feel an impending sense of regret, as if, at any minute, I'll know it was wrong to have come here in the mood I'm in. I have often felt like this: at the very moment of something starting, I want it to end, or never to have begun. Ten minutes after the guests arrive, I want them to have gone, feeling as if we've said everything we're ever going to say to each other and the rest will only be chatter. (If I'd thought I was going to be able to subject them to the relentless probe of an in-depth interview though, I'd have wanted them to stay all night. 'Nothing's as much fun for you as an inquisition,' Clare used to say to me in disgust, and with distressing accuracy.)

My casual clothes don't fool me for a moment and I doubt if my behaviour will be able to match them. Still, there is a serious purpose here: I'm on a mission of concern and support. So why the wine *and* flowers? Wouldn't one or the other have been symbol enough? Perhaps I can say the wine is for dinner and the flowers are to say 'thank you' for her attention to my injuries. (Unconvincing. A tiny posy like this is inadequate. Say nothing.)

Let's face it: it feels like a date.

The roof of the Abels' front porch has been taken down by the salvage crew, so my arrival feels very exposed—all the way to the sky. I knock.

I can hear a suppressed giggle and the sound of pushing and shoving. The door flies open and there's Laura, beaming, with Humbold and Ethel flanking her. They're all in their pyjamas, looking angelic and freshly bathed. All eyes are on the flowers: they'd have been hoping for chocolates.

'Tom's here! Tom's here!' Ethel chants raucously, almost mischievously, presumably for Ruth's benefit. I wasn't expecting the children to be here: they have certainly never greeted me so enthusiastically before and I'm . . . wary. I'd be pleased if Ruth appeared quite soon.

Humbold grabs me around one knee and drags me, hobbling, inside. Laura takes the flowers and says, as if she's the mother, that she'll put them in water. 'Hey, cool shirt,' says Ethel, fashion critic at seven.

'Come and play "Croc". You have to collect gems in your backpack. Can you play it?' Humbold hasn't let go of my leg yet and I seem destined to accompany him to his room where a computer sits on the floor, wires snaking in several directions. 'Can you wee over the side fence? I can, almost.' I think we've moved from 'Croc' to reality, but one can never be sure.

A pleasant, grey-haired woman I've seen visiting the Abels, but never met, appears at the door of Humbold's room. She extends her hand. 'Hello. You must be Tom. I'm Judith—Ruth's mother. Ruth rang to say she's been held up at the surgery. She won't be much longer, but she asked the children to make you feel at home. I see they've already started. Would you like a drink?'

'Thank you, but I think perhaps I'll wait for Ruth. It looks as if I'm going to be busy here for the time being.'

I lower myself to the floor and accept the controller proffered by Humbold. My damaged knee is not entirely happy with this arrangement.

'Watch me, first,' says Humbold, and I cheerfully comply. I'm unfamiliar with 'Croc', though clients have referred to their children's enthusiasm for it. I had imagined it might appeal to a slightly older age-group than Humbold's.

Humbold crouches beside me, leaning forward intently and shouting at the images on the screen. Suddenly, I feel myself being throttled by a small pair of arms circling my neck from behind. 'Guess who?' Ethel shouts in my ear. I don't like to disappoint her by seeming to identify her too readily.

'Laura?' I squawk through my constricted throat.

'Wrong, wrong, mister pong!' This is followed by gales of laughter. Ethel has me in the cross-hairs of her terrorist's sights; I'm her target for tonight. Laura is nowhere to be seen. Humbold is too intent on his tiny crocodiles to notice our sideshow.

'I can't breathe, Ethel. Could you let go?'

'I can't breathe, Ethel. Could you let go,' she echoes.

'No, really, it's hurting.'

'No, really, it's hurting.'

'I'll have to free myself.'

'I'll have to free myself.'

I remember being infuriated by this game when I was a child and realising, even then, that its only point was to irritate. It still works. I reach up and grab Ethel's wrists, gently pulling them apart.

'Ouch! That hurt!'

'Sorry, Ethel, but I honestly was having trouble breathing.'

'Sorry, Ethel, but I honestly was having trouble breathing.'

'Your go!' Humbold turns to me defiantly, looking like a boy who expects me to fail at the first obstacle, which I do, in spite of a transparently earnest attempt to succeed. Humbold advises me that I have been dumped in a lava pit.

Now Ethel clamps her hands over my eyes. 'Guess who?'

I'm tempted to short-circuit this by identifying her straight off, but I'm also reluctant to trigger another round of the echo game.

'Bartholomew Diaz?'

This has the desired effect. Ethel's hands are quickly retracted as if they've been in contact with a madman.

'Can you spell "fuck"? I can, almost.' ('Almost' seems to be the breakthrough word of the moment, even more fascinating to Humbold than 'fuck'.) Humbold asks me this without taking his eyes off the screen, his fingers busily jabbing at the keys on his controller.

Laura, bearing a bowl of potato crisps, appears just in time to rescue me from a spelling quiz of dubious propriety. 'Anyone want a chip?' she enquires, and Ethel and Humbold respond by descending on the bowl like wolves on the fold. Entering into the spirit of it, I, too, thrust my hand out, competing with theirs for a modest share of the action. Under this furious assault, the crisps are rapidly broken down into unappealing little fragments.

'Don't be greedy,' Laura commands. I withdraw my hand instinctively, then realise she's probably only addressing her siblings.

'Can you ride a two-wheeler?' Ethel has fixed me with a searching look, not unlike her mother's, and I realise this is more likely to be a test than an invitation.

'Well, I used to be able to, so I suppose . . .'

'Come on, then.' I was wrong. It is an invitation.

'Wait for me,' screams Humbold as we all surge towards the back door.

'You're not going out there,' says Judith firmly. 'It's too late to ride your bikes. You're all clean and ready for bed.'

'Poo,' says Ethel. Humbold is hugely amused by this monosyllabic act of defiance.

'Inside, young lady,' says Judith, with an authority that would be the envy of any drill sergeant. I'm impressed.

The children hear Ruth's key in the lock and race for the front door, whooping and yelling.

'I might have that drink now, if I may,' I say, hoping a glass in my hand will disqualify me from participating in whatever wild possibilities might still lie ahead of us.

'Do you have any children of your own?' Judith asks, rather pointedly.

I shake my head.

She smiles at me. 'They're more excitable than usual. Kids always are when they're out of their normal routine. They go a bit silly. But don't be alarmed—Ruth will want a few minutes with them and then I'll take them back to my place. Until Rich sorts himself out, I'm the back-up. Ruth says you've been very supportive.'

I shrug. It's hard to imagine how I've been supportive, except in listening while Ruth described the tip of her private iceberg, but I don't want to have a conversation with her mother about Rich. Judith seems like a thoroughly sensible woman, as calm as I'm tense: if I'm not careful, I could find myself telling her my intentions towards her daughter are honourable. 'She's lucky to have you on hand to help with the kids,' I say.

'Oh, she knows that. I keep telling her she's liberated at my expense. She used to criticise me for being a doormat to my husband and children. She doesn't say that any more. I wonder what will happen when she's a grandmother. Will she be available for this kind of thing? I doubt it.'

Ruth pokes her head around the kitchen door. 'Hi, Mum. Hi, Tom. Can you two amuse each other for a few minutes longer? I'm going to have a shower.'

There's a certain amount of squalling and clinging from Humbold when the time comes for the children to leave, but Judith takes a firm hand and herds them all into her Honda. Laura waves cheerfully to me as they go, but the other two ignore me and I understand why: I think I failed every test they set me.

Ruth is not, as it happens, in a diaphanous skirt, but she has changed into black silk pants and an ice-blue top. Her mother has prepared the dinner, and I hover in the kitchen as Ruth serves it. Then I remember the bottle of wine and go hunting for it in Humbold's room. It had rolled under the bed and come to rest against an errant bicycle wheel—not, I'd be prepared to bet, the recommended pre-opening treatment for St Henri.

'Your mother is quite a woman.' I don't want to say anything at all right now: I want to savour a situation that feels unexpectedly homely and comfortable, as well as being charged with a million volts of electrical potential. But her mother *is* quite a woman.

Ruth smiles, says nothing, and carries our two plates to the dining table already set by her mother. 'Can you fix the wine? I'll light the candles.' I like the sound of candles.

I pour the wine and carry the glasses to the table. Ruth is bending over a candle, match alight. 'Don't misinterpret this. I'm not playing *Vogue Living*. It's just that, every night since Jack's death, I've lit a candle for him. The children have no idea why— Rich won't let me explain it and he doesn't approve of me doing it, as you can imagine. Tonight, I thought we might light a second candle for Joe. Okay? So . . . this one is for Jack . . . and this one . . . is . . . for . . . Joe. There. Please sit down.'

The candles burn brightly, side by side, in the centre of the table. As soon as we are seated, Ruth reaches across the table and takes both my hands firmly in hers. Then she closes her eyes, her grip on my hands slackens and the corners of her mouth droop. She looks for all the world like someone going into a trance.

Her eyelids flutter open and, for a fleeting instant, she seems surprised to see me. 'Well,' she says briskly, as if she has managed to drag herself back into this moment from a long way away, 'let's eat. What a day.'

Ruth recounts a catalogue of the small dramas streaming through her surgery. 'I know half these people would be perfectly all right without seeing a doctor, but who else are they going to talk to? Who else is going to listen? One of them told me today that she goes to the supermarket every day, whether she wants to buy anything or not, so she can be around other people. She's stuck at home with a young baby and no family in Sydney. Another one said her husband hasn't spoken to her in three years, and I believe her. I've met him and he'd be capable of that. He's even unhappier than she is. There aren't many chirpy tales coming out of a GP's surgery, I'm afraid. But maybe today has been particularly bad. So many people seem to be under pressure, but they don't know how to name it—they don't know where it's coming from. So they think it's all to do with schedules that are too tight, or disobedient kids, or budgets that refuse to balance. I have a hunch it's all about not being taken seriously enough by someone—anyone. Even one person will do. If you haven't got that, what have you got?'

I don't know how I expected the evening to unfold: I suppose I might have imagined it would be dominated by Ruth's need to talk about the state of play with Rich. I certainly hadn't anticipated the animated tempo of our conversation, nor its easy flow. Although we speak of other people—her patients, my clients, friends, people in the news or in movies we've enjoyed—the conversation is clearly about us: we're exchanging our own ideas, feelings, impressions, reactions.

Ruth and I have touched on some pretty big themes these past few days, but the weave of her life remains a mystery to me. I know the obvious stuff, I even know a bit of her history, but I have only a fragmentary impression of Ruth herself. Those earlier conversations, about Rich and about the quality of Ruth's mothering, were like emergency sessions, business sessions, in some way not quite personal. They were also a bit like walking before you could crawl. Now, the lightness of this conversation seems to imply, we need to go back, to plant a flag marking the spot where simple friendship might have begun, and from where it might naturally grow. We are both smiling a great deal—perhaps to encourage each other, perhaps to protect this fragile encounter from the inevitable difficulty that will arise when one of us mentions Rich. (It won't be me.)

Perhaps I'm learning, at last, about the hazards of aiming too high. I'm learning how an enclosed moment—even a silent enclosed moment—can connect you more intensely than trawling through the encyclopaedia of someone else's life. For now, to my surprise, the mountains and valleys of Ruth's life seem better left unexplored. It's enough to be wandering through these gentle foothills.

Is intimacy smothered by too much information? Is intimacy a fleeting thing—tentatively constructed out of small declarations and disclosures, more imagined than realised? Are our connections harder to sustain once too much of the substructure is exposed? I don't think I could bear that to be true: how could I then make sense of the idea of relationships that are nurtured by a lifetime's gradual peeling away of the layers of self-protection, or of the many accounts of married love that grows deeper through years of inexorable coexistence, respectfully negotiated? Doesn't intimacy evolve through a willingness to share life's tiniest details?

Even here, even now, I sense there's an aspect of being a neighbour in all this. Yes, I've crossed some boundary; yes, I'm ready to receive whatever personal treasures Ruth will yield up to me. Yet I was wrong about the sense of potential. We are not necessarily *going* anywhere. She is still my neighbour's wife, after all, and I have no sign from her of anything other than a need for connection, support, friendship—though 'friendship' is a word too soft, too innocent for what I feel.

I describe, as sympathetically as possible, my encounter with the children. Ruth is amused, but realistic: 'They're behaving like little monsters at present. Humbold is obsessed with four-letter words and Ethel is a complete lunatic. Did I tell you she ran away from school? Seven years old and she ran away from school. Well, sort of. She didn't run far, needless to say. Straight into the milk bar where she and Laura sometimes buy an ice-cream after school. Still, it was a shock when the infants mistress rang me. Poor Laura takes such things very personally. She's acting as if she has to carry the whole load on her own.'

'Is Rich in touch with them? Do you know where he is?'

Foolish questions. I had resolved to say nothing about Rich, and that would have been wise. Now Ruth is dabbing her eyes and asking me to excuse her. Wanting him out of her life—if that's what she does want—is a very different thing from facing the trauma of his going. Children alter everything, as Clare was fond of reminding me.

A small pebble in your shoe, if not quickly removed, can ruin an entire walk. One indiscreet remark, carelessly made, can ruin an entire evening. It takes almost nothing to upset the delicate balance of human contact, to disrupt the comfortable flow of conversation, and to cause people who were travelling cautiously towards each other to spin off course—sometimes irrevocably. I'm determined to contain the damage I've caused.

I pick up our empty plates and take them to the kitchen. Ruth is standing by the sink, head bowed, a handkerchief pressed against her face. I stand beside her and put my arm around her shoulders. (Say nothing.) She leans into me and rests her head against my chest. (Say *nothing*.)

'Rich is never coming back, you know.'

I say nothing.

'That's the way he wants it, and that's the way I want it. Naturally, it won't be the way the children will want it when they find out.'

'Look . . . you don't have to talk about this if you don't want to. I was right out of line even mentioning it. It's none of my business. I'm sorry.'

'No. Don't apologise. You're one person I *can* talk to about the whole sorry mess. You and a couple of my girlfriends. My parents are wonderful, but they could screw Rich's neck, which isn't a very helpful attitude when I'm about to start trying to work out a civilised custody-and-access arrangement with him. Right from the beginning, they thought I was wasting myself on him, which was quite unfair. No daughter is ever quite as gorgeous as her parents think she is—and not many prospective sons-in-law are as unworthy as the bride's parents think they are, either. Rich certainly wasn't. I thought Rich was wonderful . . . Rich *was* wonderful. My parents didn't happen to agree. Well, they weren't marrying him—except it turns out that you do marry into an entire family, don't you? Now this has happened, it's all—well, you can imagine—they're not exactly saying "we told you so", but they might as well be. When things go wrong, it's never as one-sided as parents assume. I hope I won't be as unrealistic about my kids as my own mother and father have been about me.'

'Let's hope that situation doesn't arise.'

'It'll arise, all right. Let's not fool ourselves. You know the statistics better than I do. Three kids? At least one of them will have a failed marriage. No—you don't approve of that term, do you. What am I supposed to say? At least one of them will experience the termination of a marriage, the breakdown of a Relationship—capital R—or the transition from being partnered to being single. Why do we have to make it sound so neutral? One of their marriages will *collapse.* One of their marriages will fly into tiny, jagged pieces and make a terrible mess. One of their marriages will split and tear and rip and *burst apart*, and there'll be pain, Tom, *pain.* If they have children of their own, their children will suffer; and if they don't, *they'll* suffer. Oh, but they won't suffer alone—their parents will be right there alongside them, feeling all the pain with them and blaming their partner . . . and silently criticising them too, for bringing all this disgrace on their family.'

'Ruth. Hey. What is this? They're little children. Why are we talking about them like this? Come and sit down and let me pour you another drink.'

'I don't want to sit down and I don't want to have a drink. I want you to stand right where you are and keep your arm right where it is and . . . and *hear me out.* Okay? I don't *want* to talk. Oh no. But I *need* to talk, Tom. I need to talk and you're here, so you're the bunny. And, no, I'm not talking about my kids—I'm talking about *me.* Me and my parents. I don't know of a single marriage break-up that didn't suffer from IPS.'

'IPS? Not a medical term, I take it.'

'Interfering Parent Syndrome. One of my friends identified it years ago. Oh, parents can't help it. It's all well meant. But it often tips the scales in favour of a break-up when the husband and wife should be shouldering their own responsibility to sort things out. Having your parents act like an off-stage cheer squad is all very reassuring, but it can weaken your determination to work through your own problems. I've seen it with several of my friends. Back to the arms of mummy and daddy, and the poor benighted husband is out in the cold.'

'Poor benighted husband? Rich?'

'Well, no. My parents are rough on him, but not half as rough as they'll be if they ever find out the full story.'

I say nothing.

'Do you want to know the full story? Is your stomach strong enough for this? I'm sure you can guess. It's your field, after all.'

This is one invitation I know how to refuse. 'You sound like Ethel. I don't want to guess. If you want to tell me about Rich, tell me. Up to you.'

'Go on, guess. I bet you couldn't imagine what's been going on.'

Ruth is sounding sharp, shrill, as if she might be on the edge of becoming hysterical. I grip her shoulder more firmly. 'I think we should go and sit down.'

'Yes.'

We sit in her lounge room, occupying the same chairs as last time, and I wait. The next bit is a long time coming.

'He's back with the research assistant—except the fellow is now a fully-fledged lecturer. Never left him, I gather, even though he fathered three gorgeous children in the meantime.'

'Him?'

'Him.'

'I'm sorry.'

'Why are you sorry?'

'I don't know why I said that. I'm not sorry—I'm startled. Sorry.'

'Don't keep saying "sorry". *I'm* not sorry, so why should you be? I'm beside myself with rage and humiliation, but I'm not sorry. The only place for Rich to be is out of here, and he's out of here. Why should I be sorry?'

'So, he didn't tell you, back then . . .'

'He was very evasive. When he confessed that whole episode to me, he referred very carefully to his "lover" and by then it was all supposed to be over, so I didn't want to talk about it any more than he did. Once, when I visited his office with Laura, I asked him to point "her" out, but he refused. He said it was over, so what was the point? It never occurred to me to size up any of the men as the possible ex-lover of my husband. Rich had the perfect smokescreen: he talked as if he was outraged by homosexuality, and I used to chide him for being so prejudiced against gays. He used to describe some of his colleagues as members of the poke-a-bloke club. I remember asking him to tone it down—to be more tolerant and reasonable. Anyway, what difference does it make now? One of my friends claims it might even be easier if your husband discovers he's gay, rather than taking up with some other woman. "My problem is not that I'm an *inadequate* woman," she says— "it's that I'm a woman." Her husband is a notorious groper, so she knows whereof she speaks. Hard to say which would be worse. She's humiliated every time she goes to a party with him. Bastard.'

'Rich told me about a colleague whose wife had left him for another woman. He quoted the colleague as saying what you've just said—it might be easier than if your wife leaves you for another man.'

'Oh, yes, he told me that story about five times. I should have been suspicious. It was a kite he was flying for my benefit—a kind of cautionary tale. Rich's attempt at inoculation. There never was such a colleague.'

Ruth hunches her shoulders up and sucks in her breath. Then she releases it with a huge puff and almost smiles. 'Can you imagine Judith taking this in her stride?'

'She might surprise you.'

'In one way, you know, it's a relief. It makes sense of Rich's weird, obsessive behaviour over all these years. He was consumed by guilt and confusion. Or so he tells me now.'

'Do you know where he is?'

'In the country, needless to say. No surprises there. Well, sort of in the country. Depends how you define country—they're in a rented cottage in Kellyville. The next thing is going to be explaining it all to the kids. They're dying to see Daddy's new farm. He has a few chooks, I gather.'

I move across the room and perch on the arm of Ruth's chair. 'Well, if there's anything I can do . . . ferrying the kids to or from Kellyville, for instance, until you feel up to facing Rich yourself. Your mother might draw the line at doing that.'

'Facing Rich is not the problem. Do you know what the worst thing is? Something I never would have guessed. This place doesn't feel like home any more. I don't know where my home is.' There's a long pause. 'But thanks, anyway. We'll see.' Ruth smiles and squeezes my hand. 'Let's finish dinner. Mum tells me the girls prepared dessert. Brace yourself.'

THIRTEEN

'You have the look'

'You were right about Rich, you know. Only you didn't get the details right. Even you didn't pick it.'

Maddy and I are having morning coffee together during a break in the flow of clients. She always comes into my office with a plunger and cups on a tray, and performs the full ritual. 'You wouldn't get a younger woman to do this sort of thing for you, Thomas. They'd want an automatic machine, or tell you to make your own effing coffee, more likely. Some of Fi's friends seem to think being rude is a sign of their true liberation. But I'm so liberated, I'm able to maintain an interest in good manners and things being done properly, without feeling as if I've compromised my integrity.'

'That must be music to Harley's ears. It's music to mine.'

'Now let's get something straight, Thomas. I do this for me as much as for you. My little rituals are not to be confused with servility. Clear? This is my pleasure. *My* pleasure. Get it? If you enjoy it too, so much the better. But if you didn't, I'd still be doing all this for my own satisfaction.'

'My mother's definition of a gentleman: a man who uses a butter knife when dining alone.'

'Precisely.'

'Did you hear what I said about Rich?'

'I chose to ignore it. You made it sound salacious.'

'He's gay. What you once called "his entertainment" turned out to be a male partner.'

I'll give Maddy her due: she doesn't betray a flicker of surprise when I tell her this. Her hand is perfectly steady as she passes me my cup of coffee. 'Did I say "entertainment"? That was a lapse in taste. I'm not surprised he's gay though, and I'm pleased he's doing something about it. But this must be quite difficult for Ruth.'

'Very.'

'But she has you there, standing by her side, offering any help she needs. Thomas the Good. Thomas the Faithful.'

I look carefully at Maddy, unsure how to read her tone.

'Yes, I'm there. I could grow very fond of Ruth.'

'I can see that. Give it six months though. That would be my advice, even though you didn't ask for it.'

Maddy chuckles as she does when she wants me to ask her what's on her mind. It's an endearing habit that should be infuriating.

'All right, what do you want to say? Out with it.'

'Alex has met her match, obviously. She's dead in the water, wouldn't you say? Well, I would. You have the look. Alex never managed to do that to you, in spite of the bare midriffs and the poetry.'

'The look?'

'Smitten. Bandoogled, the girls used to call it. I've never seen it on your face before, not once during your various quite courageous attempts to fall in love with a procession of inappropriate women. Including Clare, by the way. That wasn't the great adventure in True Love you had hoped for, though I accept you were in lust with each other for a while. She was your foray into unhealthy dependency. This one sounds more promising. Don't rush it, Tom, that's all. Whatever she might say to you about Rich, Ruth will be grieving and if you take advantage of her vulnerability, she'll never forgive you.'

'Should I start calling you Aunty?'

'You should try to get a sensible look on your face. Your eleven o'clock will be here in a moment. Give me your cup.'

FOURTEEN

He walked into a
wall of grief

I had no idea Joe was a Catholic, though I wasn't surprised when his funeral turned out to be a huge, warm, celebratory affair, packed with reminiscences, tributes, tears and cathartic stings of laughter. Father Flaherty, clearly a close friend of both Joe and Enid's, spoke of Joe the way any of us would wish for at our passing. 'Here was a man who embodied the truth that we are not defined by what happens to us, but by how we deal with it,' Father Flaherty said. The ceremony was inspiring and comforting, even to an outsider.

I also had no idea that Enid and Joe had been married for such a short time. They had moved into the Close only a matter of weeks before Clare moved out, but none of us realised they were newlyweds.

And here's what else I didn't know. (Why should I have known? What business was it of mine?) I didn't know that Joe had previously had a complete family—a wife, two grown-up sons and a teenage daughter—and that all of them, *all* of them, had been killed in a light plane crash on a flight he had refused to take. For years they had all mocked Joe's fear of flying, but he was resolute: while his wife and children were flying to Cowra to spend the weekend with the family of Joe's eldest son's fiancé, Joe was driving the 300 kilometres across the Blue Mountains and out through the Central West to join them. It was late at night when he arrived at the farm of his future daughter-in-law's family, tired after four hours at the wheel. Instead of being greeted by the ribbing he had anticipated, he walked into a wall of grief.

It was several days before searching helicopters found the plane, buried under a tangle of vines and tree-ferns in a wild gorge near Kanangra Walls.

Enid was Joe's second wife. He was her first husband, and their marriage was still fresh when he died.

All of this was only obliquely mentioned by Father Flaherty, who assumed, no doubt, that anyone who knew Joe would have known the history. Ruth filled in the details for me over coffee after the funeral. Hearing the story on that particular day was almost too much to bear, yet Joe had borne the actuality of it. He had lived through the kind of loss you could never come to terms with and had somehow kept going. He had found enough reserves of hope to ask another woman to marry him in his retirement. He had given friendship to Upton, love and attention to the little Nguyen girls, and three years of radiant happiness to Enid, who adored him.

The storm had crashed through all that, though Enid had clearly been readying herself for an end that would have soon come anyway. Had she appeared inconsolable at her husband's funeral, that would have been easy to understand. In fact, she seemed strong, dignified and calm. If faith means anything, I suppose it means such things can be borne more easily than if death is interpreted merely as an ugly interruption or even a merciful termination. If she had conventional Catholic views about the afterlife, Enid must have been sure Joe would receive his reward. But even if she hadn't, her sense of Joe's death being part of a larger scheme might have helped. Further down the theistic scale, she might have drawn comfort from a sense of her own oneness with the universe, united with Joe like tiny ripples on the same measureless sea of being, lapping the shores of eternity.

I did not envy her her grief, but I admired her faith. My own feelings about Joe's death were a pale shadow of both, though I knew I would miss him and regretted I had been such a half-hearted neighbour. Joe added a unique dimension to the life of the Close, giving far more than he took. You could see him walking the Nguyen girls to the park, or coming home from bowls with Upton, or leaning on his front gate, Enid beside him, chatting to Alex and admiring the baby. In spite of their rocky start as neighbours, he was the only one who ever had the time to let a conversation with Mrs Spenser run its course. And if he found my politics too soft for his liking, he certainly never said so. I can't say I ever connected with Joe, never particularly warmed to him, and although I'm embarrassed to admit it to myself, I was relieved when he struck up such a close friendship with Upton: Rich and I had visited him when he first became ill, but there was some undeniable strain in it—as there usually is when the motive is duty, not love. Yet I was full of admiration for him: like Sexy, he enriched the life of the street with a distinctive presence and style.

And me? For all my sentimental ramblings about the joys of life in the Close, I wonder . . . If I've been taking more than I've been giving—and I'd be pretty confident that's the way it is—then perhaps these things go in cycles and my turn will come.

FIFTEEN

'I'm afraid you're wasting your time. They've gone'

On my way home from work on Thursday evening, I decide it might be worth one more try to contact Brian Stuthridge, perhaps even to mention tomorrow's street party to him. I have assumed his wife gave him the message about his papers being welcome in Melbourne, but I'd like to be able to close off that bit of business in person.

There's no answer at the front door, even after several knocks, so I wander down the side of the house and into the back yard. A hose is trickling onto the chipped and broken concrete path that leads from the back door to the rotary clothesline. I follow it to the tap and turn it off. The body of a rosella parrot lies on a small patch of grass, mauled and discarded by a neighbourhood cat. A white rag hangs from the clothesline: not a garment or a towel— a rag. From the house, no sound; no sign of life.

I knock on the back door, tap at a couple of windows, call out Brian's name. No response.

Brian's car is in the carport, but the radiator grille is stone cold and the doors are locked. An overnight bag is lying on the back seat, a couple of bulging manila folders poking out through the open zipper. The sun has almost set, but there are no lights on in any of the rooms in the house.

Returning to the front garden, I see Sexy O'Good across the road, also arriving home from work. I wave and she comes over to talk to me.

'I'm afraid you're wasting your time. They've gone.'

'Gone? How do you mean, gone?'

'This morning. Before we left for Joe's funeral. The police took Mrs Stuthridge and an ambulance took Brian. He was quite badly hurt by the look of him. Her face was in quite a state too.'

'But did anyone say anything? I mean, didn't you ask the police what was going on? Didn't Upton?'

Sexy looks at me steadily. 'We called the police, Tom. We couldn't stand the sound of the banging and screaming. Violet and the children were upset. I'm surprised you couldn't hear it from your place. The Stuthridges wouldn't answer the door, neither of them, so we called the police. They forced their way in and then they must have called the ambulance. So yes, we spoke to the police.'

'And?'

'You know how the police are. They wanted to ask us things, not tell us things. They had a job to do.'

'Are you saying they'd injured each other? He'd been bashing her? Was that the welt I saw on her face a couple of days ago? And then she'd turned on him? I can't believe it.'

'Tom, you're always searching for an explanation. I know you can't help yourself, but why all this speculation? You may well be right; that might be what happened, but so what? I wouldn't have a clue how or why it happened. Not a clue. And I wouldn't want to know. What business is it of ours? Why do we always feel as if we have to know everything? Not everyone knew what Joe had been through until after he was dead. That's how he wanted it. Sometimes it's better not to know. People will always tell you what they want to tell you. Isn't that right? Some of them even make appointments and pay money to see professional listeners like you. That's how desperate they can be. But if someone doesn't want to tell you, well . . .'

'Do you honestly believe that, Sexy? Don't you think we owe it to our neighbours to take an interest—to be aware when they're in trouble? You hear these awful stories about people who died alone and the neighbours didn't even notice they were missing. I mean, that can't be good. That can't be right. This is a street where we're supposed to look out for each other. I scarcely knew Brian, but he had asked me to help with his papers and things. I listened to his wife on the one occasion when she opened up. But these last few days, I mean, I saw her once, but then . . . no one would answer my knock.'

'Exactly. What were you supposed to do? Break down the door? Call the police and tell them your neighbours wouldn't speak to you? It's not as simple as it sounds, Tom. We were all conscious of Brian's strange behaviour, but strange behaviour isn't a reason to go to the police. Why is this upsetting you so much? Good neighbours give help when it's asked for—they don't interfere when it's not. He asked you to help him with some papers? Good.

I assume you did. He didn't ask you to help him with anything else, so that was that. Why can't you accept that? Come and have a cuppa with Upton and the boys. Upton needs a bit of cheering up.'

Sexy looks at me with one of her famous enigmatic looks. She doesn't expect me to offer Upton any cheer. She doesn't expect Upton to offer me any either. But she's a firm believer in the therapy of a shared cup of tea.

Upton is slumped in a chair, head tipped back and an open copy of the *Herald* spread across his knees, looking like the debris left over from a children's party—a deflated balloon lying under discarded wrapping paper. He greets me without smiling, and motions me into a chair.

Sexy produces a pot of tea and five mugs and calls the boys to come. It's an odd time of day for this little ritual, but Sexy is determined we should all pause and do something normal. 'What a week it's been,' she says, the banality of the remark just what's needed.

The boys are in the midst of an arcane argument about the precise month of 1953 when the inaugural Holden FX gave way to its more famous sibling, the FJ. I'm always intrigued when people argue over matters of fact as if they are matters of opinion. While they pore over old car magazines and various authoritative-looking tomes, my eye wanders to an envelope sitting on the coffee table in front of me. It's been torn open and the contents refolded and stuffed back into the envelope. The envelope is addressed to Colin and the handwriting is unmistakably Clare's—the familiar circles for dots over the i's, the familiar final flourishes for any words ending with a 'y' or a 'g', the distinctive purple ink and the same speckled handmade envelopes she always used. (Has nothing changed?)

I can't take my eyes off it and, although I try to contribute something to a rather desultory conversation between Sexy and Upton about the public transport arrangements for Christmas, my mind is elsewhere. Does this mean I wasn't entirely wrong about Clare and Colin? Has some kind of relationship persisted through Clare's various changes of location and men? Is this a simple friendship? (Inconceivable. What could they possibly see in each other? What could they possibly have in common?) Or is it more than that—is it a show of friendship, a smokescreen, including the regular exchange of innocent letters, to conceal something murky? Are they parties to some kind of unhealthy, sexually charged liaison that thrives on their utter incompatibility—and, for that matter, their inaccessibility to each other? (This is stupid. Why do I still care? Why can't my brain get off this treadmill?)

What I want to say is: How come there's a letter here from Clare? What in God's name is going on between Clare and Colin?

What I actually say is: 'Well, I'd better be going. Thanks for the tea, Sexy. All set for tomorrow night, Upton? I've told everyone drinks at my place at seven. Ruth has offered us the use of their new barbecue, so perhaps you could help me set that up. Rich may or may not show—I daresay Ruth's brought you up to date on all that. The music is entirely up to you. Don't forget the Nguyen girls are going to perform. By the way, did you know Ruth is something of a singer?'

Sexy sees me to the door. 'Alex and I have the salads and things in hand, Tom. Oh, I nearly forgot.' She turns and calls to Colin: 'Show Tom your letter from Clare.'

Colin hands me the envelope. I look at him quizzically, but he only stares at me. I withdraw the wad of paper and unfold it. It's a brief note from Clare, clipped to a series of printed pages about a new car museum opening on the North Coast.

The note says:

Dear Sexy, Upton, Colin & Robert —
I've been thinking of you all through this terrible business with the storm and Joe Riley's death. I phoned Tom—he seemed a bit off-the-air, which is understandable. I suppose you all are. I'm staying in Sydney over Christmas and I thought I might come out and see you—maybe even come to the street party if you're still holding it this year, all things considered. I can't even remember whether we used to have it before or after Christmas, but I'll give you a call later this week. I'd love to see you all—that's if it wouldn't upset Tom too much. (Could you sound him out, Sexy?)

Colin—
I thought this place would interest you and Robert. It will be teeming with old Holdens, Falcons and Valiants, by the sound of it. They also claim to have a P76 in 'mint condition'. That would be something to behold—even the new ones were hardly that.
Clare

'So, has she called?'

'Yeah. I spoke to her last night, but I wasn't much help. She's ringing Mum tonight to get the details. The car museum sounds like . . . yeah. Could be great, eh?'

Colin is just another young man in the grip of a passion—in his case, old cars, not middle-aged women. What would be the point of Clare asking *him* about the street party? He's probably only dimly aware Christmas Day is next Sunday. He has the deeply relaxed air of a person whose administrative arrangements are all taken care of by someone else, except for those he concocts, almost by chance, at the last minute. ('When I was his age,' Upton is fond of saying, 'we had to be home by ten o'clock. That's when he and his friends are starting to think about going out.')

'Are you comfortable with that, Tom?' Sexy's tone makes it clear that, after three years separation and considering all the circumstances, only a vengeful psychotic would be anything other than comfortable with that.

'Fine. Absolutely.' (So that's why Sexy asked me in for tea.)

Without any purpose in mind, I return to the Stuthridge's back yard and take another look around. It's that strange time of evening when night seems to fall from the ground up: although the street lights have come on, the western sky is still quite bright. Standing in the gloom, I can no longer make out the dead rosella on the ground, but the white rag is luminous on the clothesline.

Even in this half-light, the Stuthridges' back yard is unbearably desolate. The back yard might have served as a place for Brian to escape to (though many men use hardware stores and golf courses as more effective hide-outs), but it must have seemed, year after year, to be little more than a grey and formless drudge—a killing ground for cats and a place to hang wet washing. Yes, it's a personal plot of land—an integral part of the great Australian dream of home ownership where 'home' implies 'house and garden'—but it is so meaningless, so lacking in charm, it mocks the dream. The Stuthridges may as well have lived in an apartment. For how many other suburbanites, I wonder, is 'the garden' a burdensome convention—'hey, you've gotta have a back yard'—rather than a source of delight?

Does anyone ever *intend* to create a place like this—devoid of any beauty, any interest, any potential? Does anyone *choose* to live in an environment that seems so mean and ugly? Maybe your back yard chooses you. (That sounds like something Alex might say.)

Walking back home, I see that the Nguyens and Mrs Spenser haven't been idle: their Christmas lights were destroyed by the storm, but new ones are up and blazing. They believe in tomorrow and are pleased to declare it.

SIXTEEN

Worry is okay

When will you ever learn? (I'm addressing my image in the shaving mirror again and I don't much like what I see: an exhausted creature with a haunted look.)

— When your marriage was crumbling, you tortured yourself with that mad fantasy about Clare and the O'Good boys, and now you're at it again. An innocent letter, kindly meant, but no— without even testing the water, you're in at the deep end, thrashing around in a lather of raging paranoia. It's as though the last three years had never happened. Alex says you're hopeless, and, as a technical description of your current state, it's not bad.

— Okay, okay. It was a silly reaction, and an unwelcome reminder of a bad patch.

— A bad patch? Is that what we're calling it now? I thought it was the closest you've ever come to a total breakdown. Still, if 'bad patch' helps you deal with it, so be it.

— Look, occasional lapses into mild insanity can be a great comfort. You feel disengaged, slightly irresponsible, and pleasantly insulated from whatever's bugging you. That's precisely how lawyers feel when they take an afternoon off to play tennis. Staying intensely engaged all the time—that's when you put yourself at risk. When people are under pressure, some of them drink too much, or pop too many pills, or buy something they can't afford, or have an affair . . . it's not necessarily healthy or sensible, but it's quite rational and often extremely effective. Other people spend inordinate amounts of time in the garden, or take up embroidery or watercolours—the so-called 'creative outlet'. As a defence mechanism, such things work for a lot of people. The controlled descent into mild neuroticism worked for me. Can we leave it at that?

— 'Mild neuroticism.' Good one. I like 'controlled descent' too. If only.

— People need escapes, okay? We choose our own. I'm not a gardener. I'm not a basket-weaver or a sand-modeller. I'm not into yoga or Pilates or bushwalking. I'm not against any of those things. My thing just happens to be worrying. I'm a worrier. That's my source of comfort. I worry. That's my ritual, my defence, my escape.

— And you call yourself a counsellor.

— Listen, most of my clients are worriers too. We worry our way through their stuff together. I don't think I ever cure them of being worriers—maybe I help them cope with a particularly tough episode and then they go back to routine, low-level worrying. They get by. Basket-weavers get by. Yogis get by. But they have to stick with it to get the full therapeutic benefit. People with strong religious faith have to *practise* it for it to work. There's no single-dose, broad-spectrum cure for the human condition. Worry is okay.

— Is this one of your instant theories, designed to rationalise a particularly embarrassing gaffe? I don't think I've ever heard you eulogising worry before.

— You're oversimplifying again. I'm not eulogising worry. I speak in praise of the therapeutic effects of ritualised discipline. A bit of random worry won't do it. You've got to be a serious, committed worrier. You've got to have established practices. It's best to start young. Remember how I used to worry when I was walking home from primary school about whether a mad assassin would try to ram me with his car? Every single time I crossed a road. It concentrated my mind wonderfully.

— And has probably shortened your life.

— These things aren't about lengthening your life—they're coping mechanisms. People who meditate or play tennis for the purpose of lengthening their lives are into an altogether different level of neurosis. 'The world can't live without me! I can't face the thought of dying!' Well, well . . . the world got on perfectly well without me for several million years and it will cope perfectly well for the next several million after I've gone. I don't worry to live longer. I worry to stay sane—to cope.

— Tom's Paradox. I love it. Transcendence via ulcers. So today, presumably, you'll keep yourself sane with an all-day program of fully focused, non-stop worry about whether Clare is going to show up at the street party? Let's see . . . it's seven thirty. You've got almost twelve hours. You could develop a very effective little routine in that time. Perhaps you could visualise her walking up the street with her squadron leader in full dress uniform on one arm and her hippie on the other—caftan flowing and beads ajangle. Perhaps Colin and Robert could be hovering somewhere, wearing loin cloths and waving palm leaves. Nice. Then you could have a full-scale anxiety attack about what Clare and Ruth might say to each other if they're left alone for ten minutes. Or Clare and Alex. Or Ruth and Alex. Better and better.

— Are you quite finished? I don't fancy myself as the topic of conversation between any of these women.

— My point precisely. Anyway, I'll watch your performance tonight with great interest, in view of recent developments.

— Go easy on me, will you? I think I'm learning something from Ruth. I have no idea where the relationship—

— Dangerous word, if I may say so. Presumptuous word.

— I have no idea where the relationship—the *relationship*—is going, and I think that's as it should be.

— Holy Christ. Pompouser and pompouser.

— Listen, Wednesday evening was something of a breakthrough. The previous deep and meaningfuls were like neighbours' work—fixing a leaky tap, or helping out with a bit of painting, or digging a hole to plant a tree. This time, it felt as if we were starting to get to know each other. And, frankly, I think small steps—small disclosures—can be treasured even more when you realise that might be all there is. Differences tend to get brushed aside, nuances ignored, when you're both intent on the gallop towards bed. When that's not on the agenda—and I assure you it's not yet on our agenda, and may never be—you can savour everything more fully and enjoy each other in simpler, subtler ways that might turn out to be even more rewarding than sexual gratification. Anyhow, plenty of relationships thrive on undischarged sexual energy.

— How can you bear to look at yourself in the mirror while you mouth such tosh? You take the high road, by all means. Personally, I'd take the low road, and I bet I'd be in Scotland afore ye.

— Things aren't always what they seem, you cynic.

— No, but they usually are.

— Clare always talked about 'life's rich tapestry' when she wanted to sound detached. 'All part of life's rich tapestry' . . . as if everything was just another thread in a pattern you'd never discern until it was too late to matter. Well, I'm happy to declare an interest in the rich tapestry of Ruth's life, but I'm content to start with some of those tiny threads. For me, that's an improvement, isn't it—not wanting the whole story, *now, now, now?*

— I'd clap if I wasn't holding this razor.

PART THREE

Street Theatre

ONE

'Kisses all round. Once a year only. Come and get it.'

As a child, I tried to avoid parties. I had trouble facing the moment of arrival; hated playing formal games with children I was perfectly happy to play with in more relaxed settings; assumed, on the basis of grim experience, that the food would make me sick (though it was probably the stress rather than the food); was embarrassed about having to join in any singing; usually left early, often in tears. If I stayed the distance though, and found myself with one or two close friends after the tide of other children had receded, that would be wonderful—not like a party at all.

Nothing much seems to have changed. I'm waiting for the right moment to venture into my own front garden where I have set up a table with drinks, ice and glasses for people to help themselves. Ruth and the children are already there, along with Violet Nguyen and her two daughters. (I learned only today that the big one is Monica and the little one is Brigid.) I can hear Upton teasing the children: he's in robust form, or else he's putting on a remarkable show.

Everything was all right half an hour ago when Upton and I were hauling the Abels' barbecue onto the footpath and Ruth was helping me with the drinks. We were in old clothes and it all felt quite normal, like a cooperative assault on a couple of neighbourhood chores. But now the mood has changed completely. We've switched roles from being 'neighbours' (or possibly even 'ourselves') to being actors in a play called 'Let's Have a Party'. Through the window, I notice Ruth has reappeared in a long skirt that could almost be described as diaphanous and Violet Nguyen is wearing an emerald cheongsam. The children are dressed across the spectrum—Laura in cargo pants and fluoro lime singlet, Ethel in a fairy costume and the Nguyen girls in immaculate white T-shirts and shorts. Humbold, like Ethel, is in some kind of fancy dress. I can't interpret it from here, but it involves a mask.

I'll hold out for one more arrival, I decide, though when I see Jodie walk through the gate and ponder the prospect of trying to avoid talking to her about the huntsman episode—or, worse, not trying to avoid it—I decide to wait a little longer still. (Her car was flipped over in the storm, Thomas: don't forget you've got that up your sleeve.)

I recall reading about the English author P G Wodehouse's dislike of parties. Once a year, he and his wife would hire a marquee and everyone owed hospitality would be invited for drinks. Wodehouse would greet his guests as they arrived, then retreat to his study for the evening. His wife would summon him when the guests began showing signs of wanting to leave and he would reappear in time to farewell them. This has always struck me as an excellent plan.

I hear a fuss being made over the arrival of Alex and Jemma; this had better be my cue.

'Kisses all round. Once a year only. Come and get it.' Alex is doing the rounds, planting a kiss on everyone's cheek, including mine: *mwa mwa mwa*. I remember girls like Alex at those long-ago parties: they intimidated me by their heartiness, appearing to be having a whale of a time even before anything had happened. Alex's effervescence notwithstanding, we'll be relying on a few drinks to relax us, and the children to distract us, while we settle into the rhythm of this awkward little ritual—pretending that neighbours are friends. We can do a party; hey, why not?

There are office parties like this—occasions that practically guarantee an uncomfortable collision between those who can cast off their office persona, determinedly acting as if this is a purely social gathering, and those who cannot. (In an attempt to 'involve' me in such a function, a senior manager once drew me into a toe-curling conversation with his colleagues about the joys of Provence. Through endless descriptions of charming cafés, arrogant waiters, sublime meals at *unbelievable* prices, it emerged, to a general slapping of thighs, that two people in his much-travelled coterie had almost certainly eaten a meal at the same place a mere twelve months apart.)

I sidle up to Ruth, wanting to ask her whether Rich is likely to show up: this is his thing, after all. But I don't want to raise it in front of everyone else. In any case, if our street party is to have any authenticity, it should have a life of its own. We speak of it as if we want it to have become an institution. An institution? So far, it feels like six adults and five children stranded in my front garden, wondering what to do next. Even Upton seems lost for words.

'I hope Enid will come. Sexy is in with her assembling some salads. What a week,' Alex says. It is a week for saying 'what a week'. All the week's trauma and sadness can't be brushed aside for the sake of something called a street party: if we had called it something else, we might have felt better about it. (Why didn't we call it 'Christmas drinks'? I think even I could cope with Christmas drinks.)

Mrs Spenser, head still bandaged, is walking carefully along the path from number nine, bearing an armful of parcels. I go to meet her.

'Stand aside, young Thomas. This is between the children and me. Come here, Laura. You can help.'

One by one, Laura takes the parcels from Mrs Spenser's arms and hands them to each child, as directed. The wrapping paper is torn off and there are squeaks of pleasure as the children uncover items that seem uniquely suitable for each of them. Humbold, whose costume has been explained to me by Ruth—'he's supposed to be a shepherd, but he insisted on adding a Batman mask'—is enchanted by a rubber ball which he throws into the middle of the drinks table, sending several glasses flying and upsetting a jug of orange juice. Ethel's gift is a clutch of sparkly bangles that complement her fairy outfit perfectly. Laura receives a new book with characteristic radiance and is instantly immersed in it, sitting cross-legged on the grass. The Nguyen girls have been given a tambourine and a tin whistle which they press into immediate service in an uncertain rendition of 'Twinkle, Twinkle'.

'How do you manage to get it right year after year?' Ruth voices the question we're all asking.

'Nothing to do with me. Man in the paper shop gives me good advice. He's a dog lover, see? Like your friend Sam, young Jodie. Where is she?'

'Coming, Mrs Spenser, coming. Apart from her, and Enid and Sexy, we're about all here, aren't we?' It's a tentative question, and no one wants to answer it, the implications being, in their various ways, too shocking, distressing, bewildering or disappointing. Joe, dead; Chika, on remand; Rich, gone bush; Peter Nguyen, still trapped in Hong Kong awaiting the long flight home. It's unlikely the Stuthridges would have joined us, but they're not even around to make that decision.

What a week, indeed. We are like survivors.

Sexy and Enid emerge from the gate of number five, bearing large salad bowls. Ruth walks across to meet them and puts her arm around Enid's shoulder. Upton, Alex, Jodie and I stand and watch the three women slowly approaching us across the road. Enid is smiling the kind of defensive smile that could be dissolved, in an instant, by any kind of fuss being made of her: 'I'll be all right as long as no one is too nice to me,' her expression seems to be saying. Samantha, in black leather pants and a lolly-pink silk top, emerges from number four and waits respectfully on the footpath until Enid is seated in a canvas director's chair. Suddenly Upton grabs the jug upturned by Humbold's ball. 'I'll fix this up, young Tom. You pour the ladies a drink. I—I may be a little while.' The children, ever vigilant against possible outbreaks of intensity among the adults, scurry into the Abels' front garden and tumble around with the new ball. That leaves me standing here with eight women; the demographics of the street are asserting themselves, and there's still Clare to come.

Alex helps me carry the meat from Ruth's refrigerator to the barbecue on the footpath and I remark, rather awkwardly, that Clare might turn up. 'That's cool,' she says. I'm beginning to realise that Alex offers, as if it's the result of a carefully weighed judgment, the same response to almost everything I say and, presumably, to almost everything everyone else says: 'That's cool'. How can *everything* be cool? Is Cool the new nihilism? I can easily imagine reaching the end of my tether with Alex; I've almost reached it now.

She tells me that Chika won't be home for Christmas: she will visit him on Sunday morning and then go to stay with her parents for a few days. 'Where will you spend Christmas?' she asks, without any evident interest in the answer: it's a form of words you utter, her tone suggests, in the days leading up to Christmas. I'm destined to be asked the same question three or four more times before the evening is over and, although it sounds lame, the truth is that I hadn't given it any thought. Maddy has included me in her family's Christmas each year since Clare left, but she and Harley are going to Adelaide this year to spend some time with Maddy's father, now well into his eighties and in poor health. (Later, Ruth will carve out a moment of privacy to ask me if I'd like to join her for supper on Christmas night after the children have gone to Kellyville. With that prospect in view, a solitary lunch will be no problem at all.)

The one interesting thing I've learned from Alex is that Chika is still on remand, so it looks as if Chika and 'Tony' are not one and the same person after all. (Who cares?)

As I set about lighting the barbecue, Rich's black Volkswagen comes burbling into the Close. His children rush over to meet him, as if this is the same as any other homecoming. Another man emerges from the passenger's seat. Hunched over the hotplate beside me, Ruth tenses like a drum. 'He's not bringing that person here, surely? Is he? Tell me he's not.'

I can offer her no reassurance. Rich has introduced the man to his children and is walking towards us. 'Everybody, I'd like you to meet my friend Mervyn.'

'Merv the perve,' Ruth hisses in my ear. 'I don't think I can handle this. Why didn't Rich warn me?'

It is impossible not to sense that in the space of just six days, Rich has been transformed. He looks relaxed, expansive, liberated . . . *jaunty.* He is stylishly dressed in a charcoal-grey linen jacket over a white shirt and cotton slacks, instead of his normal checked shirt and stock-standard beige cords. There's a distinct spring in his step. None of this will be easy for Ruth. Mervyn moves around the group, charming everyone and radiating the kind of warmth we had so far failed to generate for ourselves but were badly in need of. Mervyn joins us as a friend rather than a neighbour, so that affects the way he is received. He is wearing a cream, collarless shirt, chinos and immaculate navy joggers. A red sweater is slung over his shoulders, the sleeves loosely knotted across his chest. In the evening light, he looks about ten years younger than Rich.

While Rich is chatting to the neighbours, and responding to the enthusiastic attentions of Humbold and Ethel, Mervyn approaches Ruth and takes her hand in both of his. I can't believe this is the first time they have ever met, but that seems to be the way it is. 'I'm Mervyn and I hope we can become friends,' he says quietly. He leaves open no other possibility than that Ruth would say, 'I hope so, too,' which she does. It is either the most civilised or the most inhibited exchange I've ever witnessed.

The change in Rich is remarkable, suggesting the release of a long pent-up desire to resolve the ambiguity of his situation. It's hard to imagine he wouldn't have been feeling some awkwardness about this re-entry, but none is evident. Perhaps he assumes the neighbours don't yet realise he's left Ruth, or that Mervyn is his new partner; perhaps he doesn't care. At a quick glance, I'd say the dominant emotion in him is relief at having at last found a way of being true to himself. He seems blithely unaware of the complications that lie in store, and who am I to speculate upon them?

TWO

'I don't know where
to look'

'Upton?'

Upton has been missing, along with the empty orange-juice jug, for long enough to make Sexy a little anxious: 'See where he's got to, will you, Tom? This is not like him.'

It's certainly not like Upton to be perched on the closed lid of my guest toilet, his head in his hands and clutching a handkerchief drenched with his own tears.

'Upton?'

He rises unsteadily to his feet, shaken by the tremulous aftershock of a sob. 'Sorry, Tom. Not like me. Not like me at all. Can't explain it . . . that bloody Samantha . . .'

'Samantha? I thought perhaps it was the sight of Enid . . .'

'Enid? How do you mean, *Enid*? Oh, yeah, I see what you mean. Enid. Wonderful woman and brave as buggery, I agree.

Yeah, Enid. How will she ever get over Joe? How will any of us? Never. No way. Man in a million. What can I say?'

'But Samantha upset you in some way . . .'

'Pour me a drink, will you. A strong one. Come and sit down for a moment. I don't think I can face the melee yet.'

This is an astonishment. Upton reluctant to face 'the melee'? Sitting in my study, it's hard to recognise him: his mouth is slack, his lids are drooping low over reddened eyes and his head is thrown against the back of the couch in a gesture of anger or frustration or despair—anything but repose.

'You and I have never had a proper conversation, young Tom. I don't know if I can trust you. Sexy tells me you're in the counselling game, so p'rhaps I can.'

Never had a conversation? This seems a harsh assessment of our encounters over the years, though we've never connected in any particularly personal way. Asking him about the authenticity of his surname was hardly soul-talk, I admit. 'Try me,' I say.

'Fair enough. Listen, you're a single bloke—how do you cope?'

'Cope? Well, I . . . You mean cooking? I'm not sure, I—'

'Sex. What you do. Do you jerk off when the urge takes you? Do you have a willing woman tucked away somewhere? Do you pay for it? What do you do? Aren't you ever desperate? What's it been, since Clare dumped you? Three years?'

'What's this about, Upton? I don't get it.' (And I don't like it much either.)

'Sexy can't stand the thought of it. Not any more. Can't stand the sight of me when I'm—you know—ready and willing. Freaks her. "Be sensible," she says. Sensible! God help me, Tom. Freezing up isn't my idea of sensible, and it wasn't hers once upon a time. "Put it away," she says. I feel as if I'm married to a nun.'

'Maybe menopause, Upton . . . you know, a lot of women go through periods of diminished desire . . .' I'm stalling for time, talking like a sex manual, and Upton's face registers a justified impatience.

'Five years? Don't give me that "diminished desire" crap. Five years, Tom. The woman has basically shut up shop. Kaput. She'd sleep in another bed if we had the room.'

I look at Upton as dispassionately as I can. Slumped on the couch, red-faced, rheumy-eyed, grossly overweight, puffing from the effort of talking, unkempt . . . it's not that hard to see how Sexy could find him less attractive than she used to. Yet he's a man with a heart of gold and I daresay he means to make the world a better place than he found it. It would be too blunt to propose some regular visits to the gym, so I stall some more: 'Do you think it's only about sex? It's rarely that simple, Upton. You must know that. Perhaps there's something else going on between you, or something else going on in Sexy's life. Maybe we should talk about this another time.'

'Listen, young Tom, I'm a desperate man. Whenever I see that Samantha, I practically go wild. Did you see that blouse, top, whatever the hell you call it? That pink thing? Practically see-through. Lacy bra, the works. Those magnificent boobs—don't tell me you haven't noticed—what's a man supposed to do? I don't know where to look. Well, I *do* know where to look—that's the trouble. Don't you ever get like this—uncontrollably randy in the face of such magnificence? When you're stuck in the desert, what are you supposed to do when you see an oasis—avert your gaze?'

This is a moment for sympathetic silence. I see Upton wants to recruit me for a bit of man-to-man unburdening, but I've never enjoyed this sort of overt talk—not at school and not now. 'Just look at their faces,' a friend of mine used to urge me when we were students together, as if that was the way to curb libidinous excess, but the warning was wasted on me: I used to *like* looking at girls' faces. 'Are you a breasts man or a legs man?' friends would ask each other. I could hardly say I was a faces man. (These days, with women mostly wearing pants, life must be very frustrating for the self-proclaimed legs men.)

'Worst of all, she and that Jodie are going out with Colin and Robert tonight. They often make up a four, even though the girls are considerably older than the boys. Nothing in it, Colin reckons—they just like going to the same places. I can tell you, if I was shut up in the van, pair of boobs like that, there'd be nothing platonic about it. But these boys, they take it in their stride. "We're just friends, Dad," they tell me when I ask them what's going on, and I *do* ask them what's going on. What are they—undersexed, or what? Am I missing something?'

It's tempting to begin at the beginning, but this isn't the moment. Upton, stumbling towards sixty, is a man utterly unswept by—and quite possibly unaware of—the teeming currents of the women's movement. When it comes to gender issues, his adopted sons are a big mystery to him, and so is his disenchanted wife. Upton is bewildered by any attempts to complicate matters that seem to him of axiomatic simplicity: Aren't men supposed to be treated like potentates? So . . . who turned off the tap and why?

'We'd better join the others, Upton. Ruth's about to start cooking. I'm happy to talk about this another time.'

'Fair enough. So . . . what's your advice? For now. Tonight. Can't you help a man out? How should I cope with . . . you know, everything?'

I fear he's going to start sobbing again if I don't offer something very specific, very quickly. 'If you can't avoid talking to Samantha, ask her about her doctoral thesis—Jodie tells me it's about the attention span of rats—and then try very, very hard to follow what she's telling you. That should do the trick. Oh, and just look at her face.'

THREE

'Can we stop this?
Can we *talk*?'

Clare and I used to play a game we called 'Bio'. We'd see a group of people in a restaurant, or a couple who passed us in the street, and we'd compete to see who could create the wildest story about them that could conceivably be true, or was at least not contradicted by the available evidence. It was like a biographical version of 'Dictionary' where you try to deceive your fellow players into accepting bogus definitions of words by making them sound as plausible as entries in a dictionary.

We'd observe a middle-aged couple strolling across a park, hand in hand and deep in earnest conversation. Clare might see them as a pair of adulterers, recklessly in love and planning to do away with the woman's husband—a ruthless, drug-crazed brain surgeon who had never recovered from a tour of duty in the

Vietnam war and who'd had an affair with an anaesthetist who then mysteriously disappeared. I might describe them as the estranged parents of three gorgeous and talented children, planning their custody and access arrangements and desperately trying, this one last time, to bring a touch of decorum into their negotiations.

Seeing Clare climbing out of the O'Goods' van and walking towards us, flanked by Colin and Robert, several bios flash through my mind. She's a welfare officer bringing two delinquents home to face the music, only to find their parents have perished in a murder–suicide pact. She's an international money launderer posing as a lingerie designer, who never travels anywhere without bodyguards. She's a nymphomaniac who keeps two young studs on stand-by, in case of urgent need. She's a United Nations relief worker who has adopted two Afghan refugees and brought them back to Australia to start a new life with her. The most predictable bio—that she has taken up with Colin and Robert where they left off, and is staggering, dishevelled, from the back of their mobile love nest—comes to me finally, and only faintly, like a dutiful echo of the old fantasy.

The truth is scarcely less probable than any of my tall tales. This startling blonde (previously a brunette, by the way) was once my wife. Three years with squadron leader and hippie have not been kind to her. I'd say she's put on weight; in fact, I'd say she has put on a great deal of weight. She is wearing pants—always a mistake for her, now even more obviously so. And, and . . . she is smiling warmly at me, that dear face glowing as it used to in the very beginning.

This is a scene to pop the eyes of even the most relaxed observer. Rich and Ruth are standing side by side at the barbecue, wearing matching aprons and dispensing steaks and sausages; Mervyn is nursing Jemma while Alex eats; Clare and I are sitting together on plastic chairs, wine glasses on the ground at our feet and plates balanced on our knees.

'The street looks a sad wreck,' she says.

There's a long pause while, I suppose, we both wonder whether the same might be said of us.

'It was good of you to come. I mean, to be concerned.'

'Well, of course I was concerned about you. About you all, I mean.'

'Of course. I knew you meant all of us.'

'No. I didn't mean I wasn't concerned about you too.'

'No. Of course. I didn't think you meant that.'

'All I was trying to say—'

'No, it's okay. I know what you were trying to say. And it *was* good of you to come. It was nice. I'm sure everyone appreciates it. I do.'

'Oh, Tom. Can we stop this? Can we *talk*?'

Well, that's a first.

The music coming from Colin O'Good's portable CD player is loud enough to mask this excruciating exchange, so we are the only ones embarrassed by it.

'Go on, then,' I say, knowing I'm being unhelpful and ungenerous.

'How do you mean, "go on". That isn't how we talk to each other.'

'I mean, when you say "talk", is there something in particular you want to say?'

She looks down at her plate of uneaten food. In five years of marriage I never saw her cry, but now her bottom lip is trembling. I reach across and put my hand, inadequately, over hers. I snatch a glance at Ruth; she's preoccupied with the meat.

'I want to say I behaved badly.'

This is about the last thing I expect to hear from Clare. I used to dream of her ringing me up and saying precisely that, and I imagined I would revel in it, agree with her, rub her nose in it and ask for details.

'We both behaved badly.' I feel content, hearing myself say it. It's about as close to the truth as I can get. There will be no recriminations—not after three years apart.

'I'm not certain you believe that, but thanks for saying it. We wasted a lot of words, you and I.'

Frankly, I had never seen wasted words as our problem, though I couldn't say, right now, exactly what our problem was. But it's clear to me that none of this matters any longer, and I'm relieved to have even that much clarity. We said too much for Clare's liking, too little for mine . . . perhaps we only said exactly what needed to be said.

'You were always the expert on life's rich tapestry, Clare. Well, I'm happy to file our five years together under T for tapestry. Are you?'

'I wish it could have ended differently, but I'm grateful to you for letting me go as painlessly as you did.'

Painlessly? Does she mean her or me? (Was the pain all mine then?)

'Anyway, there's something else I wanted to say. I didn't want to do it by phone and it's not exactly suitable for e-mail or a postcard. Even a letter would have seemed a bit cowardly.'

Good God. What now? I would once have yearned for some sign of rapprochement, but no longer. I want only one Christmas present from Clare: peace, silence, absence, distance. She has a nice face (and a nice voice, I now remember), and I'm over her. I had wondered, at least a thousand times, whether I would feel a surge or even a twinge of desire when I saw her again and the answer is: I don't. So what does *she* want?

'I think we should get a divorce. It's silly not wrapping it up properly. We should have done it ages ago, but I didn't feel like getting in touch, to be brutally frank. Also, I didn't want to marry anyone else, so it wasn't an issue.'

'And now?' (There I go, jumping the gun like an overtrained athlete. Incorrigible. I should be banned from the track. Can I take those words back, somehow, before they reach her ears?)

'Not sure. I might. Do you care?' She looks at me with mock intensity.

'Polite interest. Nothing more. You used to be a close relative, that's all.' (Better, Tom; that's better. Keep it light.)

'I think it will be easier for both of us if we do the deed while there's no pressure, and then it's . . . finished. Closure—isn't that the term? You're the psychologist.'

'I see. Closure. Okay. Sure. Why not?' There's no reason to feel unhappy about this, but I am suddenly stabbed by a sense of loss. Perhaps it's merely a recollection of the pain of past wounds. 'So, will you organise it or will I?'

'Leave it to me. I'll be in touch.' And she's gone, over to Colin and Robert, to be introduced to Samantha and Jodie.

Concerned about you all, indeed. Worried about the storm, indeed. Like to see you all, indeed. Could I come to the Christmas party? Would Tom mind? There's only one thing Tom minds: the duplicity. No, two things: the duplicity and the opportunism.

Clare waves the city-bound foursome off and takes a seat beside Upton, her business with me completed. I stay where I am, toying with a cold sausage and draining my glass. Ruth is sitting with Enid, holding her hand. The others—Alex, Mervyn (nursing Jemma again), Rich, Violet, Mrs Spenser—pull their chairs into a semi-circle and settle into the comfortable murmur of undemanding conversation: there will be no hilarity this year, not even from Upton (especially not from Upton). It's practically dark and no-one has bothered to put another CD into Colin's machine. The children are playing inside the Abels', Laura emerging from time to time to enquire when the carols will start.

Off to one side, disengaged, I look into the distressed faces of my neighbours, where the stories of this dreadful week have been etched. There are traces of many other stories, of course, most of which I will never be told. But I'll catch tiny glimpses of them in a shadow crossing a face in an unguarded moment of sadness, or in the lines etched by imperceptible fragments of memory, or in the false calibration of a laugh that doesn't quite match a particular situation's quotient of humour. Those hints will do. No one needs to know everything about anyone: what a relief it would have been to Clare if I'd understood that when I was married to her.

Rich comes and sits in the chair vacated by Clare, pointing a cautionary finger at me. '"On this subject I pray you be dumb . . . The word, for your guidance, is Mum." WS Gilbert.'

'I didn't know you were into G&S.'

'Mervyn.' Rich takes a sip of his wine. 'Knows all that stuff. Sings it in the shower. Cooking. Washing up. Everywhere.'

'Ah.'

'What do you mean, "ah"?'

(Note to self: take more care with the inflexion of 'ah'. 'Uh-huh' is safer, less threatening, more non-committal.)

'Nothing sinister, Rich. I love G&S myself, but I've never heard you mention it before. That's all.'

'You're remarkably tense, Thomas, if you don't mind my saying so. Remarkably tense. Clare rough you up a bit? Is that it?'

Rich's attempts at flippancy never succeed.

'We had a fairly terse exchange. But no, it's fine. I'm fine.'

'You know, Tom, I've never said this to you before, but I think you're a man who bottles things up. I've never heard you raise your voice, never seen you looking angry, even when you were going through all that stuff with Clare. That must have been hell, but you never showed it. Point is, mightn't you be better off showing it? Letting it out? That's something Mervyn has certainly taught me: let the passions run wild. If things get a bit tense as a result, if there's a bit of collateral damage, okay, deal with it. But at least you know what you're dealing with. Mervyn says that remaining calm can sometimes be a pathologically inappropriate response. Think about it. Staying calm can be a health hazard for all concerned, Tom.'

Rich looks intently at me, glances over to where Ruth is sitting with Enid, and looks back at me. He lowers his voice: 'I must say Ruth is a brick. She's taken it all remarkably well. As you would expect. Wonderful woman. She's known about Mervyn for some time, but me moving out last Saturday night like that was a bit of a shock. Height of the storm and everything. I can see how it might have seemed a bit precipitate from her point of view, but there's never a right time for something like this, is there? You'd know that, in your line of work.'

I suppress an urge to shake Rich until his teeth rattle. I shrug instead, then wonder if he'd have preferred me to let my passions run wild.

'Anyway, life goes on,' he says, sounding as if he's casting about for something to say.

I suppose it does, I'm tempted to say. But I remain silent. I'm confused by the mixed messages Rich is sending me. He's as irrational as the rest of us, so I take it he's saying: 'Let the passions run wild except when they might offend me . . . on the subject of *me* I pray you be dumb.' He seems to be praising Ruth for her restraint and criticising me for mine. I'm reminded of Ruth's own assessment of their marriage: that loving Rich was like applying a daily ointment. It's all rather reminiscent of Clare at the height of one of her storms, when she would urge me to be myself, to speak my mind, then savage me for being insensitive and inconsiderate if I dared take her at her word. The woman was a witch: it's only taken me three years to realise it.

(When people urge you to speak your mind, they rarely mean it. What they usually mean is, 'Tell me what I want to hear, but please make it sound convincing.')

Rich's admonitions notwithstanding, I'm confident this is neither the time nor the place to unleash the anger I'm experiencing, especially as I'm not sure who to be angry *with*. I'm shaken by Clare's news about the divorce and I'm astonished by the depth of Rich's self-absorption. But why should either of these things have any negative impact on me? The divorce is both sensible and desirable, and Rich's departure has already brought me closer to Ruth.

There's a role for civilised behaviour: in some circumstances, surely, it's healthier to repress rage than express it, so long as you don't let it go on seething and festering inside you. Anger turned inwards can easily become depression, and I've seen enough cases of that to recognise the warning signs in myself.

Rich's mind is already on other matters. He's like a dog who shakes himself dry before plunging into the next conversational puddle. 'I must tell you something, Tom. You'll love this. You remember our discussion about the student evaluation caper? My infamous five point seven rating?'

I nod, trying to rake up some interest.

'All a mistake. It was a—wait for it—mathematical error. Seven point five was the right answer, it turns out. Not that I approve of the system any more than I did before. No way. But seven point five is a darn sight better than five point seven. At least I'm back in the game. I'm not on probation. I can apply for grants. Can you believe it?'

Ruth appears beside us. 'Go and chat to Enid for a while, Rich. I want to talk to Tom.'

FOUR

We make a strange procession

There's a light on at the Stuthridges' and, as we approach the O'Goods' gate, Brian appears at his front door. He calls and waves and I go over to him. As though he's part of a bizarre double-act with Mrs Spenser, his head is also swathed in a bandage. I am surprised to see him smiling at me.

'Tom,' he says, quite distinctly.

'Brian, good to see you home again. Are you okay? Were you admitted to hospital? Is Mrs Stuthridge back home too?' (Too many questions, as usual.)

'Power of speech . . . good as gold.' It seems a slight exaggeration, but the transformation is remarkable. 'Hit on the head, maybe . . . that woman gone, maybe. I'll join you . . . listening, not singing.' He smiles as if he's made a joke.

He is very unsteady on his feet but, with a great deal of assistance, he makes it across the road and into the O'Goods' patched-up home, swathed in its own big blue bandages. He takes a tentative seat close to the front door. Alex comes over to him and kneels beside his chair, flashing her sweetest smile. Poetry is bound to be on the agenda. I move away.

Mervyn is the surprise hit of the carol-singing. He possesses a rich baritone voice, perfect pitch, and a willingness to throw himself into it that shames the also-rans like me. 'Jingle Bells', 'Good King Wenceslas', 'Silent Night', 'O Come All Ye Faithful', 'Hark the Herald Angels Sing' . . . Sexy is a dogged accompanist, but Mervyn is full of flourish, egging the rest of us on and enjoying himself hugely. Ruth is probably the only one of us not prepared to be impressed by him, though I harbour my own resentment about his presence, and about Clare's: this is not their street; their homes were not ravaged by the storm; Joe was not their neighbour; they are not part of what we have become. One way or another, everyone who belongs here feels damaged: our singing is bound to be more subdued than Mervyn might wish it to be.

Upton is our official leader, but his voice lacks its normal power: the sight of Enid Riley, bravely singing along, is too much for him—or perhaps it's the thought of Samantha, out on the town with Colin. Enid's rendition of 'Away in a Manger', sung as a duet with Laura—planned and rehearsed, according to Ruth, long before the storm—brings tears to my eyes, and to Enid's. Laura, eyes fixed on the ceiling, voice clear and strong as a siren, saves the day.

The violin item from Monica and Brigid is a testing experience for the audience, musically speaking, but its point is hardly musical: these are two little girls who had discovered that 'The First Nowell' was Joe's favourite carol and intended to surprise him with it. Monica announces that they are playing it for Joe. Some uncertain harmonies and a few unscheduled stoppages can't deflect the performance from its unerring aim at our hearts.

Throughout the carols, Rich sits on the floor with Ethel on his lap, his nose buried in her hair and neither of them singing a note. Humbold circulates like a diplomat, freshly important with the news that, come Christmas Day, he's off to see his father's chooks.

Once or twice, I glance at Clare, though our eyes never meet. I find it difficult to believe she's here, and almost impossible to believe I was once married to her. She looks too haughty for marriage.

Ruth comes with me while I walk Brian to his front door and he shakes my hand. 'Thank you,' he says, fingering the bandage on his head. There's a tone of triumph in his voice, as if to say, 'See, I *can* say "thank you"—I always knew it would come back.'

'I'll call by tomorrow to make sure you're okay,' I say, as if Brian has become my personal responsibility. Perhaps he and I will have lunch together on Sunday.

Walking back across the road to join the others as they emerge from the O'Goods' place, Ruth slips her hand inside my arm. Alex, noticing, wrinkles her nose. Rich, not noticing, reaches down and lifts Humbold into his arms.

The mood is mellow as we drift back to the Abels', where we'll clear things away, share a final drink and exchange Christmas greetings. We make a strange procession, wandering along the footpath of our desolated street: Humbold riding high on Rich's shoulders, Ethel holding her father's hand, Mervyn still nursing

Jemma and chatting animatedly to Mrs Spenser, Alex making Violet laugh, Sexy in silent sympathy with Enid, Upton with an arm around Clare's shoulder. Laura is carrying Monica's violin case and questioning her closely about the process of learning to play the instrument. (I wonder how Ruth is reacting to the prospect implied by the question, her own parents having so strongly dissuaded her from taking singing lessons too seriously.) Brigid, deprived of the pleasure of having Humbold to mother, is in a world of her own, still humming the last of the carols.

Anything could happen. I could ask Clare to come inside for a nightcap. Ruth could ask me to stay with her for support while her children farewell their father and his friend. I could offer to carry Jemma to her cot, though that seems the least likely option. Or we could go our separate ways, all goodnights said in public.

It would be best not to plan any of this. ('You think too much, Tom.' Right, Alex.)

My current working hypothesis—but don't hold me to it—is that I might do well to take each moment as it comes, examined but unexplained. I might even prefer to live that way, with no grand plans. There could perhaps be something to the idea that life's mystery is sweet, even when it's painful; trying too hard to make sense of it might be to miss the point.